Suquamish

Suquamish

Jerome V. Lofgren

Authors Choice Press
San Jose New York Lincoln Shanghai

Suquamish

Authors Choice Press
an imprint of iUniverse.com, Inc.

For information address:
iUniverse.com, Inc.
5220 S 16th, Ste. 200
Lincoln, NE 68512
www.iuniverse.com

ISBN: 0-595-18387-5

Printed in the United States of America

This book is dedicated to
The members and friends of the Suquamish Nation.

PREFACE

Suquamish has always been a place of conflict, grinding, explosive conflict of earthquakes and eruptions. It is one of God's caldrons. It is a place where the ore of life is ground up then heated under tremendous pressure until the dross is boiled away. The golden metal of souls purified, souls empowered remain. It is a place where the molten lava is produced deep beneath Suquamish by the grinding of the pacific tectonic plate against the North American plate.

Seas covered Suquamish for more than 4 billion years. At the close of the Jurassic period 135 million years ago, the plates collided with such force that the Sierra Nevada, Coastal ranges and Cascade mountains were shoved up. The plates continued to collide sending shock waves eastward over the continent causing the interior plains to lift and fall, to be flooded several times creating vast inland seas. Oil and coal beds were formed from marshy vegetation. Then 60 million years ago, the greatest collision took place buckling the floors of the inland sea and sending the Rocky Mountains into the sky.

Fossil-laden rocks that once were the mud flats of ancient inland seas rose several miles into the sky. Fossil remains of the once terrifying Tyrannosaurus Rex, the ponderous Stegasasaurus and Triceratops dinosaurs, became the perching places for modern-day golden eagles and peregrine falcons.

The ongoing collision squeezed molten lava up between the grinding plates to produce volcanoes such as Mt. Rainier that hovers over Suquamish like a sleeping giant whose periodic stirrings warn that it is not dead but is taking a little rest before roaring back to life.

A million years ago glaciers three-miles thick covered Suquamish. Puget Sound was carved out between the Olympic and Cascade Mountains by the grinding advances and retreats of these oceans of ice. Like giant millstones, they ground the basalt, metamorphic and sedimentary rocks into sand and gravel interlaced with sediment slabs of blue clay. Then about 12,000 years ago, the glaciers retreated depositing long ridges of drift that reached into the sound like hairy fingers.

Grasses crept over the gravel and rocks. Soon reeds and sawgrass populated the mashes. Birds came in search of food—mallards, cranes, and little sandpipers.

The birds exploded into the air in panic at the sound of dull thunder that rolled over the plains and up the valleys. The woolly mammoth had arrived in Suquamish. In the Olympic Mountains, the saber-toothed tiger and the cave bear fought over territory and food.

On the hairy ridges of glacial drift, droppings were deposited by passing mallards and snow geese en route to their summer nesting grounds in the far North Country. In the droppings were cedar seeds that germinated in the warm, wet soil heated by the summer sun.

Over the centuries, alder, birch, pine and hemlock joined the cedar seedlings. When humans first entered Puget Sound, the ridges and valleys were filled with huge grandfather trees like the cedars that were fifteen feet at the stump and several hundred feet tall.

Clams riding the incoming tides wiggled into the beach sands and mud flats. Razor clams and geoducks multiplied beyond count.

Fish found the plankton-rich waters of the sound ideal. Salmon, trout, lingcod and halibut with a host of other marine creatures surged into the emerald waters.

When the natural forces had done their work and Puget Sound was stocked beyond imagination with trees, food and minerals, the human creature from the far north entered the scene creeping and paddling along the shoreline, following the salmon to their spawning grounds.

One day a small hunting party arrived at the mouth of Agate Pass. They drew their dugout canoes up the gravel beach to a place of smooth sand that was surrounded by giant cedars. Their wanderings ceased. They had found what they and their kind had been searching for since their ancestors left central Asia. Salmon were in abundance, the swift silver and the mighty king. There were giant geoduck clams with huge siphons so long that a single clam fed a family of four. There was cedar bark for shelter, clothing and fuel.

The medicine men and women, after consulting the oracles and spirit guides, declared the place to be good and called it Suquamish. In the Salish language, Suquamish means "The place of clear water" that was born out of the conflict between salt water and fresh water. It was where the spirits of their ancestors who lived in the Orcas and Salmon had told them they should live. So they settled at Suquamish, as did their children and their grandchildren, for thousands of years, years beyond their ability to record.

Conflicting forces of nature made a good life possible for the Suquamish Indians. Fall rains broke the back of summer drought; winter cold froze the rain into snow and ice that fell upon the cedars sending many of the ducks and geese south and the warm spring sun brought them back to Suquamish as the forests and streams freshened and bubbled with life.

Seasons came and went during the succeeding millenniums. Salmon returned to spawn. Ducks flew by in flocks so dense that the sun was darkened. There were skirmishes between tribes over fishing and hunting grounds.

These conflicts were but preliminaries to what lay ahead. It began with rumors of strange white-skin men, rumors that were brought to the Suquamish longhouse by cousins who lived at the mouth of the Hoh River. The Suquamish medicine men and women were also seeing visions of their coming.

In May 1792, the Suquamish fishermen saw the white sails of Captain George Vancouver's "Bird-ship" as the ship was eased into the sound on the incoming tide. They did not know that Captain Vancouver named their sound after his navigator, Lt. Peter Puget. When Captain Vancouver went ashore on Blake Island to meet with the native leaders he was met by a friendly young boy. He immediately took a liking to the boy. With the coming of the white man, the great conflict of people and cultures began.

At first, the Suquamish people viewed the intruders as curiosities. But as the white people came in increasing numbers and stayed, the Suquamish people saw the white people for what they were—a threat to their way of life. By then it was too late.

Chief Sealth, who was a lad of five when he met Captain Vancouver on Blake Island, had seen the future and understood the white man's lust for the grandfather cedars, the lush valleys where herds of deer grazed and the gold of the sacred mountains. The white man lusted after brother salmon and the clams of the shore—all were in abundance beyond imagination.

Chief Sealth had come to know the blackness that was in the white man's heart. He also knew that his people were powerless to prevent the white man's progress. When the Point Elliott treaty was signed in 1855, the Northwest Indian tribes were far from being conquered.

While it is believed that most Indians, given the events of the day, were pragmatic enough to see that the "Bostons," as the white men were then called because the vast majority of the original immigrants were from the Boston area of New England, were powerful people growing in numbers.

In 1855, the Indian population, estimated at 7,500, dominated the settlers by three-to-one. Clearly, Governor Stevens needed the Indians' goodwill and realized both the threat of bloodshed and the subsequent slowing of the white settlement would occur if the U. S. Government did not deliver on the promise to compensate the Indians for their land.

"We have to do this to avoid conflict," Stevens said.

Chief Noah Sealth was variously described as "runted" and as standing over 6-feet tall in his moccasins. He was called both ugly and a man of strong features that indicated character.

Historians are unanimous in saying the Chief disdained Western clothing and wore a breechcloth and blanket. He also was a man of his word and had a powerful, persuasive manner of speaking.

He was a Chief by virtue of the position his father held in the Suquamish Tribe. Sealth spoke only in Duwamish, the language of his mother's tribe. He refused to use the Chinook trade jargon. No word of English is known to have passed his lips.

Governor Issac Stevens, who became Washington's first territorial governor when the territory was created in 1853, also served as superintendent of Indian affairs.

Stevens, a small man often described as a "human dynamo," embarked on a whirlwind campaign to negotiate treaties with all the tribes in Washington Territory. His goal, and he thought it a proper one, was to send the Indians peaceably off to reservations in return for modest amounts of money and guarantees of traditional food-gathering rights.

The Point Elliott treaty, written in English, was translated verbally to the Indians via a 300-word working Chinook Jargon, and then into Lushootseed and Straits Salish. Language problems, cultural differences and Stevens's haste, all contributed to the misunderstandings that have persisted to this day.

On January 22, 1855, Chief Sealth, then about 68 with 12 years of life remaining, addressed a gathering of over 2,000 people at Mukilteo, estimated to be one-fifth of the total population of Western Washington. The meeting was called by Territorial Governor Isaac Stevens to approve the Point Elliott Treaty. His friend, Dr. Henry Smith, translated Sealth's words.

Some historians have questioned the translation. But Smith always swore to its accuracy. Certainly the ideas and the pure poetry are as compelling today as when the Chief held an audience transfixed with these words:

"It matters little where we pass the remnant of our days. They will not be many. The Indian's night promises to be dark. Not a single star hovers above his horizon. Sad-voiced winds moan in the distance. Some grim fate seems to be on the Red Man's trail, and wherever he goes, he will still hear the approaching footsteps of his fell destroyer and prepare stolidly to meet his doom, as does the wounded doe that hears the approaching footsteps of the hunter.

"A few more moons, a few more winters—and not one of the descendants of the mighty hosts that once moved over the broad land or lived in happy homes protected by the Great Spirit will remain to mourn over the graves of a people once more powerful and hopeful than yours.

"But why should I mourn at the untimely fate of my people? Tribe follows tribe, and nation follows nation, like the waves of the sea. It is the order of nature, and regret is useless. Your time of decay may be distant, but it will surely come for even the white man whose God walked and talked with him as friend with friend cannot be exempt from the common destiny. We may be brothers after all. We shall see.

"We will ponder your proposition and when we decide we will tell you. But should we accept it, I, here and now, make this the first condition; that we will not be denied the privilege, without molestation, of visiting at any time the tombs of our ancestors, friends and children.

"Every part of this soil is sacred…Every hillside, every valley, every plain and grove has been hallowed by some sad or happy event in days long vanished. Even the rocks, which seem to lie dumb and dead as they swelter in the sun or darken in the rain along the silent seashore, thrill with the memories of stirring events connected with the lives of my people.

"And when the last red man shall have perished from the earth, and the memory of my tribe shall have become a myth…these shores will swarm with the invisible dead of my tribe; and when your children's children shall think themselves alone in the fields, the store, the shop, upon the highway, or in the silence of the pathless woods, they will not be alone.

"At night, when the streets of your cities and villages will be silent and you think them deserted, they will throng with returning hosts that once filled them and still love this beautiful land.

"The white man will never be alone. Let him be just and deal kindly with my people, for the dead are not powerless.

"Dead—did I say?

"There is no death.

"Only a change of worlds."

The cultures continued to clash and churn, rip and heave. By 1995, only 832 remained of the once numerous and proud Suquamish people. The grandfather cedars have been cut down and floated over to the Port Madison sawmill. Only scrub cedars that were not worthy of the ax or saw remained.

Shortly before my arrival, the Suquamish tribe had begun to assert its primacy within the boundaries of its 7,486-acre reservation in ways that alarmed the estimated 5,000 non-Indian landowners within its borders and the more than 6,000 neighbors surrounding its borders. Tempers and emotions on both sides had risen to the flash point.

In the small Catholic cemetery located in the center of Suquamish there are twin canoes painted brightly with red and black ceremonial markings and mounted on cedar posts. This marks the grave of Chief Noah Sealth. It is a beautiful site that has a clear view of the city that is Chief Sealth's namesake.

I watched the visitors approach the grave with reverence. It was a good thing to do, to show respect for such a great leader. But I had come to know, as the Suquamish people had always known, that though the body of their great chief was buried there, he was not dead.

I knew that, in spirit the Old Man could see the future.

I asked, "Will there be an end to conflict? Will there come a time when humans live in peace?"

The Old Man smiled in his crazy twisted way, a sheepish grin of a trickster.

"Take care of today and the future will take care of itself," he replied.

"But will there be no end to conflict?" I insisted.

The Old Man sighed deeply.

"Conflict is a gift from God. Conflict is necessary. Change comes with conflict. Water needs the conflict between heat and cold to change from rain to rivers and oceans then back to the clouds to cleanse itself of pollution. The process of change brings clashes and storms. Without conflict of opposing forces, the earth would disappear. It is according to God's plan.

"Into this caldron that we call life on earth our souls are repeatedly flung until, through conflict, the dross is driven out. Conflict refines as well as destroys. God has given people the freedom to decide how long it will take to purge their souls of selfishness that breeds fear, hate, greed, envy and lust.

"As long as the outer world abides, there will be conflict. But, when you solve the great riddle of your soul, your inner conflict will end. Have you solved it?"

INTRODUCTION

Have you ever watched yourself walk by? Perhaps you've seen your reflection in a mirror or store window. But, have you heard yourself speak as a separate person, distinct from your Ego perspective? Have you come to know yourself, not as others know you, but as you really are?

Charlie Frankson came upon himself sitting on a beached log beside Agate Pass late one afternoon in mid-August of the year he arrived at Suquamish. He sat among driftwood driven upon the beach by the Nor'westener that had come rippin' and roarin' out of the Gulf of Alaska the previous winter.

He was just sitting, doing nothing, saying nothing, just looking out over the waters of Puget Sound. Though the Seattle skyline blazed in the afternoon sun his gaze went beyond, beyond even snowcapped Mt. Rainier that dominated the southern end of the sound.

The man Charlie observed was a different sort of man. He was a nice man, who blended into the crowd of the nondescript, to be swept along by life's tides like flotsam and jetsam, being pushed and shoved by forces beyond his control. There wasn't to be found in him any of the charisma of a take-charge, do-it-my-way, assertive macho male. He was more like soggy toast in milk.

As he talked he gestured with hands that hung loosely from his wrists in an effeminate way that accentuated the impression of a soft, gentle person who didn't want to offend anyone.

Charlie had seen him around the village many times before. He felt an acquaintanceship with the man though they'd never spoken. There was always a smile on his lips, a twinkle in his dark-brown eyes and a friendly wave as they passed. But when Charlie sat next to him on the beach that day he gave no acknowledgment of Charlie's presence.

Charlie was totally unprepared when the man on the log began to speak as if in a trance, addressing an unseen audience that was gathered before him…

CHAPTER ONE

I'd watched the great sentinel bear throughout the long dark night wheeling around in the same place, keeping a wary eye on Orion, the hunter. I was happy to see Dawn rise from her bedchamber, and with rosy fingers on the Eastern Mountains, lift the curtain to begin a new day.

As the sun rose, a burst of energy flashed between the mountain peaks. Streaking through the mists of Puget Sound, it plunged into the crystal hanging in my cabin window. Thence to be transformed into colors, that performed a swirling rainbow dance across the ceiling and around the walls before continuing on—to where?

I couldn't comprehend its whereness. Nor could I comprehend this awesome fact—the burst of energy, that had entered my cabin and danced on my walls, had been present at the beginning of the universe and will be present at its end. By divine grace, I'd been permitted to savor the moment of its passing.

I touched the crystal again and watched other energy bursts dance about in their beautiful colors. I could distinguish seven colors, but perhaps there were more that I could not see. Nothing was permanent; yet everything was eternal. The passing of the energy burst had brought happiness to my heart like she did when she came. I wondered if she would come again. Would that be the morning she would appear again at my cabin door?

Sometimes while waiting, with the morning mists draping over my shoulders like a cape, I imagined myself a medieval knight waiting for his lady love to steal to his side, she who lived beyond the magic seas in a world not accessible to me.

I didn't know if she'd come that morning. Still I hoped that I'd catch the flash of her smile and the sparkle of her green eyes as she danced through the door once more. Many mornings had come and gone without her. Why did I torment myself with such waiting?

She said, "I may come; and then again, I may not."

But she always said that, knowing I'd be waiting when she did come. With each fruitless wait, another piece of my heart was lost. Would the loss be replaced with wiser tissue or would my heart shrivel up into a cold, hard, lifeless thing?

She warned me fairly, but I refused to listen.

I cursed the fatal compulsion that was ever prompting me to draw the veil from women of her kind, and cursed the natural impulse that gave it birth! That compulsion was the cause of half—no, more than half of my misfortunes.

She taunted, "It's not my fault that my sexual energy drives you mad. If you can't handle it that's your problem, not mine."

Why couldn't I live alone and be happy? But she wasn't happy, and I wasn't sure that I'd be either. Was I a fool to love a modern woman? But then, she wasn't modern. She was as ancient as the beast. I hated myself for loving women who were as elusive as the burst of energy that danced through my crystal.

I'd waited with my heart shrouded in love-fog though she had said, "I don't know whether I'll come or not."

Still I waited faithfully for her coming.

I knew that about myself and hated myself for the knowing. Such self-knowledge was too painful to be kept for long, so I quickly pushed it aside and replaced it with the memory of how she purred so softly as we held each other in exhausted embrace, "I love you. Always remember that I love you." Those were her words but did she mean them?

The urge would boil up within me to leave and never to wait again. But I didn't; I couldn't.

God knows she was a cruel woman. She was cruelest when she did come—as she did that morning last week. Was that a loving smile or a smile of conquest?

Our previous times together had been filled with blazing passion. I loved the way she played the instrument of my body with magical hands. She took me to unknown realms. She never promised anything beyond the moment. I knew that her power over me was complete each time she vanquished the beast and it retreated into its lair.

Such times of passion were followed by times of warm affection, with quiet nestling in each other's arms as I shared the intimate things of my heart freely and without fear of rejection or recrimination. She encouraged me to bare my soul as I did my body, without fear or shame. So I spoke the secrets of my heart, confident they'd remain locked securely in our little castle beside the misty sea.

But she was a cruel woman. She enticed secrets from my heart only to use them like stilettos to attack my vulnerability.

She lived in a fantasy world in which she would journey across the misty waters to her waiting knight who would sweep her into his arms and carry her off to his castle by the sea. There she could act out her fantasies, free to play whatever role the moment inspired—sometimes the seductive vamp, sometimes the virgin princess.

I was sensitive to her moods, as she was to mine each responding without inhibitions. There was time for all things. There was time for the erotic pleasures of lovers. There was time for the gentle snuggling of friends. I thought myself to be her perfect lover and friend though I knew I could never be her mate.

She lived in two worlds separated by the waters. On the other side was her perfect world, a respectable life with wealth and station surrounded by husband and children. She was a professional woman, successful and respected. On this side dwelt her lover. I thought she was content with her two worlds but I was mistaken.

I thought ours was a mature love. With the desperate urgency of youth long passed, I thought it was an autumn love, a time to harvest the wise fruit of a lifetime.

That morning she wore a red dress, shear, long, imprinted with orange flowers and stood in the doorway that opened onto the deck. With arms raised she gripped the upper casement allowing the gentle sea breeze to mold the silky fabric over her body as her long auburn hair streamed down her back. Standing thus, with legs spread apart, the morning light silhouetted the fullness of her mature figure, the curve of her waist, and the sweep of her hips. A shaft of light guided my eyes to her rain forest.

She knew that I was watching her and loved the power her body had over me. I hated myself for being under her control, for being her plaything.

Why? Why did I put myself through such torment? Was it the passion? Ah, yes, the passion, the exquisite passion, fleeting, raging though it was. But I thought there was much more than passion. There was the sensitivity that enabled me to communicate the deep things, the troubling things of my life, the joyous and happy things. As soul mates, I sensed that she knew all that, born of the fellowship of like spirits walking together along the spiritual path, the sacred path, as soul mates.

We had sat naked, facing each other, sharing the communion of bread and wine, and inviting the Holy One to join us as we journeyed back into the eons of our togetherness and forward into the future seeking where our final consummation was to occur. We'd shared the deep mystery that binds a man and woman.

"Men are such fools," she suddenly shrieked. "They're nothing but macho egos hanging between legs.

"But yours...."

Pointing at my littleness, she laughed again.

Her laughter rang in my ears as she swept out the door leaving me to contemplate my smallness of flesh and weakness of character. She was still laughing as she waved triumphantly and drove away in her white

Mercedes to a destiny neither she nor I could have imagined; though on reflection it was inevitable.

I viewed myself a nice man, a gentle man. Why was I continually getting involved with sadistic women? Why couldn't I be a raging bull instead of a sacrificial calf?

The throbbing in my head called me from a fitful sleep, from the recurring nightmare in which I rode a gray horse across a wasteland devoid of trees and water. Driven beyond all hope of return, I found myself thirsty and exhausted at the edge of a deep dark canyon. I leaned forward in my saddle to peer fearfully into a bottomless pit. I jerked back when I felt a strange dark urge within me to leap forward over the canyon rim and into the darkness. Just as I was about to fling myself into the void, I was called back by the beating of the drums.

BOOM…boom. BOOM…boom.

With each beat of my heart, another surge of blood pounded into my brain. I wished it was another hangover but it wasn't. Remembering yet another time of wine and sorrow, the wine was supposed to drown the sorrow, to let me forget her in a dreamless sleep, but it had been a cheap red wine. I could no longer afford the vintage Cabernet Sauvignons of the past. Hangovers from the latter were soft throbs not the loud booming that came from cheap red wine.

BOOM…boom. BOOM…boom.

Clasping a pillow around my head, I tried to press out the throbbing and the memories but like flashes from a strobe light, the nightmare kept piercing my defenses.

It was always the same. I would be sitting quietly on a gray horse like the legendary warrior who had journeyed to the end of the earth searching for the passage to the sunset paradise and had found nothing but a lonely wasteland and a cold, impassable sea. I, too, had failed in my quest.

Like the warrior, I faced a crisis in which my mighty visions showed their other, destructive faces; inner turmoil, despair, and depression were now my companions.

BOOM…boom. BOOM…boom.

I looked down at the gray horse that had carried me to my rendezvous with futility. Across my saddle I held a lance that was stained with the blood of slain enemies. Expecting a hero's glory, I found only disillusionment. By the ancient law, the shadow of death now hung over me like a black vulture following the scent of death.

BOOM…boom. BOOM…boom.

The throbbing in my head continued to grow louder and louder until I flung away the pillow and staggered out onto the deck unmindful of the beautiful sun that had lifted out of the eastern mountains and now rode majestically over the waters of Puget Sound. Though my blurred and sensitive eyes lacked appreciation, the sun's warmth softened the ache in my heart.

Still, the throbbing continued, growing louder and louder. Then I stopped and listened. The pounding was no longer just in my head. It was resonating from the tall hemlocks that embraced my little cabin. It echoed from down the street.

The booming of the drums vibrating through the village cast a magical net over me and drew me away from my little blue cabin and down Angeline Avenue into a mass of people gathering around the large concrete pad in the center of town.

Drum teams had come from various Pacific Northwest tribes, some as far away as southeast Alaska and Arizona, to celebrate Chief Sealth Days.

I stood near the host team as its leader, a village elder, stiffened his back and struck his drum sharply with a leather-tipped beater, ignoring the hostile glares that came from the tribal members standing nearby. They were angry because he had included two women in his drum team, a traditional man's role, and white women at that.

BOOM…boom. BOOM…boom.

His team quickly blended their beats, raising the volume and resonance.

BOOM…boom. BOOM…boom.

When the leader's voice was raised in praise to the Great Spirit, his team joined in.

"Hi ya ya ya…Hi ya ya ya."

From the surrounding crowd, women and girls dressed in bright native costumes edged their way onto the pad with shuffling steps. They flowed into a serpentine circle, each dancing their personal dance, some lightly tapping with their toes, others shuffling, some stomping firmly, some bent over. One woman lifted her shawl-covered arms like eagle wings to swirl about the sky on tiptoes. In one corner of the pad, a solitary man dressed in white danced the dance of the whooping crane with jerking steps.

"Hi ya ya ya…Hi ya ya ya."

Around and around, they danced to the beat of the drums and the chanting of the singers unmindful of the blazing sun that beat down upon them bringing rivulets of sweat that dripped from their faces and soaking their costumes.

"Hi ya ya ya…Hi ya ya ya."

The native people of the Suquamish nation sang and danced and drummed in honor of their great chief, Chief Sealth.

Suquamish, a small village across the Puget Sound from Seattle, is Chief Sealth's home. Once Chief Sealth had a 900-foot longhouse on the beach at Agate Pass but, in 1870, the soldiers came and burned it down. A grave in the local Catholic cemetery contains what remains of the chief's physical body. Wood carvers have told Sealth's story on a totem pole that looms high over the Village Square. With the passing of the years, the story of Sealth's life has acquired the mythological proportions of a god-like being with great courage and strong medicine, of wisdom born of inner vision, of compassion and brotherhood.

It was a hot weekend. The yearly celebration held in Chief Sealth's honor was in full force. It wasn't long before the heat took its toll on the performers and spectators. In the shade of the barbecue pit, where salmon steaks sizzled over alder coals, two paramedics from the village fire station were treating an old man for heat exhaustion.

On the street the underarms of the tribal policemen's shirts were stained with sweat as they directed the steady stream of cars and motorcycles weaving their way through the village, passengers and drivers gawking and clicking their tongues at the throbbing drums and sensuous dancing.

Most of the good, white residents who lived in the expensive waterfront homes stayed away to avoid the noisy celebration. But a few were drawn downtown, partially out of respect for Chief Sealth's memory, but mostly by the numinous power of primitive wildness.

I recognized two women. The youngest was in her 60's and her mother nearly 90. I'd encountered them while walking along south Angeline Avenue. Beside them stood a woman with short brown hair, who struggled on a crippled left leg to fend off the jostling crowd.

In front of the Tides-Out Saloon, the minister of the Suquamish Bible Church, with his pretty young wife at his side, thumped an open Bible and, with a raised finger, exhorted the indifferent patrons as they flowed in and out of the saloon with the inevitability of the tides.

Scanning the milling crowd on the far side of the pad, my eyes met a pair of dark eyes fixed upon me causing me to stop to exchange a moment of acknowledgement before the woman with an outstretched red shawl swirled between us. But when she had passed the dark eyes were gone. A month would pass before I'd encounter those eyes again.

"Who are you?"

The shrill demanding voice welded me to the sand. I searched the shadows beyond the small beach fire but could see only a long cedar log with chips beside it and a blue plastic tarp rigged over it.

I stammered my answer, "Frankson."

"That's not your name," came the gruff reply. "That's your father's name. That's your family name. But who are you?"

I called out my first name, "Charlie."

Again the shrill voice demanded, "That's the name your mother gave you. But who are you?"

"I don't know who I am." I whimpered in frustration.

"Isn't it about time you found out?"

The old man, who rose from behind the huge log, had dark eyes above a bridge of white teeth set in a round moon-shaped face. His gray hair, once coal black, hung to his shoulders.

An old olive-colored army blanket hung over the old man's head and shoulders and due to his shortness, drug on the sand. The blanket was as ancient as his weathered face.

The old man then shuffled over to the fire and sat, motioning with a gnarled hand for me to sit on the opposite side of the fire.

There was something compelling about the old native that brought words to my mouth; and in no time, I poured out my story and why, in the fog of anesthetized emotions, I'd been walking the beach searching my soul for answers that wouldn't come when I came upon the beach fire by accident.

"There are no accidents," the old man replied softly. "I was told you'd come tonight."

"Who told you? How could they have known?"

"The Great Spirit knows everyone's path for he marked them all before the earth was formed."

The old man tossed more driftwood on the fire.

It was an especially beautiful fire. The salts and minerals absorbed from the sea added a rush of colors, hues of blues, and reds and greens to the yellow-white flames which, like ballet dancers, leaped and swirled on a pyretic stage.

I'd been like a piece of driftwood bobbing on the surface of life, which was sometimes calm and peaceful, sometimes whipped by violent storms—but always, always beyond my control. Now I was tossed up on a beach in a place called Suquamish. Why?

I hadn't spoken of it often; when pressed I had given the replies acceptable to my parents, my teachers and others in authority over me. But no matter how others viewed me, an inner voice kept whispering that I was more than that—I was more than a man, more than a husband, more than a father, more than a teacher, more than all the other vocations I'd tried. All my life I'd been searching for my true self like a knight searching for the Holy Grail. But I remained entangled in the brush and vines of other people's perceptions.

"Perhaps you can help me find my path?" I asked.

The old native's reply was slow in coming as he quietly tended the fire while considering his answer.

The evening had wrapped us in an aromatic mist of musty seaweed, rotting carcasses of indigenous fowl and fish and crustacean, all blended and salted by the sea air and served up as an exotic dish of shore smells which saltwater sailors stretched their nostrils to catch when returning home from a long sea voyage.

"Yes," the old man said. "It's time for you to walk your path. Listen to the voice of your inner guide. She won't lead you astray.

"In the outer world She-Who-Hates-Men brings chaos and unhappiness. Such a one will not help you to find your path. Only She-Who-Loves-Men can show you the way."

"How do I find such a woman?"

"You must die!…Oh, don't be alarmed! Death is part of life. It's the second important event in your life."

"What's the first?"

"The first what?"

"You said death was the second important event in my life. What's the most important event?"

"When you're born again. Do you see them?"

"Who?" I asked, looking around and behind.

"Can't you see them? Right now, around this fire, spirits are gathering.

"They're the poor souls who can't let go, who are addicted to this world like some people are to tobacco, or to strong drink. Learn to distinguish your true guides from such spirits. Do you see them now?"

Straining I began to see faces materializing in the darkness just beyond the soft swirling smoke. At least, I thought I did.

I was about to speak when the old man held up his hand for silence.

"Listen," the old man whispered, cocking his headfirst one way then another.

I strained to listen but heard only the soft lapping of the incoming tide and the muffled rumble of a car passing over the distant bridge.

"I don't hear anything," I replied softly.

"That's because you've adopted white man's ears. To hear the spirits you must believe in them. White men don't believe so they can't hear. But you're not a white man.

"You'll find your path when you solve this riddle: When is a man his mother's daughter? When is a woman her father's son?"

The old native struggled to his feet and with shuffling steps disappeared around the big cedar log. I jumped up to watch his going but when I looked he was gone leaving me to stare into the dying embers and to ponder the riddle—When is a man his mother's daughter? When is a woman her father's son?

CHAPTER TWO

My thoughts went back several months to that July Sunday morning when the sun rose brilliantly hot. A blanket of sticky, humid air hung over Port Madison Bay as Joe Old Coyote and his friend, Tom Proudfoot, pushed their rubber Zodiac boat away from the Suquamish shore and began paddling due east.

Joe watched Point Monroe slide along the Seattle shoreline to the southeast until it lined up with Alki Point.

"Drop it…now." He said softly.

Tom guided the unwinding yellow line as the anchor sank quickly to the bottom.

"What's the depth?" Joe asked.

"Twenty-four-and-a-half fathoms."

"Good. We should be near the canyon rim."

Joe looked at his diving watch. It was 11:35.

"Let's go. We've less than an hour before the tide turns."

Tom threw over two large, orange mesh bags. Joe slid a red flag with a white diagonal stripe into its base on the boat's prow.

With professional attention to details, the men adjusted their black wet suits, slipped on air bottles, pulled masks into place, tightened the straps of their diving lamps, checked each other's air regulators, then flipped backwards into the calm waters with the ease of black seals.

The red flag with a white diagonal stripe jerked abruptly then returned to its slow lazy waving in harmony with the soft swells.

The divers followed the bright yellow line into the cold darkness down to the gravel bottom unaware of a presence that was waiting in the watery silence, a creature whose ways have long been veiled in mystery and legend. Its bright red form had materialized out of the milky plankton-filled waters as it prowled the canyon rim. Its yellow-green eyes glared upward focused on the black intruders as they descended into its realm on strings of bubbles.

The creature's eyes followed the black intruders as they settled to the bottom and picked up their bright orange mesh bags.

The complexity and capacity of the creature's brain enabled it to survive more by intelligence than on instinct. So it waited, hidden among the bulbous seaweed and algae, waiting for its dinner to come within its grasp.

The creature had an arm spread of thirty feet and a weight of six hundred pounds. By any measure, it was a true colossus.

Its eight arms were fitted with suction cups to clamp onto its prey with unbreakable holding power.

Since ancient time, folklore and fable had cast the creature in the role of a blood-thirsty killer which waited in ambush for ships as large as Captain Nemo's *Nautilus* and unsuspecting divers such as the two who now approached following the searching beams of their twin headlights.

Joe Old Coyote pulled up so quickly that his partner bumped into his back as Joe then hand-signed the danger lurking just ahead. The initial reaction of fear, born in primeval times, eased quickly as Joe's intellect again took control. His survival instincts said move away. His intellect reassured him that, contrary to fables, the giant pacific octopus, which appeared in his light beam, was really a shy, retiring creature. Its gentle nature was contrary to its reputation as a man-eater. Joe knew that the octopus preferred to haunt the groves and canyons of its undersea domain seeking the crabs and scallops that comprised a large part of its diet.

The divers, suspended in the murky haze of the emerald waters, were silhouetted against the soft sunlight filtering down from the surface. They were momentarily hypnotized by the creature's eyes fixed upon them and by the rhythmic pumping of its mantle muscles as it breathed sea water in through a vent behind its head and out through a siphon beneath its neck.

Slowly Joe brought his hands together in front of his face mask like the way he prayed each Sunday morning at the St. John's Catholic Mission with his family. He bowed his head slowly in an act of honor and petition.

After a long period of suspended time, the octopus, with a powerful contraction of its mantel muscles, pushed water through the siphon with the force of a jet engine and slipped over the canyon rim into the darkness below, its trailing tentacles beckoning them to follow.

Joe tapped Tom's shoulder. They swam over the rim and disappeared into the blackness of the deep canyon formed by the scouring of retreating glaciers.

Like two spermatozoa entering their mother's womb, Joe and Tom descended into the deep marine canyon; instinctively following their probing beams.

As they descended beyond the tidal depths, they entered a world unmarred by the forces scouring Agate Pass, a silent world where seaweed flourished.

The hollow rasping of their steady, rhythmic breathing told them that they were in a hostile place. The trickling bubbles of expended air ascending to the silvery surface above reminded them from where they had come and to where they must soon return. They were intruders here, a violation by alien beings. Conscious of that violation, Joe and Tom slowly entered the mother's realm where swam the fishes in abundance, where the fishermen dropped their hooks and set their nets.

But Joe and Tom were not interested in fish on that dive. In their quest for a much larger quarry, they paused to watch a drama enter upon the stage of their light beams.

A giant nudibranch, which looked like a cobra dressed in white flowing robes, raised its full length up off the ocean bottom and arched its body to strike from above. But the anemone was too quick. Sensing the oncoming strike, it jerked back inside its tube trailing its tentacles like a retracting brush, which formed an impenetrable barrier against the nudibranch's jaws. In their homes, made of slime and sand, the anemones were safe from all but the most carefully mounted attacks. That anemone was safe…for now. But the contest between the two species would be replayed again, often yielding no more than a few stray tentacle tips.

So close was the relationship between the giant nudibranch and the anemones that the predators used the tubes of their prey as the anchor for their eggs. But few among the young nudibranches were likely to survive the perils that stalk their world.

No bottom predator was more to be feared than the giant sunflower seastar, the next to make its entrance onto the lighted stage. Growing to more than three-feet across, it was a monster among seastars. And the giant nudibranch was careful to avoid it. Fortunately for the nudibranch, when it found itself in a pinch, it could summon the power to swim. And swim it did in a majestic undersea ballet with graceful dips and turns and curls, which would have, been the envy of the finest ballerina.

The undersea world was a watery maze of islands and channels, a jigsaw puzzle of habitats. That diversity of habitats helped to account for the variety and abundance of life to be found in Port Madison Bay.

As Joe and Tom continued their descent, they passed great clusters of cloud sponges, among the most ancient of animals in the sea. At seven feet in diameter, these, too, were giants, living plankton filters, fixed for life to the rocks on which the colony had settled thousands of years ago. The sculptured chambers of the sponges made ideal condominiums for a host of small sea creatures, among them juvenile rockfish who found refuge in the many nooks and crannies. Like a chandelier in an old-time movie palace, a colony of sponges gave splendor to the cold dark waters.

And deeper still, fans of Georgian coral uncoiled their feathery pollops to fish in the rich green depths.

Joe reached to slow Tom's descent as he pointed his light at an outcropping of rocks, as they became spectators to yet another Dionysian tragedy in progress.

The giant octopus stealthily approached the egg nest guarded by a male lingcod. Despite its strength, the octopus was cautious in its choice of an opponent. With single-minded devotion, the male lingcod guarded the eggs. The lingcod eggs would make a fine meal for the octopus and it would seize any chance to steal them. But the father of the brood was more than ready to defend its own. Repeatedly, the lingcod darted in and snipped at the octopus's arms. A quick-change artist, the octopus paled to ashy white, a signal to its opponent to get ready for trouble. But the battle was one-sided. The lingcod was eager for the fight.

Snip…snip…snip, the lingcod darted in to bite off bits of the octopus.

Soon escape became the sole objective of the octopus. With a jet of ink, the octopus laid down a smoke screen to confuse the fish and cover its retreat. The precious eggs were safe…for now. But just in case, the ling-cod escorted the octopus away and delivered for good measure one final nip as a reminder not to come that way again. The wounds acquired in the brief battle would not trouble the octopus for long. In its lifetime, which with luck might stretch to up to five years, there would be many battles and many opportunities for prey.

Joe and Tom resumed their descent.

Late that afternoon a storm with dark clouds surged through Shelton gap and swept down Agate Pass like a massive beast. In fits of angry temper, it struck out with white-hot lightening and emitted rolling growls. The air snapped with ozone invigorating me as I walked along the beach. The incoming tide rushed passed me on its way to do battle with the oncoming wind.

A strange flotilla surged past as it was swept up Agate Pass by the incoming tide. The empty rubber boat, stern first, led the way. Like the colors of a cavalry charge, its red-and-white flag was extended against the rising wind of the approaching storm. Following close behind were six bright orange air bags bucking against the counter waves. Joe and Tom were struggling to guide something beneath the surface, something massive with a will of its own. Whatever it was, it was firmly in the grip of the powerful, surging tide.

"Hi there, Joe," I called, waving to catch Joe's attention.

"Hi," Joe answered while kicking as hard as he could to keep the contraption in mid-channel.

"What on earth are you doing?"

"We're moving this up to the Tribal Center."

I couldn't keep up with the surging tide. Soon the flotilla had passed, heading toward the bridge.

Joe fell to thinking about the first time he'd come upon his discovery. Two years previous he'd been exploring for lingcod along the sharp face of the canyon, going deeper with each succeeding sweep as if being drawn by some unseen force. Then it loomed in front of his light beam as he saw that the nose of the long, dark, encrusted thing was wedged under a rock ledge.

His first impression was that he had come upon a World War II torpedo, perhaps one that had gotten away from the Navy's nearby Keyport testing facility.

With that possibility in mind and knowing the danger that it might go off with the slightest jolt, he left the thing undisturbed.

Later, in his capacity as a scuba instructor, he appealed to the Navy to make sure the area was free of lost torpedoes before taking his students into the deep waters of Port Madison Bay.

Lt. Riggs, the young public information officer at Keyport Navel Station, sat behind his desk.

"Navy records do not list any torpedoes being lost in Port Madison Bay. The Navy takes pride in having recovered every torpedo it has test fired. Port Madison Bay is a long way from our test area. Besides, they're fired in the opposite direction, toward the Keyport reservation."

Reassured, Joe started to get up to leave.

Lt. Riggs raised his hand for him to remain seated.

"That's not to say there might not be a torpedo of Japanese origin. It's well known that Jap subs operated off the Washington coast in the early part of the war. It's doubtful that any succeeded in penetrating the inner sound. But there's always the possibility that one might have slipped in to survey the shipyard at Bremerton and the Boeing bomber plant just south of Elliott Bay."

Joe imagined how a Japanese sub might have fired a torpedo at a ship coming or going from the shipyard. Since no torpedo attacks had been recorded, it must have missed. Once its batteries had been spent, the torpedo settled into a downward angle, becoming wedged under the rock ledge. There it remained for nearly 50 years hidden beneath layers of barnacles and ocean slime.

Lt. Riggs added, "The chances are remote since the whole sound was surveyed in the years immediately following the war. But it wouldn't hurt for you to be alert. Tell your divers not to mess around with anything that might remotely look like a torpedo. Let us know and we'll send Navy divers to check it out."

In the two years since, Joe had been drawn to the thing repeatedly. In visions and dreams it rose up out of the deep and called to him. He dove repeatedly, usually alone, violating his own safety instructions and slowly examined it. Then he carefully scraped away the layers of barnacles exposing its inner nature.

"The tide's slackening," called Tom. Both men were near exhaustion. "We'll never reach the beach in time. We should beach it and wait for the next high tide."

Joe had been watching the approaching storm front. The thought of a summer storm tearing down Agate Pass kept him kicking. Such a storm could carry his discovery away, returning it to the depths from which they had labored so hard to retrieve it. His eyes glazed over with determination not to let that happen.

"Keep kicking," he shouted against the wind, which whipped white foam into his face.

"It's hopeless," called Tom. "Give it up, Joe. We'll try again tomorrow."

"It won't be here tomorrow," shouted Joe.

Rain began to beat into his face.

"I'm heading for shore," called Tom as he swam for safety.

Joe didn't respond. He continued to kick his exhausted legs with the determination of a crazed man. He fought against the slackening tide and the growing wind, which rose up to bar his passage. The wind caught the float bags and was shoving everything backwards, back down the Pass, as if the great mother had summoned the wind gods to recover the treasure stolen from her womb. Joe kicked and kicked until he kicked himself into delirium. It was too much for him. The winds and the tides had won. He collapsed in defeat as the flotilla was swept backward down the Pass.

I wiped the rain from my unbelieving eyes as the Pass came alive with black-and-white backs, as a pod of Orcas breached and dove in irregular harmony on their way up the Pass.

I couldn't recall ever reading about Orcas coming through Agate Pass before. Why now? Perhaps they were chasing a school of salmon. But for some reason I felt they were there for another purpose.

Looking up the Pass, I saw Joe's exhausted body draped over something floating just beneath the surface of the raging water. Then a marvelous thing happened, something told in ancient legends but not believed nor expected to recur in modern enlightened times.

Later Joe would tell his wife and two sons how a small pod of Orcas appeared out of the storm to surround the thing with its floats and pushed it through the water with the power of tugboats.

"The waters rolled away in foaming white wakes," Joe exclaimed.

When the Orcas reached the beach in front of the Tribal Center, they deposited Joe's treasure on the sand, which locked it firm against the receding tide.

Above the roaring storm Joe's exhausted mind heard the squeaks and shrills of good-bye as the Orcas pulled away. Joe waved.

"Good-bye and thank you, my ancestors."

As his weary eyes watched the pod breaching and leaping its way back through the Pass, faces of ancient chiefs and warriors appeared in their markings. Joe knew that his ancestors' spirits lived in the Orcas. Soon the pod disappeared into the gathering darkness of Puget Sound and an echo floated up the Pass, "You're welcome, my son."

"Somehow they're involved in what's going on," said Joe.

"What is going on?" Asked Sue, his wife, who stood beside her husband looking at the huge barnacle-encrusted deadhead lying on the sand like a beached whale.

Later that evening, with his family gathered around the hulk, Joe explained that in the mid-1800 nearby Port Madison had been a vast lumber center. Northbound sailing ships carried ballast bricks, which were used to build the cities of Port Townsend and Victoria. They returned with lumber for the emerging cities along San Francisco Bay.

Port Madison was a large and prosperous lumber and shipbuilding city when Seattle was still the little whorehouse of Puget Sound.

Logs from surrounding cedar and hemlock forests were gathered into holding ponds in nearby Miller Bay prior to being floated across to the mill. Some of those containment booms transported as many as two hundred logs, each five feet or more in diameter and a hundred feet in length.

Occasionally, a log would lose its buoyancy, become water logged, and sink beneath the surface. Some would float around the sound just a few feet below the surface. The mosquito fleet of ferries and tugs, in spite of sharp lookouts, were constantly hitting those deadheads. In time, the deadheads would absorb enough water to sink to the bottom.

After scraping away the barnacles, Joe realized that he had come upon just such a cedar deadhead. The bottom of Puget Sound was covered with deadheads. They were part of the marine landscape viewed by every scuba diver and became collectors of fishermen's lures.

But Joe's deadhead was something special. It was a log with numinous power, which wouldn't let itself, be ignored. It had haunted Joe's dreams and disturbed his thoughts. Always the dreams were the same. He saw it come free from its murky grave and rise slowly through the swirling waters until it broke the surface. It would remain on the surface for a few moments as if it was waiting for him. Then it would descend again to its place beneath the rocky ledge. Its spirit was calling him. He knew that he had to bring that log to the surface.

"What are you going to do with it?" Sue asked, shaking off the cold shiver that surged through her body as she surveyed the dark hulk covered with dripping seaweed. It reminded her of an evil sea monster. She was convinced that no good would come from it.

"I don't know," Joe replied.

"Why don't you ask the elders?" Sue suggested.

CHAPTER THREE

Late the next day Joe and his friend Tom returned to the beach lugging bundles of long willow poles. They selected a level spot on the beach above the high-tide line. Working silently they reverently preparing their sacred place.

Tom began to scoop out a shallow oblong pit while Joe circled the pit by shoving poles deep into the sand. Working together, they bent and tied the poles to make a frame over which they spread a blue plastic tarp. The sweat lodge was complete.

The chainsaw screamed as Joe began cutting firewood from the drift logs nearby. Soon an enormous pile of split wood appeared on the beach beside the fire that Tom had started.

Beside the fire another pile grew. There were rocks the size of cantaloupes that Tom and Joe carried from the brush where they had been hidden following previous use.

Over the next six hours repeated firings created a large bed of white-hot coals. Tom began to place the rocks on the perimeter of the coals while Joe rolled an empty oil drum to the opening of the sweat lodge. Stringing a garden hose from a faucet at the Tribal Center, Joe filled the barrel with fresh water.

All the activity was done quietly and reverently following the sacred way of the Suquamish people. Only after the preparations were completed and the two men sat tending the fire did they speak in lowered voices.

"Do you think they'll come?" Asked Tom.

"Yes," answered Joe.

But Joe's confidence began to waver as the dark shadows crept down the beach. The darkness deepened into night and still they sat alone tending the fire that heated the round stones until they were white hot.

Finally Joe said, "It's time to begin."

He undressed and was about to crawl under the tarp when I appeared. "I'm glad you came," said Joe. "Come, join me."

I'd met Joe Old Coyote shortly after my arrival in Suquamish. Native legends fascinated me so, when I saw a notice on the post office bulletin board that the public was invited to a small pow wow at the Tribal Center featuring the tribe's storyteller, Joe Old Coyote, I jumped at the chance. After the pow wow, I sought him out and quickly found a friend. Joe was quick to introduce me to the customs and stories of the Suquamish Tribe. When it came time for Joe to hold his sweat lodge ceremony, he was kind enough to invite me.

When Joe turned and crawled into the dark chamber, Tom scooped up a hot rock with a cradle made from the yoke of a green sapling, carried it inside the lodge, and placed it in the inner pit. Tom continued to add hot rocks until the pit was full. I undressed and crawled into the hot and stuffy lodge.

Joe took a dipper from the water bucket that sat just inside the entrance flap and slowly poured fresh water over the white-hot rocks. The water sizzled and bounced on the rocks before exploding into suffocating clouds of hot steam. Joe sat back, cross-legged, and began to softly chant the ancient songs of his people. I adjusted my legs to the same position but remained silent.

Tom Proudfoot, as the sacred fire keeper, tended the fire with wood and stones, periodically adding hot stones to the growing pile inside the lodge and retrieving the cooled stones. On request, he refilled the water bucket from the barrel, all the while keeping watchful guard against any who would disrupt the sacred ceremony.

As the hours passed, others began to appear silently out of the darkness and disrobed. Before entering the sweat lodge, they sprinkled pinches of tobacco into the fire as a gift to Grandfather. In all, there were three men and three women, some old; others in mid years; all joined the sacred ceremony with reverence and respect.

As each took their place inside the five-foot-high lodge, Tom would drop another hot rock into the pit then closed the flap so that no light or air leaked in.

Joe continued to pour water on the rocks, increasing the smothering heat and steam. We stayed inside the lodge, that was much more sweltering than any steam bath. Though we were cloaked in sweat and gasping for cool, clean air, the ceremony, which could last up to 10 hours, had just begun.

Some sat cross-legged on the sand; others leaned on their hands and knees with their faces almost touching the ground. The incandescent glow of the rocks and the sparks of sprinkled cedar were the only interruption in the blackness. A pungent smell of smoke and sweat clung to our bodies and stung our eyes.

For the next few hours we sweated, prayed, sang, yelped, moaned, shook rattles and banged on drums to purge our personal demons.

As the temperature continued to rise and the sweat poured off my body, I began to gasp for air. I became light-headed and wondered when the flap would open again. The muffled voices, sounds and thoughts of the circle, which were my only foothold to consciousness, began to fade into the steam clouds.

In the distance I heard the call of a raven, its caw caw caw echoed off the high canyon walls of concrete, steel and glass. At first the street was empty but gradually, as I adjusted my eyes to approaching night, the street began to come alive with dark, dirty men, women and children. I stood at a street corner, suitcase in hand, looking up and down the street.

Walking up the street, I saw a crudely painted sign, illuminated by cheap floodlights, MOVIES 25 CENTS, and below in smaller letters, Adults Only, and below that, a row of large X's. In spite of the many porn shops along the street, I saw no one entering or leaving.

The street began to come alive with buses and cars, their engines roaring, spewing exhaust. Ahead I heard voices of people milling about.

The people were from the bottom of life's barrel. Their dirty clothes reeked of urine, vomit, and body odors. Their eyes were blurred with alcohol and drugs. Many were native Americans. Most were men in their 20's and 30's, a few appeared much older. Some women were sleek, young and pretty, but most were fitting counterparts to the men.

I struggled to hold back a surge of revulsion. Looking at that human vermin, I tried to see the Christ presence in each face. That was the mental exercise I'd taught in my self-help seminars.

"Physician heal thyself," a voice called out.

Again I strained to see if I could detect anything faintly resembling Christ in the face of those pitiful, desperate and dangerous creatures. The pearl of a divinely given soul had been wasted among those swine and had been trampled under their hooves. Trying as hard as I could, I could not see Christ in those twisted, pox-marked, grimy faces.

"Hey, Mister, I'll do anything you want for a couple dollars. How about it? Do you want to go?"

She had appeared out of nowhere, sticking her thin, peaked face into mine, blasting away with a breath sour with wine. She wore a black wool overcoat, which hung loosely from her thin shoulders. She blocked my way while awaiting my answer; her blood shot eyes pleaded for acceptance. I stepped around her feeling dirty just being near her.

"No!" I said, with a shake of disgust.

It was difficult to say no to the cute, smiling girl who was next to appear. I guessed that she was about fifteen though dressed much older with bright red lipstick, dark eye liner, wearing an equally bright red cotton dress which hung loosely from her slender hips while her tightly fitting bodice displayed her finest budding asset.

"Hi!" She said in a soft seductive voice as she stepped from the side of the building.

"Do you want to go?" She purred.

"No…Thank you, anyway."

A flint-like hardness quickly replaced her friendly, seductive smile as she turned on her heel to resume her hunt.

I turned into the lobby of a run-down hotel and took a room for the night. I realized my mistake as I stepped through the open elevator doors when a big Black Hand reached between the elevator doors and tripped the safety bars, reopening the doors. Wedging his huge body into the small elevator, a big black man gave me a smile, which sent shivers up my back. I felt my body tightened with fear as my nostrils sucked up a mixture of musk cologne and the sweet marijuana smoke. I returned a quick smile of acknowledgment to the tall, muscular man in his early 30s whose white teeth and eye balls glowed not two feet away in the dim light of the elevator.

For the first time in my life, I experienced the fear, a constant companion of women, the fear of being trapped in an elevator and at the mercy of a strange, potentially overpowering man. My stomach twisted with cramps.

I remembered how very confident I'd been when I left the bus station. My steps had a bounce to them. I'd felt fine even as I entered that elevator. But suddenly my legs had become compressed springs, twisted tight by the pumping adrenaline, ready to let loose at the first move by the black man.

"Where're you from?" The black man asked.

He appeared friendly enough perhaps too friendly.

"Anchorage," I replied.

"Where's that?" He asked.

"In Alaska."

"Wow, man, that's way up north ain't it?"

"Yes, it is."

The black man caught my eyes dropping to the center of his chest where "Hang Loose, Baby" was boldly lettered on a sleeveless gray sweatshirt. I recognized the Hawaiian greeting of extended thumb and pinky over curled inner fingers. But, on second glance, I saw it was the view of a woman on her back, legs spread, exposing her privates. I quickly looked away, but not quick enough. The black man had caught my stare and smiled knowingly.

My hands felt cold and clammy as I tightened my grip on my gray suitcase. Edging a step closer to the control panel, I located the emergency button out of the corner of my eyes. I wondered if anyone in that skidrow hotel would respond in time. Even the desk clerk hid behind barred windows, his eyes flitting to the entrance door monitoring the comings and goings by remote control door locks. The best I could hope for would be that the desk clerk would call the police, that is, if the emergency button actually worked. But even if it did, the police would arrive too late, long after the black man had finished with me.

"What room did they give you?" The black man asked.

Was the black man edging a bit closer to the door? Was he getting ready to block my escape?

"It's 401, I blurted out, giving the wrong floor number.

"Oh, that's a great room. It's right next to mine. I'll show you the way."

"Thanks," I mumbled as my mind raced for a way to escape.

My heart stopped with a thud as the doors opened on the fourth floor.

"After you," the black man said politely with a wave of his arm.

Stepping out into the hall I fumbled for my key.

"Oh, I made a mistake. I'm on another floor," I said, quickly stepping back into the elevator just ahead of the closing doors.

Between the closing doors, I could see the black man standing in the hall smiling broadly. I realized that he would watch the floor indicator and run up the stairs, where he would take a position in the hall ready to jump me.

The jerk of the elevator as it stopped abruptly pulled me back to my immediate problem, finding Room 501. The hall lights were out. The desk clerk had told me to turn to the right and go down the hall to the last door. If I had any sense at all, I would've turned heel right then. But the elevator was gone. I couldn't go down the stairs for fear of meeting the black man coming up. That meant I had to try for my room. It was something like a B horror movie. My muscles tensed as I passed each door. At any moment I expected a door to suddenly bust open and a hand reach out for me. I walked softly, listening for the slightest sound.

My imagination ran wild. I'd read that men were raped just as often as women. My God, what a thought! I'd considered being robbed, even getting mugged, but raped? That was a woman's fear. Still, my friends always said I crossed my legs like a woman. Perhaps some fagot mistook one of my mannerisms. Do I walk like a queen? Did that black man mistake my interest in his sweatshirt? The humiliating rape scene in the movie *Deliverance* flashed vividly to mind. Would I submit as easily? And then, there were the stories of brutal gang rapes in prison.

My hands shook as I slipped the lock and quickly closed the door behind me, half expecting the black man to come crashing in after me.

Drawing a deep breath, the full impact of my dirty, musty room hit me. So this was their best. Austere wasn't adequate to describe its barrenness.

The best and completely out of place, thing in that room was the fresh, real, yellow rose, placed artfully in a water glass braced by white baby's breath and green leaves. Its fragrance helped to offset the stink of the dirty socks left in the dresser drawer, a gift from the previous guest. Through the white-curtained windows street noise blasted up a mixture of buses, cars, shouts and screams.

Primeval fear gripped me as I dropped on the bed. My racing imagination transformed every creak and groan of that sad, old building into robbers, thieves, muggers and rapists looking for ways to break into my room.

As I lay upon my bed, lumpy pillow crunched under my head, alternating waves of chill and sweat rolling over my body, sweat beads forming on my face, sheets cold and clammy, the sounds of street and alley amplified, I drifted in and out of fitful sleep.

Suddenly my body jerked with the realization that something was wrong. Looking about the room, that was softly illuminated by the streetlights, I saw that everything was gone, my suitcase, even the color TV that didn't work. Stumbling around the room, I could see how the thief had entered. There was a flat roof outside the opened bathroom window.

Looking out the window, I saw someone wearing a filthy, dark overcoat running toward me over the roof.

"What a rip-off! This camera don't have a lens."

"That's not my camera," I replied. "Besides that's a Polaroid. It has a built-in lens."

I grabbed the overcoat and pulled my thief through the window and into the bathtub. As we struggled, I pulled off the thief's heavy coat.

We rolled onto the floor and across the room. I threw my thief on the bed. I was amazed by his lack of physical strength. He was small but wiry. Pinning my thief's arms, I saw twin bulges on my thief's chest. Tearing open the shirt, two breasts flopped out. I pulled back.

"Go ahead and fuck me if that's what you want," she snarled.

Her filth and smell nauseated me.

"Why don't you take a bath?" I replied.

Obediently and silently, she drew the bathwater, took off her stinking rags, and slipped into the tub. She appeared to be in her late 30's or early 40's but it was hard to tell. Her hard life had aged her beyond her years.

"My God, I'd forgotten what a bath was," she sang out from the soapsuds, luxuriating in its warmth.

"Where's my suitcase? I want it back. There's nothing in it but personal things."

"Oh, it's sitting just outside the window."

As she got up, I saw her body for the first time, free from grime and grease. There were huge bruises, all black and blue, on her back and buttocks. Her breasts were covered with small round scars, some red and festering.

"You've really been marked up."

"Every way you can imagine, I guess."

"Who did this to you?"

"Men."

Seeing the confused shock on my face, she added:

"What the hell, they pay good."

"You mean you agree to such abuse?"

"Sure. As long as I get paid in advance."

"What's the small round marks?"

"Oh, I've this John who gets his rocks off by playing a little game. First he strips me, then he gags me and ties my wrists and hangs me from the ceiling with my feet just off the floor. As I hang there, slowly turning, he lights a cigarette and sits for a long time in the dark just smoking. It's weird seeing that red glow turn bright and then go dim. When he's ready, he snuffs the cigarette into my body."

"How much do you get paid?"

"Twenty dollars. He usually buys a pack worth."

"A dollar a cigarette?"

"Yeah."

"How can you stand it?"

"Women can endure a lot more pain than men. We just mentally go tripping off to other places while our bodies are being used. How do you think we endure men poking into us?"

"But, why? Why do you live like this?"

"I like it," she said. "Besides, I've many friends around here."

"You like being beaten up and tortured by some psycho? Don't you realize the next time he might snuff you?"

"Maybe…But that'll be all right too."

"Is that all the value you put on your life?"

"Hey, man, fuck me or let me go, but don't preach at me."

In the dimness of the early morning hours, reality and fantasy were mixed; my mind confused the two. How long had she been gone? Perhaps she was never there. I tried to focus on the face of Christ. That was what I'd told my daughter when the night people visited her, 'Visualize the face of Christ and repeat the Lord's prayer.' Now it was my turn.

"Our Father which art in heaven…"

"Get away from me, you bastard," a woman screamed from an alley below.

"…Hallowed be thy name"

She continued to scream as I heard the dull sickening sound of fists striking flesh.

"…Thy kingdom come, thy will be done"

"Help me! Oh, God, won't somebody, please help me?"

Her pleading screams echoed through the canyons below.

"…On earth as it is in heaven."

Who was she?

"…Give us this day our daily bread."

Was she high on drugs or drunk or just crazy?

"…Forgive us our debts."

Was a customer out of control?

"…As we forgive our debtors."

Had she been on her way home when some beast dragged her into that alley?

"…Lead us not into temptation."

No one came to her aid.

"…But deliver us from evil."

I expected to hear the sound of police sirens.

"…For Thine is the Kingdom."

Still she screamed.

"Please, stop…Don't do that! Oh, God, won't someone help me?"

"…And the power."

But no one came to her aid.

"…And the glory."

And neither did I.

"…Forever and ever."

But I was a stranger there, just passing through.

"…Amen."

Her soft distant sobbing floated up from the silent alley. Street noise and creaking buildings faded as I slipped away into deep peaceful sleep.

CHAPTER FOUR

The dark-skinned men and women ignored my distress. They continued to pray and sing, purging their personal demons with loud, uninhibited cries.

Tom stood by the doorflap listening for the call from within "More rocks,"…"More water."

When Tom opened the flap, light from his fire turned the dark interior into an eerie gray mist. A slight wisp of fresh air seeped in before the flap was dropped and the dark humid world returned.

As the participants finished their individual rituals, prayers and songs, they crawled out of the lodge in a clockwise motion, steam rising from their naked bodies in the cool night air.

I stood on the beach, oblivious to the sharp wind whipping off the mountains. I watched steaming bodies being doused with cold water from the barrel while others plunged into the frigid waters of the pass. Steeling my nerves, I ran down the beach and flung myself into the icy waters to wash away the accumulation of sweat and sand. I emerged invigorated and refreshed.

A short, fat woman, whose enormous breasts hung down over her full belly, slipped up beside me as I came out of the water. She reminded me of the rotund little fertility goddesses found in early stone-age graves. She spoke as we dried ourselves by the fire.

"Visions can be very confusing, can't they?"

"Yes, they can."

"I'm Morning Star. Your vision was depressing."

"What do you mean? Did you see my vision?"

"I was the raven you heard. We all participated in your vision. The grandfather asked us to help you."

"What grandfather?"

I began to shake, not from the cold air, but from the realization I was involved in something outside my conscious control. My hands shook as I started to dress. Morning Star placed her hand gently on my arm.

"The ceremony isn't finished. We're only taking a short break.

"Your vision showed you that the women whom you've drawn into your life have been reflections of your inner woman. Your inner woman was the woman you met in that hotel room. Before you can have a healthy relationship with outer women, you must have a healthy inner woman."

"But, how can I heal a vision?"

"You can't. You can only help the vision woman to heal herself. You can do that by remembering what she reveals of herself in your dreams and visions. Your inner woman wears seven veils; six remain."

Morning Star smiled when she caught me looking at her breasts.

"Being naked is neither a barrier nor an excitement when you accept yourself as the Great Spirit created you, as a sexual being, male or female. Nudity is natural and good. It's bad minds that see nudity as evil.

"Before we resumed our ceremonies, things were really bad around here. You could cut the tension and the bad feelings with a knife. It took a while to work things out.

"It's true that many of us have spent most of our lives in prison. Many are addicted to drugs and alcohol. The sweat lodge ceremony helps us to survive and defeat the demons that would destroy us.

"Peace of mind and patience has come to me through sessions in the sweat lodge. Before, what I did I did to, and for, myself. Now, I do things for others and stop centering everything on myself.

"I used to mark off the days and hours until my next drunk, my next man.

"I've always been a square peg in a round hole, but now I've a direction, a goal. Oh, sure, sometimes I'm scared, but I know I can make it now. Our ceremonies are something I can hang on to."

A middle-aged man with a large extended beer-belly joined the conversation. His dark eyes sparkled with an Inner Light. His smile was big and wide and accepting as his name, Bigjim.

"These rites are necessary to maintain pride among our people," Bigjim said. "In my home, when I was growing up, we weren't allowed to speak our native language. When I fought in wars overseas, I got away from the ways and lost my traditions and self-respect. Some white Christians say our ways are barbaric and pagan, but it's the same. It's religion. And we have to keep up the traditions. It's all we have left."

Amana, a slim woman whose eyes danced with the light from the fire, spoke up, "The sweat lodge ceremony is meant to be conducted on nature's time, orchestrated by what feels right. White people are held prisoners to schedules that must be adhered to."

When our bodies had cooled, we re-entered the sweat lodge. Tom Proudfoot replenished the pile of hot stones inside.

Sweat poured from my face as the steam clouds swirled around my head. Soon I returned to the world of dreams and visions.

This time I was a young boy playing in a hayloft with my best friend, bounding about the fresh-cut alfalfa. The sweet smell engulfed me. For a seven-year-old boy, it was a time of youthful innocence, a time of cowboys and Indians, a time when consciences were free from the adult baggage of guilt and remorse.

My friend's older sister stuck her head up through the trap door.

"What ya doin'?" She asked.

She wore a flour-sack dress.

"Just playin'," I answered casually between leaps. She was just a girl, an older girl, so I didn't think of her joining in our fun. But recently she'd appeared whenever we were playing in our secret places.

She climbed up on the ledge and jumped. When her dress flew up over her head, I saw that she wasn't wearing underpants. Girls were a mystery for me. I'd heard that they didn't have a thing like boys.

"I've got a great idea," she said. "Let's play house. I'll be the mommy and you be the daddy."

"What can I be?" My friend asked.

"You can be our son and go outside and play for awhile. Don't come in 'til I call you," she answered while leveling off a place in the hay.

My friend climbed down out of the hayloft.

I stood wondering what kind of game was playing house. Then she dropped to her knees in front of me and undid my belt. Unbuttoning my pants, she pulled down my underpants.

"My, you've got an itty-bitty thing, haven't you? Let's see if I can get it to grow."

The pleasure confused me. It was strange and new. My confusion grew when she pulled me down onto the hay.

"Now you do something to me," she instructed as she laid back and pulled up her dress.

"What should I do?" I asked innocently.

"Don't you know anything? Here," she said, grasping my hand, "Put your finger there…."

"What the hell are you two doing up here?"

A large, bull like man leaped up through the trap door. In a flash he grabbed the girl by her hair and pulled her back through the trap door. I followed at a distance, confused by the shouting and screaming, as the bull-man pulled the young girl up the path to the house.

The bull-man turned and shouted at me.

"You go home and don't you come back until you clean up your dirty mind."

I didn't know what a dirty mind was. I hadn't done anything. She did everything.

The girl's screams drew me to the bedroom window. Peeking inside, I watched the bull-man tear off the girl's dress and tie her wrists to the bedpost. Drawing his belt, the bull-man began to strike her naked buttocks. When she twisted in pain, he lashed her budding chest.

The whack of leather on flesh froze me in place. Repeatedly, the bull-man swung with all his fury raising long red welts on her body. Over the girl's screams, the bull-man shouted, "I'll teach you, you little slut. You want to know what it's like, I'll show you."

The bull-man dropped his pants to expose a huge erection. He untied her wrists and threw her on the bed. Leaping on her, he tore into her.

Then a strange thing happened, something that I've never understood not even when I became a man. The girl stopped screaming and kicking and threw her arms around her father's neck in a loving embrace. After a few violent thrusts, the bull-man stopped. Rolling over, he cradled her head on his hairy chest and lovingly stroked her long brown hair. On the girl's lips was a strange smile. Was it a smile of conquest?

I started for home, terrified by the violence and the bull-man's hugeness and confused by the resulting smile on the girl's face.

When I came around the corner of the house, I met the mother sitting in her rocking chair on the front porch, calmly shucking fresh-picked sweet peas.

"Your mother started her peas yet?" She asked in a casual and friendly voice.

"I think so," I answered.

"Best get home and help her, don't you think?"

"Yes, ma'am."

That was the day sex, violence, guilt and pleasure were added to my emotional caldron where they'd fester for many long years. The bull-man had wounded me as surely as if I'd been struck by his belt, leaving me to enter adulthood as a sexual and emotional cripple.

As my consciousness began to return to me in the sweat lodge I heard the little boy crying out in the fading distance, "But it wasn't my fault. She made me do it."

Another veil had fallen.

Back at the fire in front of the sweat lodge, we were assembled for another break. It was like the soft blowing of a wind over a placid pond masking the deeper bonding of spirits occurring beneath the surface.

Everything appeared to be spontaneous, without plan or schedule. Beyond the idea that a council was to be held, no one knew exactly when it would start. That could be soon, or it could be hours later. Whenever the spirit moved, they would begin. Meanwhile, everyone spoke, silently and reverently, sharing what was going on in their respective worlds.

Off at a discrete distance in the dark shadows in clumps of two and three, young men surrounded the meeting place. It was their responsibility to protect the sanctity of the ceremony.

Joe Old Coyote was a humble man, broad shouldered, in his mid-thirties, with an oval face framing dark black eyes, and a warm friendly smile. He sat cross-legged on a red blanket with a gray wool blanket over his shoulders, resting his arms in his lap and occasionally sipping coffee from an insulated mug. He wore his black hair straight and full to his shoulders and tied in a tight pigtail.

He spoke in a slow, even voice, occasionally clearing his throat of a minor catch, perhaps from nervousness at speaking in front of such a distinguished group of medicine people.

"My elders, I've invited you here to inquire of your wisdom. What should I carve on my totem pole? It's a sacred task and I seek your advice."

He looked around at the fire-illuminated faces.

"We've the good fortune to have with us one of our brothers who has just returned from Hawaii. He has studied with a keeper of Hawaii."

On Joe's left sat a tall man with a solid square body. Joe handed him the speaking stick. The man nodded his acceptance of the invitation to add his voice to council.

"My spirit guides have told me down through the years that all the forces of the earth are natural and whatever these forces do, that's what they're supposed to do. Man has to fit with nature. Nature is not going to fit with man. It's very important to know that.

"The creator forces in Hawaii are the great volcanoes. These great volcanoes were the ones who made the islands. The islands wouldn't be there if it weren't for the volcanoes. And these are part of the creative forces, the natural forces.

"According to the volcanoes, the time is at hand for major changes to come upon the earth. The forces which were part of the original creation are being called back into action at this time.

"Ancient prophecies of the Hawaiians have spoken of this time. That's why I've been walking and waiting quietly upon the earth.

"Until now, I haven't spoken to anyone about these prophecies except native Hawaiian people. That's because the spirit told me that this was what I was supposed to do.

"I've seen all the powerful changes that are coming upon the earth. I've seen them in dreams, in visions, and I've been told that the time has come for me to start reaching out to all human beings. And this is my work. It may not be the work of other medicine people, some of you maybe. Some others may be doing this now, and that's good. I hope you are walking the sacred path in the real manner because that's necessary. I hope you understand the whole of things and not take one little piece and run with it. It's time to speak up. I walk the earth in a sacred way.

"Our brother has asked, What story should his totem tell? He must walk the sacred path and listen to what the spirit tells him. Perhaps the spirit will tell him that since the little sister, known as St. Helen's, has spoken, the big brother, Mt. Rainier, will soon answer. And when the big brother speaks, all the land to the west will be swept into the sea.

Scientists speak of great earthquakes of 7 or 8, even 9 on the Richter scale. But the spirit says the coming earthquakes will be 10 and 11. That is all I have to say at this time."

I asked for the speaking stick.

"I understand what it means to walk in a sacred way. I walked across the North Country for twelve years searching for my sacred stones. These are the stones that I use in my medicine wheel ceremony. Only when my spirit was ready did the correct stones speak to me. In search of my sacred stones, I walked across the frozen Bering Sea into Siberia, across Siberia into northern China, retracing the ancient migratory paths of our ancestors. These are the sacred stones through which our ancestors speak to me. They will be buried with my body upon my death."

CHAPTER FIVE

The third veil fell during the next sweat lodge session. It came about in this fashion.

I found myself in a raspberry patch. I was about five or six-years old and the lush ripe, red raspberries begged to be picked and popped into my mouth. Their delicious juices flowed down my throat and stirred my taste buds to cry, "more, more."

The pleading grew louder as I worked my way down the tall rows. When I reached the end, I discovered the pleadings were coming from inside the abandoned body of a 1927 4-door Dodge sedan. It had been cut off its chassis when my father made a homemade tractor called a bug.

A bug was a poor farmer's tractor made by welding the front portion of a car chassis, including engine, transmission, and wheel assembly, to a truck rear end. The bug's versatile gear range enabled it to pull wagons at highway speed or plow at a slow powerful pace.

The body would be set aside to enjoy a short life as a children's playhouse before wind and weather reduced it to a rusty hulk.

Our Dodge body had rolled curtains, which could be pulled down to make a secret hideout for the mysterious imagination games children, play. The soft, velvet cushions and seats were great for bouncing on. Occasionally a quiet nap could be had upon them.

I quietly edged my way up to the car body. I could hear bouncing and movement inside. I tried to peak in but the curtains were drawn tight. Muffled giggles and movement continued. The kids inside were having fun and I wanted to join them. I tried the door handle but it was locked.

"Who's out there?" I heard my older brother call.

"It's me," I answered.

"Go away and play somewhere else."

"What'cha doing in there?"

Then I heard whispering.

"Better let him come in and do it or he'll go and tell," whispered a girl. I recognized the voice of my aunt who was eight years older than me.

"Oh, all right," answered my brother as he opened the rear door and pulled me inside.

Quickly my pants and shorts were down. My aunt laid back, pulled up her dress, then spread her legs. The smooth canyon walls guided me into her rain forest, which rose up around me dwarfing me as I was pushed into its wetness. Her hands spread the dark brush revealing the opening of a cave.

In my fear, I imagined sharp needle teeth lining the cave walls and flowing back into the depths of the tunnel. The pulsing cave reminded me of a fish gasping for air.

I panicked when she took my little thing and pressed it into her gasping tunnel. I fought to break free, to escape its deadly teeth. I wiggled and squirmed until at last I was shoved out the door. My aunt's disgusted voice rang in my ears.

"He can't do anything. He's too tiny."

SunDog spoke at the next council fire. Adjusting his crossed legs to better cradle his large beer-belly, he took up a small drum while closing his eyes, softly began to tap its surface. The soft thump resonated around the fireside.

Thump…Thump…Thump he tapped, matching the beat of his heart, blending and harmonizing the vibrations within and without, ever mindful that drums were the great Father's gift to his people.

Thump…Thump…Thump…Thump.

The tuning process continued for several minutes then Sun Dog opened his eyes and cleared his throat.

"The end of the Myanian Nine Tells occurred in '92. We're now entering the next realm of the thirteen heavens and it's time for all people to prepare themselves to walk in a sacred manner upon the earth. This is the time when we'll become aware of what is to happen. And it'll be part of our work to make people aware.

"This is a very difficult task. It's difficult because there are people who divide life into two parts. There is one part that is separate from the creator and another part that is religious. How can this be? There is but one creator and there is but one life. We are the creator's children. We can't deny our heritage. This we know. This must be told on your totem."

Following a long period of silent meditation, Morning Star, the little fat lady, spoke.

"Sun Dog speaks the truth. All people are related. To realize that everything is alive and everything is connected is at the heart of our spirit. Black Elk, the medicine man of the Lakota people, has said, 'Peace comes within the hearts of men when they realize their relationship, their oneness, with the universe and all its powers, and that the center is really everywhere. It is within each of us.' Your Totem must tell this truth."

Tom Proudfoot added his voice to the council fire.

"It's important that we share the gifts of life. This is the way we keep the old ways alive. This means more than words. It means sharing with those in need, honoring life and working for peace and mutual understanding."

There was a nodding of heads.

Bill Eagle, the oldest member present, unwrapped the deerskin bundle he had brought to the council. He was the keeper of the sacred pipe. The long smoking pipe, decorated with small white and black feathers, was filled with tobacco and lit. After several long draws he passed the pipe, stem first, to his right. With the passing of the pipe, he spoke.

"Let the sacred pipe go before everyone as they follow their own path. There are many, many paths, as many paths as there are people, yet all paths lead back to the great Father. This is the Father's great love for all his children; that they return home. The great Father has placed a secret path within each person's heart.

"The importance of dreams and visions we all know. The dream world is the real world. Dreams reveal the secret wishes of the heart. Our lives depend on the satisfaction of these secret heart wishes.

"There is a Mohawk prophecy, which says, 'In the beginning, our Creator gave all the races of mankind the same songs and the same drums to keep in touch with Him, to keep faith. But people kept forgetting. In the fullness of time, the spiritual traditions of all the peoples—they are the same—will be united again in a great gathering of their secret leaders. And they will gain power to remake the world. Something of this must be told on your Totem. That's all I have to say."

Joe thanked Bill Eagle for his words then invited me, a visitor from the Inupiat people of northern Alaska, to speak.

"I bring greetings from the Elders of Finger Point to our red brothers. Our white friends also should take hope from what I've been commissioned to bring. The Elders have instructed me to share our prophecies with all who will listen. The time is very, very short.

"Our ancient ones spoke of the time when the white man would bring a new religion to the Inupiat people. The white man would bring word of He-Who-Walks-Upon-The-Earth. The Inupiat people were to merge what was best of the ancient teachings with the best of the teachings brought by the white men. The coming of this new religion would proceed the great earth cleansing. This would enable those who listen and act to survive into the New World.

"Our elders speak of this generation as a people with great brains and small hearts, as a people who live by reason and will die without feeling what it is to be alive.

"According to our Elders, the time has passed when mankind can prevent the cleansing. The forces of cleansing have been unleashed. From deep within space, from the direction of Uranus, there is a burst of energy coming, which will soon impact upon earth.

"It will strike with such force that the earth will be knocked off its axis causing the poles to shift. The North Pole will be moved to what is now the central Mongolian desert, and the South Pole will be moved to what is now the southern tip of South America. The shift will occur in less than six-hours' time.

"There will be violent earthquakes of greater magnitudes than ever have been upon the earth. There will be volcanoes, tidal waves, rising and dropping of whole continents; storms with hurricane winds will swirl around the planet. The ice caps will melt raising the ocean levels by fifty feet or more before receding as the polar caps re-form around the new poles.

"There will be world-wide pollution as the atomic reactors are broken open releasing their radiation. Lethal chemicals will be spread across oceans and continents destroying all life that contacts them.

"One-third of mankind will die within the first hours following impact. One-third of mankind will be shocked into a catatonic state and will die unless rescued and brought into the healing centers, which are even now being prepared. The hope of survival will rest with the remaining third who will come through unharmed.

"The Elders of Finger Point say that those who wish to survive must prepare themselves while there is yet time. Such preparation will involve the cleansing of negative thoughts and then surrounding ourselves with the positive life forces of protection. One way that may be accomplished is through the Seventeen-Day Rite of Passage which I've come to teach all who will listen.

"The unseen forces are working great changes in the earth and its people today. Those who are quiet and unpretentious, the meek ones, will be the makers and the keepers of the coming age. It is they who will bring light and understanding to mankind. Do you hear that, white man? Indeed we are about to witness the fulfillment of the prophecy given by He-Who-Walks-Upon-The-Earth, 'Happy are the meek for they shall inherit the earth.'"

Joe asked, "Do your Elders know when this impact will take place?"

"Soon, very soon," I replied. "All who sit around this council fire will be present for the cleansing. But as to the exact day and hour, they haven't said. They did say the Astronomers would discover its coming a few hours before impact. That will be the warning for the survivors to enter their caves."

SunDog asked, "Should we all prepare caves?"

"As the Spirit directs."

"How long must we be prepared to remain in our caves?"

"Seven years."

"And those outside the caves, those who will be in a catatonic state, what will happen to them?"

I looked within for the answer but when none was given, I made a suggestion.

"My brothers and sisters, I don't know. But let us go into the sweat lodge. Perhaps it'll be shown to us."

The council agreed and was preparing to re-enter the sweat lodge when a white woman, wearing a dress of orange floral print and holding a red leather New Testament, suddenly appeared at the council fire. She had slipped so quietly along the shore shadows that the guards didn't detect her approach.

She shook the Bible at them and shouted, "In the name of the Lord Jesus, I implore you to give up these satanic rituals and save your souls from roasting in hell."

She closed her eyes, held the Testament in front of her eyes and called out, "Cover your nakedness and accept the way of salvation that God has prepared for all sinners such as you."

When silence greeted her pleadings, she peeked around her testament to see a circle of naked brown bodies with dark brown eyes locked upon her.

Illuminated by the light of the campfire, the manhood of the men were clearly visible to her. Self-consciously, she clutched the Testament to her chest and tried to avert her eyes but wherever her gaze fell, there was another sexual organ, each larger and more threatening.

The ancient serpent of her nightmares was stirring again, rising like a king cobra preparing to strike and sink its teeth into her flesh and fill her with its evil poison. Multiple serpent heads began to weave back and forth with tongues licking the air for her female scent. The larger the organs grew, the more her body trembled. She was losing control. Nothing was going the way she'd planned.

She felt something slip from her body. Looking down, her eyes widened in horror. Her dress had dropped to the ground leaving her naked and exposed to terrible, lusting brown eyes, probing eyes that searched every point and crevice of her body.

Terrifying screams uncontrollably emitted from her throat when she saw that her breasts and buttocks were covered with small, round, festering sores. Primeval fear poured out of her throat as she turned and ran naked into the darkness, down the beach, back to the safety of her waterfront home leaving her orange floral print dress in a crumpled heap on the sand beside the council fire.

Amazement consumed my confused mind when the council continued as if nothing had happened, taking no more notice of her abrupt appearance, and her even more hasty departure, than of a passing spirit.

"Don't be surprised," whispered Morning Star. "Native Americans have been harassed by white Christians since they first stepped on the eastern shores of this continent. We've survived by developing an ability to make them invisible."

Joe Old Coyote, as if having paused momentarily in mid- sentence, nodded to me in appreciation.

"I thank you for your counsel. I've taken into my heart all that you've spoken. Let us return to the lodge to meditate on these things. Also, remember the needs of our brother who visits with us."

Soon I was lifted inside a spiraling column of steam. The fourth vision began to form in the gray mist.

As a fat, young boy in his early teens, I stepped through the stream mists into a locker room. I was the last to leave the showers. The older boys, by pre-arranged signal, had left ahead of me. The older boys were always pulling tricks on me. When I saw them standing in a corner of the locker room looking at me I knew something was up.

"Hey, fatty, come here," demanded a tall boy, four years my senior, who was standing naked in the corner with other boys.

"NOOOO," I screamed at the top of my voice. Snapping my eyes open I saw the men and women in the lodge looking at me. Morning Star, who sat beside me, reached over to pat my shoulder in reassurance.

"Don't be afraid. This is the fourth veil," she said softly.

"No. I don't want to re-visit that time."

"You don't have to if you don't want to. But sooner or later, in this life or another, you must bring this experience to your conscious remembrance. If you don't, it will remain beneath the surface like a cancer, festering and distorting your present life. Let it come forth and thank the Father for the remembrance, and it'll be taken from you."

Joe Old Coyote's voice came to me through the steam clouds, "Don't be afraid. You'll not be alone."

I settled down and the vision resumed.

I turned to leave, but two strong boys slipped up behind me, grabbed me by the arms, and shoved me into the corner.

"How about giving me a blow job?" The leader asked with a smile as he waved his stiffening member.

"No way," I answered.

The two boys twisted my arms behind my back, bending me forward.

"Now don't you dare bite me! If you do, we'll break both of your arms."

Other boys began fondling my chest.

"He's got tits just like a girl."

They laughed as the leader pulled my mouth into position.

"Hey, he's got a nice rear end. Let me at it."

"Save some for the rest of us."

Jeers and laughter filled the locker-room.

When they were finished, I was let go. When I stood up, tears streamed down my cheeks to mingle with the white fluid oozing from my mouth with still more fluid dripping down the inside of my legs. I looked around and caught my brother's eyes in the back of the crowd. My eyes pleaded for help, but my brother turned and walked away.

I sobbed uncontrollably into my hands.

When I regained my composure, Joe asked, "Do you know why they did that to you? Was that why you were afraid that the black man in the elevator was going to rape you?"

"I suppose there is something about me that's feminine suggesting that I might be gay. Men have propositioned me many times. Once two men in an elevator fondled me but such propositions only repulsed me. To be raped is the ultimate male humiliation. Nothing is as humiliating as being transformed into a woman."

Morning Star placed a comforting arm around my shoulders.

I continued, "I've never understood why my brother didn't help me."

"That's his burden," Morning Star said softly. "What do you feel about that experience now after these years?"

"Anger…Anger like a woman would feel if that happened to her."

"And because of that experience, you know what a woman feels when she's raped and abused…You learned a very great lesson, a lesson few men can understand.

"But there is another lesson from that experience you must take to heart. You must learn that you don't have to let abuse destroy your life. If you dwell on the past, it'll destroy your present; but by ignoring your past, it'll repeat in the future. You had to bring it to your conscious remembrance so that you can thank the Father for the experience and forgive those who raped you. When you do that, the healing begins for the inner woman."

The fourth veil had fallen with the fifth close behind. They came in thunderous waves like surges of a hurricane.

When the calm eye of the storm arrived, Joe dipped and poured. The temperature rose above 120 degrees Fahrenheit and the humidity reached saturation point. Breathing became labored as the oxygen was replaced with carbon dioxide.

I began to sway from side to side then in a circular pattern, clockwise. My head began to open at the top. I felt my mind float up and away, away from the present time and the present place, up and away it floated, up into the clouds, up into the jet stream. I felt myself being swept away to another time and place. Whether in the past or in the future, I did not yet know.

"What do you see?" Asked Morning Star.

"I'm holding a ring in my hand, a plain band of white gold with a small solitary diamond."

"What kind of ring is it?"

"It's an engagement ring."

"Do you recognize it?"

"Yes."

"Tell me about it."

"During my first year in college, I met a girl. She was not pretty. Her elongated face was covered with freckles and she had straight red hair, which she cut close just below her ears. She was a junior and played the pipes in the college bagpipe band. When she marched, the kilts accentuated her bowed legs. As I said, she was not very pretty.

"Who really can explain why we are drawn to certain people? Surely, I wasn't drawn to her by her physical beauty, but drawn I was. Soon we were deeply in love…or so I thought.

"I was having trouble passing my German class. We would sit by the hour in the student lounge as she drilled me with flash cards. With her help, I passed but just barely.

"In time, we talked of getting married someday after I graduated. During the following spring and early summer, I set aside enough money from my part-time yard work to buy a small engagement ring which I planned to give to her on the Fourth of July."

"Did you give it to her?"

"No."

"Why not?"

"When I drove up to Duluth to give it to her, she told me she'd changed her mind and didn't want to marry me."

"Did she give you a reason?"

"I don't remember."

"Is it you don't remember, or that you don't want to remember?"

"Why ask me? You know the answer."

"Yes, I do. But you must bring it back to your remembrance."

I gently stroked the small diamond on the ring. After a few strokes, the ring began to grow. The more I stroked, the larger the ring became. As the ring grew, the smaller I became until I began to slip into a huge hole. I saved myself by grasping the diamond while my body dangled in empty space.

"And because of the small size of your penis she broke off the engagement?"

"Oh, she gave other reasons but we both knew that was the real reason."

"Hi Yaaaa," screamed the wild warrior as he threw back the flap and leaped inside. Crouching, with lance point first, he continued to scream and shuffle while thrusting his lance before him until he came to me. The wild warrior, eagle feathers tied in his flaring hair, stripes of black, red, and white paint streaking his face, chest and arms, anklets of White Sea shells rattling with each lunge. When he jabbed his lance at me, I threw up my arms for protection and cringed in terror against the back of the lodge. I drew myself into the fetal position and cried out like a baby babbling childish gibberish. The wild warrior stood over me, his dark threatening body silhouetted against the blazing campfire, until slowly he drew back his lance and with a quick, powerful thrust drove it deep into my heart.

CHAPTER SIX

Clara Goodwill whispered into her phone as she peeked through her lace curtains, "Do ya see 'm?"

"Yes, he's been there ever since the police and ambulances left," Honey replied.

Honey Linquist lived two houses away and was Clara's best friend and neighbor for the past twenty-five years.

An Indian was standing in the street in front of the house next door. His head was bowed.

He was wearing faded blue jeans and dirty Nikes, a red flannel shirt with the sleeves torn off at the shoulders and a deerskin vest patterned with yellow and blue beads. Around his neck hung two turquoise necklaces. His long black hair was pulled back and tied into a ponytail. Two white feathers with black tips dangled from a red bandanna tied around his forehead. A green serpent was painted on his cheeks and arms.

His arms hung limply at his sides. In his right hand, he held a small, dark rattle made from a dried gourd. Periodically, he'd gently shake the rattle and slowly step dance to a subdued chant.

"He looks so sad," said Honey. "I don't understand. How could such a person have known the Duggans?"

"I think he's one of those witch doctors. You know those filthy Satan worshipers I told you about that meet down on the beach. I bet'ya they caused this terrible tragedy."

"But why does he stand there looking so sad?"

"Lord only knows. I'm going to call Pastor Jerry right now. We've got to do something."

Dr. and Mrs. Richard Duggan of Seattle owned the large waterfront house next door. They used the house for an occasional weekend retreat, during holidays, and in the summer. When their thirty-foot Catalina sailboat wasn't moored to its float in Agate Pass, it was stored in the boathouse.

From her front windows, Clara had a clear view up and down Angeline Avenue. From her rear windows, she could observe the beach and the Duggan's back deck with its hot tub.

From his bedroom window, Henry, Clara's husband, also had a clear view of the Duggan's hot tub. With Clara's bedroom on the opposite side of the house, when opportunity presented itself, he had quietly watched Sara Duggan lounging in her hot tub. It was her custom to take her hot tub in the nude.

One evening, in the twilight of sunset, Sara had caught a slight curtain movement in the window of Henry's darkened bedroom. A smile came to her lips as she continued her soak. From then on, whenever Sara was in her hot tub, she knew Henry would be at his window, a pleasant experience for both. But it ended abruptly that morning.

That morning, Clara Goodwill, being an early riser, had seen a man slip into the Duggan house just as the sun was coming up. An hour later, she saw a second man enter.

It was midmorning when Sara Duggan drove up in her white Mercedes and swept into the house, her orange floral dress blowing in the wind. A few moments later she staggered out clutching her neck desperately trying to stem the gushing blood. She staggered a few yards up the driveway before falling. Like an accusing finger, a stream of dark, red blood trickled down the asphalt to the front door. The next instant Clara was on the phone dialing 911.

After all the activity, and with the ambulance and police gone, a strange Indian had appeared in front of the house. Clara could feel her heart racing as she reached for her Valium.

The funky village of Suquamish was a mixture of old stores and ancient traditional places. It was a place time seems to have stopped and been frozen at the year 1915.

A few years before 1915, the Port Madison Indian Reservation was opened to limited non-Indian settlement by the Federal Acts of 1904 and 1906. These Acts authorized the State of Washington to supervise the sale of inherited allotted lands and allowed the government to declare original Indian owners "competent" to sell their land.

In 1915, land developers began offering the individual Indians deals they could not refuse. The Goodwill waterfront property, as was all the property along Angeline Avenue that fronted Agate Pass, was acquired by that sale.

When I arrived in town, emotions and rhetoric between Indians and non-Indians had reached the flash point. Clams were the issues causing much of the conflict. When the State of Washington issued title to those waterfront lots, it also included the beach in front of each lot down to the low-tide mark. That meant the traditional clam beds of the Suquamish Indians, the clam beds guaranteed to them by the Point Elliott Treaty of 1855 was transferred to non-Indians. Soon the beaches were posted with signs proclaiming Private Property No Trespassing.

Nineteen fifteen was also the year Cafe Angeline opened for business in a new frame building; its one room was filled with the sweet aroma of fresh cedar sawdust. Over the succeeding years, the aroma faded with the drying of the lumber; its cracks filled with dozens of coats of paint.

Cafe Angeline was named in honor of Chief Sealth's oldest daughter who had earned her whiskey and bread from sailors and roustabouts on the Seattle waterfront. When her pearls had lost their luster, the swine pushed her aside and trampled her under their hooves. She finished her days as a Seattle raglady living in a little beach hut filled with dirty rags. She died alone in her blanket bed.

Directly across from the cafe was a white frame building that once housed the ticket office for the ferry that made twice daily trips to downtown Seattle. The ferry service had been discontinued with the construction of the Agate Pass Bridge in 1946. The building was unused except for an occasional community meeting. Hard times had fallen on the tollhouse and the cafe as it had on Princess Angeline herself.

The Tides-Out Tavern leaned against the east wall of Cafe Angeline while the west wall was supported by 2nd Hand Rose, a struggling used-goods merchant who held open for business in the old Mobil gas station. Tides-In Tavern was across the street.

Main Street Suquamish consisted of one block centered on the Post Office. JC's Market was next to the Post Office. The Tribal Justice Center, housing the Tribal Police and Courts, was next to Tides-In Tavern. The Volunteer Fire Station was further up the block. JC's Market had been recently sold to a Korean family.

While Cafe Angeline was the gathering place for the natives and near natives of Suquamish, respectable white people preferred Karsten's restaurant in the new Suquamish Village Shopping Mall on the hill.

Dining at Karsten's was an upscale event. White table linen, silver service and fresh flowers were at each table. Waiters wearing white shirts with black vests, black bow ties, and black trousers silently moved about in the soft light of flickering table candles. It was a place patrons could dress up and dine to the accompaniment of live dinner music and dance a few turns in the arms of their favorite partner.

Visitors to Suquamish were unaware of the division of commerce along religious and ethnic lines because their money was eagerly sought by both.

Those who preferred the casual lifestyle gathered at Cafe Angeline. It was a small place with a seating capacity for thirty. Small was its charm with the rustic atmosphere of a scattering of modern antiques and large original Kmart prints on the walls, and booths covered with red plastic.

Customers felt comfortable wearing jeans, flannel shirts, sweats and tenny-runners. Its laid-back pace allowed the customers to nurse their coffee while engaging in the heated conversations of the day.

"I hear Doctor Johnson is raging on about the Koreans buying JC's," I said to a friend, Jane Austin, in the next booth.

Russ Tate, Cafe Angeline's current owner, picked up his ears in passing and slid into my booth.

He asked in a lowered voice, "I don't think the tribe is going to like that. What do you think?"

I looked him straight in the eyes and said, "I'm surprised more people haven't noticed the large number of Asian-American families who are buying houses and moving their families here.

"I think it's even more wonderful if they own businesses here. Family-owned-and-managed businesses have the best chance for success in this small community."

Russ said, "I thought I heard you call Carl Johnson, Doctor. I didn't know he was a doctor."

"He's not. What I really said was DogTurd Johnson. When I say it fast, it sounds like doctor. I've been calling him DogTurd to his face since I came here but he's too dumb to know it."

"Why do you call him that?"

"He's paranoid about dog turds in his yard. He jumped me one day about my dog, Lady. When I asked him how he knew it was Lady who dumped in his yard, he told me he knew the turds of every dog in town, hence DogTurd Johnson."

Sunny, the cafe's only waitress was a thin woman in her mid-forties with long black hair neatly combed back and tied into ponytail. She entertained her customers by wearing tight protest T-shirts that maximized her petite braless figure.

That day Sunny's T-shirt display was on behalf of double hull tankers. In ribald fashion, her chest was highlighted with two black circles strategically placed around each breast. The legend beneath read: Two Are Better Than One, and beneath that was a second—plea, Double Hull Tankers Now.

Sergeant Lewis of the Tribal Police had stepped inside the door and was looking for a free booth. He was about to leave when his eyes caught me waving from the back booth.

Earlier that morning, Sergeant Lewis had been sipping his morning coffee in Cafe Angeline when his radio beeper went off. The customers had fallen silent as they listened to the dispatcher's scratchy voice squawk out a coded message. Sergeant Lewis had quietly gotten up, tossed a dollar on the table and went out to the police car parked in front. At the closing of the door, suspended conversations had resumed in mid-sentence.

I smiled warmly at Sergeant Lewis' approach, extending my hand in greeting.

"Come, my friend, join me for a cup of coffee."

"I was planning on something more substantial than just coffee," came the reply.

Sunny appeared at our table with a coffeepot and empty cup. She immediately filled the cup and handed it to Lewis while topping off my cup, all in one smooth continuous motion.

"Anything else I can get you?" She asked.

"I'd like a Swiss cheese omelet and hash browns with whole wheat toast and do you have orange marmalade?"

"I don't think so but I'll check."

At Sunny's departure, I leaned forward and softly asked the question buzzing around the village.

"I hear there were two people killed over on Angeline Avenue this morning. Is that true?"

"Not quite, one dead and the other at Harborview Hospital in critical condition. I doubt if she'll make it. I was the first officer on the scene.

"I found Sara Duggan laying in the driveway with her throat cut. The paramedics arrived shortly after I did but I had to hold them back not knowing what was going on. A witness said there were two men inside the house. I waited for the Sheriff's Department to arrive before letting the medics check out Mrs. Duggan. The Medivac copter picked her up at the elementary ball field and took her over to Harbor View in Seattle."

"What did you find inside the house?"

"We found a man in a bathtub laying in a pool of blood. His wrists and neck had been cut. It appeared to be attempted murder and suicide."

"Was the dead man Dr. Duggan?"

"No. It was someone from Seattle."

"Maybe he was robbing the place when Mrs. Duggan surprised him?"

"Maybe, but I don't think so."

"Why not?"

"We found a key to the house in his pocket and there was no sign of breaking and entering."

"Here's your Swiss cheese omelet," said Sunny, as she slipped the plate in front of Sergeant Lewis. "I came up with some orange marmalade for you."

"Hey, that's great! Thanks a lot."

I'd seen Sunny duck out the back door a few minutes earlier. I suspected that she rushed over to JC's Market to get Lewis his orange marmalade.

"You don't seemed convinced it was attempted murder and suicide," I said.

"Oh, it wasn't."

"How do you know?"

"The coroner determined the man in the tub had died at least two hours before Mrs. Duggan came home."

Pastor Jerry, having a sixth sense about Satanism, responded quickly. His credentials as a Satanologist had so impressed Clara that she'd convinced the search committee to invite him to become the pastor of Suquamish Bible Church.

"We've got to have a pastor who knows how to fight Satan," pleaded Clara.

Pastor Jerry had trained under The Reverend Doctor Pat Litchfield, the California divine who laid claim to being America's leading expert, investigator and exposure of Satanic worship.

The four members of the neighborhood watch committee were present when Pastor Jerry arrived.

"This is to be expected," said Pastor Jerry with deep concern in his voice and serious lines on his face, a skill he'd learned at Bethel Bible College in St. Paul, Minnesota.

"Kitsap County is a particularly fertile ground for Satan. Every aspect of the area appeals to cultists who gravitate to sites where the surroundings are conducive to their evil practices thus shortening the time needed to capture and control the population.

"I've studied and catalogued the weak spots in Kitsap County and the facts are bad news for the Christian residents of Suquamish."

Clara, Honey, Betty and Mary leaned forward in rap attention.

"To begin with, Kitsap County is a pentagram; its five sides are bounded by Snohomish, King, Jefferson, Mason and Pierce Counties."

"You've forgotten Island County on the north," said Mary Wilson, a petite graphic artist who lived across the street from Honey. She was the only committee member who dared to challenge Clara's strong-handed leadership.

"What do you mean?" Asked Pastor Jerry, his voice laced with irritation.

"On the north corner Island County borders Kitsap County."

"Oh…Well, that's of so little significance I discounted it. Besides Satan uses clever tricks like that to hide his pentagrams. The pentagram is a very important symbol used by Satan worshipers. All within this cursed area are in danger, trapped by pioneer lawmakers who didn't know what they were creating."

"Oh, dear," anguished Honey, her blue-gray eyes widening with each revelation.

"Evidence of rampant satanic symbolism recurs in the figure six in every aspect of county life. There are three county commissioners, and three city commissioners, for a total of the accursed six. Kitsap elementary schools contain grades kindergarten through fifth, which totals six."

"Oh, dear," shivered Honey.

"Each of the six school districts have total classes of 6-6-6, a truly satanic number. The middle school starts with grade six which is the start of trouble for youngsters too innocent to know the significance of how this will warp their lives and shape their destinies."

He went on to point out that Highway 3 entered the county and left the county, the two three's equaled six, and that shrimp were one of the county's natural resources. When cooked, they resembled the numeral 6. Total number of letters in the Suquamish Port Madison Indian Reservation was thirty-six, which was six times six.

"Oh, dear," whined Honey.

Mary Wilson was counting the letters as she quickly printed the name out on her notepad.

"I count thirty-seven."

"What?" Asked Pastor Jerry. "What are you talking about?"

"You said there were thirty-six letters in Suquamish Port Madison Indian Reservation but I count thirty-seven."

"Oh…that…may be the case," stammered Pastor Jerry. "But it's close enough to make my point. In addition, you should know that Satanic graffiti frequently uses the letter 'F', which is the sixth letter of the alphabet," said Pastor Jerry, receiving a knowing nod from Clara.

"And I don't need to tell you what four letter word begins with F."

"Oh, no," agreed Honey, shaking her head from side to side.

"It's Satan's favorite word. Kitsap County is rife with F's. Consider the Farmer's Market, a primary local gathering place for cultists."

Pastor Jerry lifted his voice into the canter of his favorite televangelist, "Then there are firs, and fish, and farms, and ferns, and forests, and fires, and fiddle players, and families, and fast food, and fire stations, and fireplaces, and firewood, and ferries."

Honey raised her hand hesitantly like a schoolgirl shyly seeking permission to speak.

"Yes, Honey, what do you want?" He asked.

"I hear there are two fairies living on the other side of town."

"Oh, yes," replied Pastor Jerry enthusiastically. "There are those creatures, too. They're the devil's handmaidens. Decent people can't even speak of the vile things they do behind closed doors."

Tongues clicked and heads wagged in disgust.

"Certain colors are significant to Satan worshipers," he continued, "among them are red, yellow and green."

Clara jerked to the edge of her chair and shouted. "That Indian witch doctor was wearing those colors."

"There you have it," said Pastor Jerry with a wave of his hand. "Consider further that logger's hats and suspenders are red as is every stop sign in the county. All school buses are yellow, as are most students' pencils and rain slickers. From the air or ground, the county is predominantly green as are the highway signs."

"And I'm wearing a red bra and panties," sneered Mary derisively.

"Really, Mary" said Clara, freezing Mary in an icy glare of disgust.

Pastor Jerry tastefully ignored Mary's derision.

"I became interested in Kitsap County when a former FBI agent told me it was a primary satanic center."

"That just goes to show that even the FBI can employ idiots," Mary whispered loudly to the woman sitting beside her.

Pastor Jerry didn't respond. He was beginning to suspect that Mary was a Satanist sympathizer.

"My in-depth study has proven he was right. Consider this fact. There is an epidemic of missing children in this country."

Looking directly into Mary's eyes, he continued, "Satan worshipers all over this country are kidnapping little children and bringing them to the Suquamish Reservation so they can be sacrificed in vile Satanic orgies. Unspeakably horrible things are done to the bodies of those little boys and girls before they are sacrificed. There are scores of little bodies buried in the backwoods of this reservation, as many as twenty little children in one grave.

"And then there are those fetuses they collect from abortion clinics which they cook in iron stewpots and eat on Witch's Sabbath."

Pastor Jerry leaned back in his chair to allow the full impact of his shocking revelation to sink in.

"I know it's inconceivable, but it's true."

Mary Wilson responded, "If it is true why haven't you presented your evidence to the police so that the perpetrators of such terrible things can be arrested and punished?"

"The Sheriff Department says they have no jurisdiction on the Reservation. And that's another thing that has to be changed."

"You're mistaken. In the case of a suspected felony, the county and state law enforcement personnel may enter an Indian reservation. If you were told that they didn't have jurisdiction, it was because they didn't believe your story."

Pastor Jerry's face reddened with anger. Now he knew that Mary was one of them. She would have to be included in the great cleansing.

Suddenly, Clara's face brightened at an insight, which came to her like a divine vision.

"Those pornographic magazines and videos down at JC's Market are part of Satan's plans. Pornography is as addictive as hard-core drugs like cocaine and crack."

Mary broke in.

"I go into JC's all the time. They only sell Playboy, Penthouse, and some nude magazines. Surely you're not calling those magazines pornographic?"

"According to the Bible, nudity is a sin," answered Clara. "Is that not right, Pastor Jerry?"

Mary swung back before Pastor Jerry could answer.

"What constitutes pornography is a very relative thing. If the women of Suquamish Bible Church had entered any 19th Century church dressed as they do today, they would have been driven out as fallen women. In fact, back then, if a woman exposed her ankle, she was being very risqué, something a Christian woman wouldn't do."

While Mary was talking, Clara began to wring her hands frantically, looking up; her eyes widened as her vision grew.

"Men read and watch that filth while smoking marijuana and drinking the devil's brew. And soon they're caught in Satan's net to be drawn deeper and deeper into the slime pit of debauchery…and…and…."

Her voice rising with each insight.

"Soon they're forcing their…their filthy things into women…and little boys and girls."

"But, what can we do about it?" Asked Honey frantically.

Clara carefully studied the eager faces hanging on her every word. In a deep, serious voice, she replied, "We can picket JC's Market. Like the ancient martyrs, we can sacrifice our bodies by blocking the doorway. We can carry protest signs. We can keep it up day after day and…." shaking her finger in the air, "And with the help of the Lord, we'll defeat Satan right here in Suquamish."

"I'm out of here," snapped Mary collecting her notepad and pencils. Standing up, she turned to the blonde woman beside her. "Betty, are you going to stay and listen to this madness or leave with me?"

Betty, not wanting to offend anyone, was horrified at being put on the spot. She dropped her eyes to stare at her fingers and nervously picked at her chipped nail polish while everyone waited for her decision.

Speaking in a soft resigned voice, she said, "It's time for me to get back to Bill. You know how panicky he gets when I'm gone too long."

Betty limped out of the room.

The confrontation left Clara and Honey frozen in shock. But Pastor Jerry quickly recaptured the momentum.

"Ladies," said Pastor Jerry, his voice heavy with concern. "We must pray for those women. I fear Satan has captured their souls."

Clara and Honey joined Pastor Jerry in kneeling at their chairs, their heads bowed and fists pressed against their foreheads as they prayed silently for the lost souls of Mary and Betty. When finished, they quickly resumed their talk of formulating their plan of battle.

"You've an excellent idea, Clara," said Pastor Jerry. "We've got to go on the offense. Satanic practices are growing all over this village. I've recently learned that there's a witch's coven that meets in the grove beside the cemetery at each full moon, and there are spirit-dances secretly being held at the Tribal Center."

Clara jumped up to add, "Don't forget the witch doctors meeting down on the beach. One of them is carving a devil's pole. He's rigged a blue tarp so I can't see what it is but I hear it's nearly finished so we don't have much time."

"I agree," said Pastor Jerry, his voice filled with excitement. "This Sunday I'll call a meeting of concerned Christians who want to drive Satan out of Suquamish. I'll propose we hold the meeting at the church Wednesday evening following midweek services."

When the 911 call came over the radio, Sergeant Lewis rushed out of the Justice Center and ran up the street to be confronted by a small group of men and women who were blocking the entrance to JC's Market. They had chained themselves to the door and were chanting, "Porn must go." "Porn must go."

When Sergeant Lewis tried to move them away from the frontdoor, Clara shouted in his face, "We've got the right to protest against filthy pornography."

Picket signs were waving in the air: JC'S Sells Filth, Christians For A Clean Suquamish, Porn Merchants Are Satan's Disciples.

"You're on private property so move away."

Pastor Jerry was about to step into the argument when a deputy Sheriff's car wheeled around the corner with blue lights flashing and sirens blaring. Pulling to a screeching stop, two deputies jumped out and plowed their way through the agitated crowd.

"What's going on here?" Demanded the senior deputy.

Sergeant Lewis attempted to explain but the deputies brushed him aside.

Addressing the crowd, the senior deputy said, "All right, ladies and gentlemen, if you want to protest, you'll have to do it off private property. Now move away from the door."

Seeing the padlocks and the chains, he added.

"Either you peacefully unlock your chains or we'll use bolt cutters."

The protesters stood their ground.

"Mike, get the bolt cutter."

A few snips later the chains dropped away and Pastor Jerry picked up a sign waving it up and down to the chant, "Porn must go." "Porn must go."

Other people began to circle the protesters. Over the chanting of "Porn must go" a counter-chant was gaining breath. "Censorship, No; Freedom, Yes."

In the midst of the shoving and shouting, Pastor Jerry glanced across the street and saw a man standing quietly wearing a sandwich board sign inscribed with Nietzsche's prophesy: Those Who Cast Out The Devil Will Find Themselves In The Swine.

A temporary truce eventually came to the satanic battlefront in Suquamish. The salivating TV crews that infested its streets and forests in search of the buried little bodies promised by Pastor Jerry had gone away. Mercifully, the absence of cadavers led to the disappearance of the investigative reporters and the electronic airheads who came to record grieving next-of-kin exhuming the rotting bodies of their missing children.

But, the serenity was to be short-lived. Another wave of bad tidings was about sweep over our bucolic paradise.

The fulfillment of Nietzsche's prophesy began to unfold when a Polaroid photograph slipped out of a damaged envelope and fell at the feet of the Postmistress.

Dominique picked it up intending to put it back into the envelope but, when she glanced at the picture, she caught her breath. Turning the envelope over, she recognized the sender's name.

Whether by intuition or impulse, fate or choice, Dominique was alone in the post office so she quietly slipped the photograph into her apron pocket.

CHAPTER SEVEN

Fot Choy had warned me that he would come.

When I heard his "Hello" from outside my door, I knew what to expect.

Earlier in the morning, while I was meditating, a cold shiver had wiggled up my back.

I felt his coming when I shuffled the 32 cards of Fot Choy and laid them out. There she was, the queen of spades, sitting in the house of callers.

A broad smile dominated his face, fixed permanently in place like a clown's mask. It was the smile he had learned from his professor of evangelism at Bethel College, who had told him that, "A warm smile is a great weapon for a Christian warrior."

The broad fixed smile was seen at all conventions and gatherings of evangelical Christians. The more gifted ones conveyed the impression of sincerity with their smiles. Whether true or false, only God could judge a man's heart.

The gaining of church members was important to Pastor Jerry. It was a deadly serious battle. When he stepped into the doorway, I was prepared.

He shoved his hand forward offering a handshake and said, "My name is Pastor Jerry Hanson from the Suquamish Bible Church and I'm visiting our neighbors and friends."

When I didn't take his hand, he nervously pulled it back and reached into his pocket to hand over a pamphlet.

I had just put in a long stint debugging a new astrology program on my computer so a mental change of pace was welcomed. I swung back in my chair and smiled. "What can I do for you?" I asked.

Pastor Jerry almost leaped at this opening.

"I've come to tell you about the way of salvation. You realize that God loves you, don't you?"

"Oh, yes, I know that God loves me and I love her."

"Do you realize that God's Word says, 'All have sinned and come short of the glory of God,' Romans 3:23?"

"I know that's what Paul, the Christian Pharisee, said."

"But do you know that you can't save yourself from the eternal fires of hell? God's Word says, 'For by grace are ye saved through faith....'"

I completed the quotation, "'...and that not of yourselves: it is the gift of God: not of works, lest any man should boast.' Yes, I know that and your fourth and fifth points as well."

"Then you're a born-again Christian?"

"Yes, I've been born again many times."

Pastor Jerry pulled back as a grave look came over his face.

"I see that you've not been truly saved then."

"Oh, but I have. I've been saved in quite a few other lifetimes as well as this one."

"So you believe in reincarnation?"

His voice became tense.

"Yes, indeed, as it was taught by Jesus."

I watched the red rise up his neck like the steam gauge on a fired-up boiler. He drew himself to full stature and cast the ultimate lance of authority.

"There is no scientific evidence to support New Age concepts such as reincarnation," he replied.

"I agree, and did you know that there is no scientific evidence for any of the key Christian doctrines such as the Immaculate Conception, the Virgin Birth, the miracles of Jesus, his Resurrection and Ascension, that Heaven and Hell are outside the test tube as is the existence of the soul and life after death? Nor is there any scientific proof that there is a God.

So when you turn to science for theological support, you're hoisted with your own petard."

Pastor Jerry fired back, "There are many Christian scientists who have proven the truth of the Bible."

"But not one of your Christian scientists can prove, by scientific methods alone, that the soul exists."

We were like two medieval knights, each clad in the shining armor of our perceptions, astride huge stallions of ancient thought, charging at each other in our individual lanes of destiny. The outcome would be in the hands of God.

"The Bible is clear, 'It is appointed for men to die once, and after that comes judgment....'"

Again I finished the quotation, '...so Christ, having been offered once to bear the sins of many, will appear a second time, not to deal with sin but to save those who are eagerly waiting for him.' Hebrews 9:27 and 28. Priscilla wrote a marvelous defense of reincarnation, didn't she?"

Pastor Jerry hesitated.

"Who's Priscilla?" He asked.

"You're a teacher of the Bible and you don't know that Priscilla, a woman and the first Bishop of Corinth, wrote the book of Hebrews? Obviously, there is much you don't know about the origins of the Bible."

"I know God's simple truth that hasn't been contaminated by clever men."

"Have you read the Egyptian *Book of the Dead*?"

"No, I read the Bible and that's enough."

"I'll loan you my copy should you want to read it sometime. It's not about the Pharaoh's journey to the gods but a ritual pleading to the gods that they won't require the Pharaoh to come back as a slave in his next life."

"The Bible teaches us to reject all such teachings as myths."

"But, Pastor Jerry, everyone has their mythology. You have yours and I have mine. It's the stuff all people live by and much the better for it. It's not the reality of the branch that determines its worth but the quality of its fruit."

Pastor Jerry's voice took on a sharp and emphatic edge.

"Reincarnation isn't taught in the Bible."

"Oh, but it was taught by Jesus. Jesus said that John the Baptist was the reincarnation of Elijah."

"That's not true. Jesus said, 'The spirit of Elijah was with John the Baptist.'"

"Now, I see that you also bear false witness. The Greek text is clear, Jesus said that John the Baptist was Elijah. As Jesus told Nicodemus, 'You must be born again.'"

"Jesus was talking about the need to be born again spiritually, not reincarnation."

"So you agree with me then. For when you say I must be spiritually born again you're acknowledging that my soul has lived before."

"You're twisting words to suit your pagan philosophy. The word of God is clear to those who are saved."

We paused to gather our breaths and also our thoughts for the next charge. Pastor Jerry looked about my cabin then said in a soft, friendly voice, "I see you have a nice computer. What do you use it for?"

"I'm a novelist," I answered, not releasing my eye hold.

"What kind of novels do you write?"

He'd taken my bait and I began to reel him in.

"I write about modern-day mythologies and cults like your Bible Church."

The response was quick and firm.

"Our church is not a cult!"

"You're followers of a religious leader, are you not?"

"We are not. We only follow the Word of God."

"And what do you understand to be the Word of God?"

Pastor Jerry pulled out a small red Testament and tapped it emphatically with his index finger.

"This is the Word of God."

"Ah, besides being cultists, you're also idolaters."

"How can you say such things?"

"You've made a graven image of that book. The very book which states that there's only one Word of God and he is the Lord Jesus Christ. The first commandment is quite clear, 'You shall have no other gods before me.'"

"Again you're twisting words to your evil purpose just as Satan quoted scripture to serve his evil purpose."

"As cookbook fundamentalists, you are like the Pharisees of old. You pick biblical texts that support your doctrinal recipes and ignore everything else as you chant your party line like zombies without intelligence."

"Now I know that you're under the influence of Satan."

Pastor Jerry fell to his knees with prayerful hands clasping his Testament.

"I beseech you, for the love of God, give up the errors of your ways and accept Jesus Christ as your personal Savior."

"Get up, young man. I accepted Jesus as my personal Savior long before you were born. That's why I recognize your lying and idolatrous teachings."

Pastor Jerry stood up and dusted his knees.

"I know that I speak the Truth. It's you who don't know the Truth."

I glanced at the pamphlet in his hand.

"I also see that you engage in false advertisement."

"What do you mean?" He snapped.

"Your pamphlet says your church is friendly. By your conduct today, I can see that it's far from being friendly."

"We don't welcome Satan into our midst if that's what you mean."

I closed my eyes, looking up to heaven with clasped hands to my forehead, I mimicked Pastor Jerry by twisting my face in anguish as I prayed.

"I pray, Lord, that you might reveal to Pastor Jerry the errors of his ways before it's too late, that he may be saved from the fate of those who lead little ones astray."

Pastor Jerry, choking with anger, turned on his heels and stomped off.

"Pastor Jerry," I called after him.

"What do you want?" He snapped.

"You forgot to shake the dust from your shoes."

The old man leaned in through the open window and asked, "Why did you do that?"

He had been listening from the sundeck.

"Those people scare me," I said. "In their lust for power, they make civil matters into moral matters. That's the way it's been with their kind throughout human history.

"Have you forgotten, old man, that it was white Christians who betrayed you, then stole your land, debased your women, killed your warriors, enslaved the survivors on this Reservation; and then in a final insult they burned your longhouse, all in the name of Christ and manifest destiny?"

"No, I haven't forgotten. But to remember with hatred lowers your spirit to their level."

I was not to be put off the scent.

"Preachers are the worst. They're temple whores who prostitute themselves for fame, power and wealth—for Jesus' sake, of course."

The old man replied, "I've known good preachers like Henry Smith who gave up everything to serve the weak and the poor."

"So have I, but they're few and without influence in the halls of ecclesiastical power. Missionaries to social lepers are ignored by headquarters."

I waxed pensive for a few moments as I gathered my thoughts.

Then I said, "I remember how southern preachers justified the slavery of non-white races as the will of God. They said it was God's will that the slaver's whip should cut the cross in the backs of rebellious slaves to teach them that Jesus loved them.

"As a protector of the true faith, St. Augustine, a great fifth century Latin father, ordered the slaughter of a whole city. Because he disagreed with the theology of their bishop, hundreds of innocent babies, children, mothers, fathers, old men and women were cut to pieces with Roman swords and their homes burned to the ground...slaughtered for the love of Jesus. An oxymoron if ever there was one.

"In the name of the prince of peace who taught his disciples to judge no one and to turn the other cheek, the sword has been raised repeatedly to save the sinner's soul by cutting off his head.

"In 1244 AD at Montsegur they burned two hundred men, women and children to death in a faggot fire to save their souls.

"In Germany the Nazi brown shirts launched their ethnic cleansing of the *auslanders* and *untermenchens* in the name of a white Christian Germany. Today the white Christian brown shirts of the far right have undertaken the ethnic cleansing of America as they attack abortion clinics and gays. Assault, murder, arson, intimidation, denial of civil rights are again the weapons of choice."

The old man answered, "Yes, all that's true. But if you're not careful, hatred will make you like them. Come out to the deck. It's such a beautiful afternoon."

We adjusted the deck chairs so we could look eastward over the sound. The afternoon sun highlighted the hulls and superstructures of passing ships with their gaily-colored pennants.

The *Victoria Clipper*, blazing white in the late afternoon sun, passed swiftly before us inbound from Victoria. Soon the gray mass of the super-carrier, *U.S.S. Nimitz*, slipped majestically past on the incoming tide en route to her homeport at Bremerton, her arrival timed to transit Rich Passage at high tide.

The old man finally spoke.

"The old ones say that there were once very wise gods who walked the earth. They were the ones whom, in their great wisdom, chose to be born of powerful human parents. In their supreme wisdom, they chose to have vast skills as hunters and leaders. By sheer force of their wills and hard work, they acquired many horses and had many wives who bore them many sons and daughters.

"The wise gods who walked the earth had strong medicine. They made themselves chiefs. They were so powerful that they controlled everything in their world. They defeated all that fought against them and made everyone their slaves.

"The wise gods would look down from their lofty mountain homes upon the squirming masses of poor people and ridicule them for not being gods. But they were jealous gods and destroyed any that would try to climb up to their high station.

"The day came when the mightiest of the wise gods who walked upon the earth cried out, 'I'm the greatest God. There is no other God like me.'"

After a long pause, I asked, "What became of those wise Gods who walked upon the earth?"

The old man said, "Oh, they died and were sentenced by the Supreme God to be reincarnated as poor and weak slaves.

"Why do you think the rich and powerful and their minions are so opposed to reincarnation? Could it be that they don't want to hear that in another life they'll be required to reap what they've sown, to experience what it's like to be treated the way they have treated others? Do they really think they can mock God?

"We've a custom known as Potlatch. It's a festival where great men are honored for their generosity and compassion.

"There is nothing wrong with wealth and power as long as God receives the glory and all people benefit. We own nothing, not even if we have treaties and certificates issued by the state and affirmed by the courts. We're only temporary stewards. The great Father teaches us that our wealth and power should be used for the welfare and happiness of all people not just for the privileged elite."

I added, "That's what Jesus taught, but today few people take such teachings seriously. Oh, when it comes to saving their souls, they take Jesus seriously but sharing their wealth with beggars in the street is out of the question.

"Today, pig ethics prevail. That's when the biggest and strongest piglets get to the full teats first and suck them dry while kicking the weaker piglets away. It's pig ethics pure and simple."

"You sound like a socialist or even a communist."

"Compassion for our neighbors is what I'm talking about. Compassion that inspires us to help our neighbors who have fallen into the slime pit by giving them the use of our ladders of education and skills so they can climb out instead of keeping our ladders for ourselves and ridiculing them for staying in the slime pit. By helping our neighbor, we're helping ourselves. For no one can enter the kingdom of God alone, we must all enter together, arm in arm."

The old man's dark eyes fixed on mine.

"Is there another reason why you dislike Pastor Jerry and his people?"

"It's their hypocrisy."

"Aren't you being too harsh in your judgment?"

"Not any more than Jesus was."

"What do you mean?"

"The only people Jesus criticized were the Pharisees. He compared them to whitewashed tombs. The Pharisees outwardly appeared righteous but within were full of hypocrisy and greed.

"He warned his disciples to beware of the leaven of the Pharisees."

The old man asked, "And what was that?"

"It was the inflation that comes to the ego when people see themselves as sole possessors of the truth. In their arrogance, they elevate themselves into the select group of the saved and like Pastor Jerry, relegate all that do not agree to the legion of the damned. They assume the judicial function that belongs solely to God."

The old man said, "They claim the authority of the Word of God."

"Many things are found in the Bible but for a Christian, all must be measured against the yardstick of Jesus, his life and teachings. Read and you will find that he had compassion for everyone.

"It's Pastor Jerry's lack of compassion that tells me he is a hypocrite. Just wait and see if he doesn't have feet of clay."

The old man laid a gnarled hand upon my shoulder and said, "My son, that may be true but don't become like them. Hatred is a flaming stick that burns both the hand that holds it and the one that is struck."

With these words the old man stood up and slowly walked away.

CHAPTER EIGHT

The full moon peeked through the mountain curtain like an anxious maiden. Her long silvery arms reached across the waters to embrace me as I sat on the deck with my eyes closed. Her numismatic power, that has captured the attention of man and animals for eons causing wolves to howl and tides to flow, also called forth man's dark side and his love side.

Long into the night I waited. Then I felt his presence as he settled in beside me with a grunt. I didn't open my eyes, not wanting to break the spell.

"Before you can live, you must die," whispered the old man in a voice as soft as the summer breeze that rose off the sound during the evening hours.

"What do you mean? You're not suggesting I commit suicide, are you?"

I was fearful that the voice might be hers in disguise, that voice, which came to lunatics telling them to kill themselves and others.

"No, my son, suicide only postpones the inevitable. It's a divine law that, what we sow, we must reap, if not in this life, then in the next. God will not be mocked by deathbed conversions or man's theology. No…what I'm talking about is another kind of death that you must undergo at Spirit Point."

"But that's a restricted area. Non-tribal people aren't allowed."

"True, but I've persuaded my brothers to grant an exception for you."

With a pack on my back, a shovel in one hand and a pick in the other, I struck off through the second-growth forest of the Suquamish Indian Reservation. It was dusk and the shadows were deep along the foot trail that led through the dense undergrowth that arched over the trail like a pristine tunnel, leading to what? I didn't know. Inside my pack were items the old man had given me; a small drum wrapped in my bedroll, eagle feathers, a crow wing and a rattle with a tip of horsehair…sacred things needed for the ceremony.

I plunged deep into the forest of hemlock and cedar trees knowing that I would reach my destination when I reached it and not a step before.

'What kind of place am I looking for?' I asked myself out loud or in my mind; I didn't know much less care.

'I don't know,' I answered. 'But spirit will tell me when I get there.'

The full moon slipped into her blood red gown of total eclipse soon after she had risen above the Cascade Mountains to the east.

My mind flashed to a childhood experience where I stood upon the roof of our house to watch another lunar eclipse.

"A bloody moon means that war and death are about to break out on the earth."

Emma Nyquist's dire warning had shocked me.

It was the first lunar eclipse that I'd ever witnessed so I was terrified by her prophecy because Emma was a solid member of the Baptist Church.

The Baptist Sunday evening services were evangelistic and preceded the youth fellowship. I'd heard many dire prophecies that the world was about to end, the Second Coming of Christ was about to take place at any moment, and so forth. The "acceptable" Christians, which were those who believed as Emma did, would be snapped up into the clouds to meet the Lord.

Those who remained would have to endure the destruction of the world by a wrathful God. The lunar eclipse was a divine warning for all sinners to get on board the salvation train.

But that wasn't the only reason I'd attended the Baptist Sunday evening services. At the time, I was infatuated with Alice Templeton who was also a good member of the Baptist Church.

Alice believed all weapons should be used to win a soul to Christ. She knew she was blessed with special weapons and didn't hesitate to use them. When she turned them on me, I quickly fell yammering at her feet. With her powerful weapons, she compelled me, though I was a Presbyterian, to attend the Sunday evening services and the youth fellowship.

To compel is the wrong word. She cast a spell over me that convinced me that I wanted to attend because it was the most wonderful thing in my young life. However, it wasn't the services that were wonderful. It was what followed.

On the way home, Alice would take me by the hand and lead me into a darkened corner where she'd guide my hands over her weapons, the most wonderful weapons in our school. That was all she'd allow but it was enough to keep me in faithful attendance each Sunday evening and yammering at her feet…until that day I looked up and discovered she had forsaken me to seek another convert. Thus I experienced the humiliation and heart-pain that came from loving a Circe woman, an enchantress who turns men into swine.

When overhanging branches blocked the trail, I stopped to ask permission to proceed.

In the deepening twilight, I held the string at arm's length to allow the small crystal to swing and twist freely. Slowly it calmed its movements and came to rest pointing straight ahead. Permission had been granted.

I lost track of time as I slowly worked my way through the dense forest, pausing, listening, turning slowly, and then moving on.

The strange and wonderful thing was that, in spite of the brush, the tangled weeds, the scratchy blackberry arms, my feet found smooth walking as my boots followed an ancient path. But where did the path lead? I still didn't know, but I was convinced that Spirit would guide me to the sacred place.

The brush pulled back and there before me was an ancient fire site. The fire pit was covered with leaves but I'd been told it was a power site, a place where the spirits of the ancient ones had been gathering to counsel seekers of countless generations.

'This is it,' I whispered with the soft voice of one who stood within a holy cathedral.

A quick glance around the site revealed why the Suquamish Indians had chosen to include that area in their reservation. Its beauty was breathtaking and the place was filled with power.

A hundred feet beyond the fire pit was the edge of a high bluff from which, the Puget Sound spread before me, ablaze with the light of the full moon, now free from the dragon's grip. Silver mountains reached toward the stars. On my right was Mt. Olympus. Directly south was Mt. Rainier. To the east were the peaks of the Cascade Mountain range. Before me the lights of Seattle danced across the waters to my feet.

I was not alone.

A chill went up my back when a heron screamed as it rose from the water's edge a hundred feet below. It's long, slow beating wings reminded me of an ancient pterodactyl.

A bat flicked past the tip of my cap.

I inhaled deeply then exhaled with a quick blast.

'This is the place. The Spirits are present.'

A fire pit was in the center of the clearing. I carefully swept back the leaves and twigs before expanding the ring of stones.

'Which direction should it be?' I asked.

At first I thought the grave should lay along the north-south axis to intersect the east-west energy flow, but when I asked my crystal, it came to rest in the east-west axis. In that position, with my feet to the east, I would face the rising sun of a new day, the time of re-birth.

When the area cleared of leaves and twigs was large enough for me to lay prone with a foot or so to spare on all sides, I was about to swing the pick to begin the decent.

"Wait," said the spirits, "You must conduct a little ceremony. Beat your drum and chant a song to the guardian spirits of this place. Also, remember that, unless you secure the Mother's permission, you'll be raping her."

I sang my song of petition.

When the sacred song was finished, I stood with bowed head waiting for the Mother's response. When she invited me to enter her golden triangle, I began to dig.

I swung the pick and shoveled as layers of dirt, four to six-inches deep per sweep, were picked and shoveled out of the hole.

As I picked and shoveled, thoughts began to form.

Descending into the earth was like entering the Mother's vagina to seek her womb, the place where I was to kill myself.

Having read extensively in Campbell and Jung, I recalled the concept that vaginal death was a primeval male fear. Each penetration stirred the primitive fear that man's vital life fluids would be sucked out by the female. That fear was so deeply ingrained in the male subconscious that some men preferred the celibate life to risking death in the female.

Religious men have always had a great problem with sexual energies. With some, the fear of vaginal death brought on impotency and premature ejaculation. Men, such as St. Augustine, not recognizing the male's primeval fears, saw sin in sexual desire and identified its source as the female vagina.

Consequently, religious zealots down through the centuries have sought to repress and deny the sexual energy. That which man fears, he seeks to destroy; what he can't destroy, he'll subjugate. At the root of sexual repression is fear, fear that the female will suck out the male's vital life fluids and he'll die.

But the old man had emphasized, "A man must die to be born again. If he isn't born again, he can't enter the kingdom."

I remembered that such thoughts had been a great mystery to Nicodemus. He could only ask the Master, "Can a grown man enter a second time into his mother's womb and be born?" The man of

Consciousness can not understand this mystery and must therefore ask, "How can this be?"

Christian baptism originally carried a similar meaning as the ancient burial rite. Paul wrote to the Colossians, "You were buried with him in baptism, in which you were also raised with him through faith in the working of God, who raised him from the dead."

Not only was baptism a sacrament, which symbolized a rebirth of spirit, it also symbolized physical rebirth. Again as Jesus told Nicodemus, "That which is born of the flesh is flesh and that which is born of the spirit is spirit." The process of repeatedly being born again of flesh and spirit was the way we enter the kingdom of God. That was the great mystery of which Paul spoke when he said we must all "work out our salvation with fear and trembling."

These were my thoughts as I picked and shoveled my way down into the ground beneath the ancient fire pit.

I was about to jump down into the freshly dug grave for another session with the pick when I took the small crystal from my pocket and held it over the pit, allowing it to swing freely.

It told me that another six inches would do it.

When the grave was finished, I entered it dressed in gray pajamas with red stripes and wearing fur-lined slippers. Over my body, in successive layers, I laid a red blanket, cedar bows, a gray blanket tipped with three white ermine tails.

Along the interior of the grave, I dug out niches for crow feathers, eagle feathers, crystals and burning sage. Before closing the grave, I spread a third blanket over me like a coffin lid.

Deep within my grave, I wiggled into a comfortable position then paused for a moment of silent prayer asking the white light of Christ to protect me and keep me warm through the bone-chilling morning hours.

As I settled into my solitary grave, I was prepared for spiritual encounters. I glanced at my watch. It was 11:30 P.M.

It wasn't long before even my mind was subdued by what pressed in upon me to wring the very life from my body. Scratchy arms emerged from the dirt walls to pull and tear at my hands and face; snake-like roots wiggled in to entangle my feet. The sounds of movement below and at my sides grew as I was pulled deeper into the mother's womb.

But it wasn't flesh and blood that pursued me. It was fear fed by my runaway imagination. However, imaginary fear is just as real as any other fear because the resulting panic is powerful.

I struggled to conquer my fears by recalling the time when I was about to leave on a dangerous trip as an Inupiat Shaman. Father John, an old episcopal priest of the village, taught me how to battle the spirits who seek to destroy us.

"When they come upon you, close your eyes and visualize a white light growing inside your heart. Keep it growing until it encloses your body within a cocoon of white light. Then visualize the loving face of the Christ before you with his smiling reassurances that, in His presence, there is nothing to fear. Do that and you will always be safe."

"Come here, my son," she whispered.

I was a young boy of eleven standing in my parents' bedroom closet. My mother had caught me rummaging in my father's World War I knapsack.

She had appeared without sound and was standing near her bed. She wore a loose-fitting housecoat that wrapped around her full figure. She extended her beckoning arms with a loving smile.

"Come here and show me what you have in your hand."

She sat on the bed and patted where she wanted me to sit. In the process, her robe came loose exposing to my eager eyes the mysterious female breasts, which had heretofore been hidden beneath layers of cloth and lace.

Tentatively I moved to my mother's side. She took my hand in hers, turned it palm up, and gently brushed my clenched fingers open. They opened slowly to expose the secret locked within.

"Do you know what that is?" She asked.

"No."

"Do you want me to show you?"

I shrugged my shoulders.

"It's time for you to learn about such things."

She took it from my hand. Then she gently laid me back on the bed. With nimble fingers she unbuttoned my pants and slid them off, easing my embarrassment by stroking my rumpled hair. The closeness of her fullness brought life to my body. She eased away my protective hands and gently encouraged my growth. When full and erect, she rolled the condom over it.

"You must always wear one of these whenever you make love to a girl. You know how to make love, don't you?"

I shook my head nervously from side to side.

"It's time you learned."

The scene shifted. I was standing over a hole in the ground frantically jabbing a little stick into the hole. Repeatedly I rammed and thrusted until I fell to the earth exhausted. I rolled onto my back.

When I looked up, my eyes were met by a sad and solitary eye peering back at me from a crack in the door, its steel black iris fluctuating with emotion. The single eye remained locked on me for an eternity before, blinking away tears, it closed and the sad face of my father turned away.

I ran to the door and called after him.

"It wasn't my fault. She made me do it."

My father stopped, slowly turned around and looked sternly into my eyes.

"But you wanted to do it, didn't you?"

I doubled with pain as the blow struck, twisting my innards into knots of steel.

Blinking back a flood of tears, I answered weakly and for the first time in my life, "Yes."

BOOM!

The shock wave struck with the force of an exploding howitzer. Milliseconds later a pyrotechnic display burst overhead. Like an exploding flower, thousands of spitting, sputtering, spiraling, miniature flares blazed briefly in the black sky.

Animal passions came alive with the pyrotechnic orgy. All thought of personal safety was cast aside as bottle rockets, big Macs, dancing Betty's, M80's cracked and flashed and boomed like a summer storm.

I found myself standing near the concrete pad at town center. Men and boys, girls and women, were rushing out to throw their offerings on the altar of a huge exploding bonfire.

The first blast was followed in rapid succession by hundreds of multi-size rockets. There were little wizzers that quickly disappeared, big roarers that lifted off like space shuttles to burst into a canopy of multi-color flares: red, white, pink, lavender, green and blue flares each with sparkling tails creating patterns of palm trees, exploding dandelions, and cascading waterfalls.

SWISH!

A large rocket flashed from the bank behind me. I ducked instinctively. Looking back I saw the knoll on which Chief Sealth's totem stood silent watch. I saw families sitting on blankets; young children, couples, young and old. I was shocked that people would set off fireworks in the midst of their families. It only confirmed the madness that had taken hold of the crowd.

A steady stream of late comers joined the festivities until several thousand or more were packed around the pad. Bodies pressed and shoved as they surged ever closer.

Errant rockets momentarily split the crowd and struck the cars parked around the pad perimeter. Like Stoic warriors, the cars stood with chests uplifted to accept the flaming lances that smashed with the force of bazooka rockets leaving black, ugly burns on their white gleaming chrome.

Dogs panicked and ran frantically through the crowd, maddened by the noise amplified a thousand times above human hearing.

A woman screamed, "Someone grab that dog!"

A large, black mongrel, his tail alive with exploding firecrackers, dashed between legs, howling in terror. The crowd howled back in delight at the sight of a hysterical animal trying to flee from its own exploding tail.

Like a scene from some horror movie, uplifted faces glowed with the brilliant flashes, mouths open, eyes wide as the pad flashed and the sky boomed and crackled.

Following each overhead burst, I heard the ascending erotic moans of a woman nearby.

"Oh...Oohh...Ooohhh," she moaned.

I couldn't help but sneak a peek at the young couple lying on the grass beside me. Cradled between his drawn-up legs she sat looking up, her back against his chest, his arms beneath her arms, his hands cupping her breasts. Her moans increased in pitch and intensity as she was lifted in ecstasy.

"Oh...Oohh ...Ooohhh."

Then I saw him. In the blinding flashes that had the intensity of a hundred strobe lights, I saw him. He was dressed all in white, a loose white shirt and white slacks, white socks and white shoes, and appeared to float through the crowd. In one hand the white dancer held a small flat drum, in the other a beater.

I watched enthralled as the man in white weaved his way through the melee holding the little drum above his head and beating it like a Spanish dancer. When the white dancer reached the pad, he stopped then began again to slowly beat his drum, bending and stomping in Native fashion. Faster and faster he beat; faster and faster he danced, around and around the exploding fireworks. I could hear the dancer's high-pitched chanting in the midst of the chaos.

Around and around he danced and chanted like the devil's cheerleader, fanning the crowd's insanity as the fireworks roared and flared and thundered. His dance became more ridiculous and obscene as the frenzy of the crowd grew.

A chill ran up my back at the sound of the fiendish laughter and pink glaring eyes of the white dancer. For an instant it was as if Satan himself had come to participate in the orgy. For an instant, framed by the flashes and glares of exploding fireworks, I saw the white dancer stop and look straight at me. His eyes glowed red as they filled with hatred. They glowed and flowed then plunge into my brain, which exploded as the fireball struck.

The stench of burning sulfur filled the dark, quiet grave. Wisps of black smoke curled up from the smoldering blankets. Deep from within the bowels of the earth in the soft pleading voice of my mother came the whisper, "I'm sorry, my son. Please forgive me."

"I do...I do forgive you, Mother...Father, will you forgive me?" I asked.

"I forgive you both," answered my father. "Now, at last, can you forgive yourself?"

Silence settled over the grave.

CHAPTER NINE

Far off in the morning fog, I heard the deep-throated squawk of a black heron. Like a primeval pterosaur it laboriously struggled, with beating wings and dangling legs, to lift its long body into the air.

The dew dripped from the trees and shrubs. It was so heavy and thick that the morning sun, in spite of its brilliance, could only cast the world in gray shadows.

As the gray fog swirled and ebbed before my eyes, strange, muffled whispers came to my ears. When I tried to get up, pain forced me back, back into the softness of white billowing clouds. But even the clouds were filled with needles that sent sharp pain surging up and down my body, a body battered by waves of fever and chills.

Hands appeared out of the fog! Beautiful long slender hands reached out to wipe my sweating face with cool clothes and tuck warm blankets around my shivering body. They were gentle hands, caressing hands, soft and white feminine hands. The nurturing fingers held cups of cool water and hot broth to my parched lips.

A woman's face would appear in the fog, leaning over me. Sometimes the face had hazel eyes. It was a happy face with a smile that framed perfect white teeth. Around the face hung long brown hair.

Sometimes the face had blue eyes and a thin smiled on full lips. Close-cut blonde hair bounced when she laughed. Though the faces changed, the loving hands were constant as I drifted in and out of sleep.

"Good morning, it's 7 o'clock. Do you want some breakfast?"

The old man stood beside my bed. His smile revealed tobacco-stained teeth that were worn and broken from long and hard use. Two upper front teeth were missing. When I nodded, he went back and squatted in front of the opened fireplace. The small, smokeless fire crackled within. A small salmon mounted on a willow rack was roasting beside the alder fire.

"How did I get back here?" I whispered through parched lips.

"I brought you."

I tried to get up but my strength was not up to the task. The old man propped me up on two pillows.

"It's quite a beautiful sunrise, isn't it?" The old man said as he dished up my breakfast.

Indeed it was. It was one of those mornings when I wished time had a pause button so I could savor its sacred beauty.

Shafts of light bathed the deck as the sun ate its way through the fog. Overhead, crows squawked their greetings to one and all. And I knew, to the very depths of my soul, that this was still God's world.

Turmoil may continue outside my cabin but within there was peace because the battle for my soul was over. I'd died and was born again.

"How's the fish?" Asked the old man.

"Great. I didn't realize I was so hungry."

"I'm not surprised. You haven't eaten for four days."

"Four days!...You mean I've been out of my head for four days! My God, what happened?"

"You died...It was a good funeral pyre. And you were singed a bit during your rebirth. I had Betty take care of you during your recovery."

"I...I don't understand. Who's Betty?"

"She's a friend of mine and could be a good friend to you if you'd like."

"I remember two women. Who was the other one?"

"I don't know. As far as I know Betty was the only one who came to nurse you when I was away."

The old man fell silent as my eyes began to droop. When I dropped off to sleep, he slipped out, to return in the evening to fix supper and spend the night.

During the days and nights that followed, I gradually increased the time between sleeps as my body recovered.

It was a time to explore each other's minds.

One morning during breakfast I said, "I've listened to hundreds of native prophecies told by storytellers from Northern Alaska to Southern Arizona and points east and west. All speak of a great cleansing about to come upon the earth that only a few people will survive.

"The stories have the same theme. White man will finally destroy himself, and the red man will rise again."

Picking his teeth with a long fish bone, the old man thought long thoughts before responding.

"Yes, I suppose that's true. Oppressed people usually find hope in some future event where their oppressors will be overthrown."

"Natives smoke the sacred pipe, perform the sacred ceremonies, drum their drums, dance their circles, and chant their songs but after the last smoke has dissipated and the voices and drums fall silent, they pack up their cars and pickups, and return to civilization. Nothing can stop the oncoming of civilization…."

I stopped in mid-sentence when I saw that the old man was distracted by something.

When the old man stirred to his thoughts, "There is a man in this village who ventured into the underworld and became familiar with the dark force. He has fallen under its control."

"Who's that?" I asked.

"You've seen him around the village. He wears many disguises. Sometimes he's a white man in a business suit, other times, he's an Indian in blue jeans. I've seen him take the form of a Christian woman attending the Bible Church. Not long ago he was an Indian witch doctor."

"Was he the one who attacked me in the sweat lodge?"

"Yes. The village is filled with rumors, whether true or not I can't say, but it's time for you to confront the wild one."

"Me? Why should I get involved?"

"You're the only one who can stop him."

"Stop him from doing what?"

The sound of gravel crunching underfoot cut short the answer. There was a loping gait to the footsteps, the gait of one who walked with a limp.

"Come in," I called at the knock on the door.

Betty Coleman's face broke into a broad smile on seeing me sitting in a chair.

"Oh, it's wonderful to see you up. How are you feeling?"

Betty's housedress gave ordinariness in her appearance. She would go unnoticed in a supermarket checkout line until you saw her eyes. They were a pale, sky blue with a tint of azure that sparkled as she talked. Her long eyelashes flipped with joy. That is what you saw in her face, joy. She bubbled with joy. There was an inviting magnetism in her eyes that drew me in and swallowed me whole.

"Just fine, thanks to you. The old man has been telling me what a fine nurse you are."

"Practice makes perfect."

The old man explained, "Since her husband's stroke, Betty has been at his side day and night. He's a very demanding patient."

"How about me? Was I a demanding patient?"

"Not at all. You were sleeping most of the time so I could slip in and out without any fuss."

"Did you have a friend with you once in awhile?"

"No, why do you ask?"

"Oh, nothing really, except I remember seeing the face of two different women."

Betty laughed.

"Ever since my accident, I feel like I'm sharing this body with another woman."

"What accident?"

"Five years ago I was in a car accident. The paramedics thought I was dead, but when they got me to the hospital, the emergency room doctors discovered I'd come back to life."

Patting her left leg, that was several inches shorter and had a slight twist at the ankle, she said, "Other than my leg, I thought I had recovered nicely until the first night after I was discharged. I was dropping off to sleep when a stranger climbed into my bed. I was so terrified I screamed and shoved him out. The stranger claimed that he was my husband. Ever since, I can't shake the feeling that my body belonged to another person."

She threw back her head and giggled, "Maybe you saw my other face."

I smiled and said, "Both faces were beautiful. Thank you very much for your care. Soon I'll be getting out and about. Perhaps I could come by your house for a visit."

"No," Betty snapped in a panic. "Don't ever come to my house."

The old man spoke up, "Betty's husband has become very jealous since his stroke. It would make things very difficult for her if he knew that she talked to other men."

I said, "Well, maybe one day I could be walking along Angeline and you might just happen to be out for a walk. We could have a little neighborly chat. What time do you usually go for your walk?"

"After his lunch Bill takes an afternoon nap between one and two."

"What a coincidence, that's when I usually take a long walk."

Glancing nervously at her watch, Betty said, "I must go now."

Entering her home, Betty was greeted by Bill's shrill voice calling for her from the front bedroom.

"Where have you been? I've been calling you for hours."

"It's such a beautiful morning I went for a walk on the beach. Are you ready for your morning coffee?"

"No! Get in here and clean me up. You were gone so long I shit in my dipper."

Betty brought a basin of warm soapy water and washrags. No matter how often she cleaned him after a mess, she was always repulsed.

"I suppose you went over to the antique store to talk to Glen. That man is a real womanizer. He wears more beaver trophies than any man in this county."

Betty didn't respond as she finished the cleanup.

"So it was him!"

"Don't be silly. I told you I went for a walk on the beach alone. Do you want your coffee now?"

"Yes," he snapped in a voice as precise as a Prussian General.

It was always the same, constant accusations and suspicions. But Betty had constructed an invisible shield that shed the abuse like water off a glass bubble.

Bill Coleman depended on Betty for everything now. But it was not always that way. Before his stroke, Bill was a tall handsome man with an athletic body, like a Gary Cooper some said. But unlike Cooper, he was never a quiet man.

Cafe Angeline used to ring with his tirades against the Federal government and the Indians. Like once on the day after the weekly Kitsap Herald came out:

"Did you read that Goddamn editorial in the Herald yesterday?" Bill shouted in the Cafe.

A shocked silence came over the packed room.

"That young editor has the balls to tell us that everything will be all right if everyone just acts nicely. The problems with the Indians will go away."

As usual, the Indians outnumbered the non-Indians in the cafe. Their narrowed eyes revealed their awareness of what was coming.

"This sounds great but is extremely difficult to accomplish when lawsuits are being filed by the tribe to gain jurisdiction over us non-Indians who have no voice or vote in their government."

Bill wheeled down the aisle to confront the booth filled with Indians.

"Put yourself in the shoes of those of us who own waterfront property. We have to pay thousands of dollars to the legal defense fund to prevent the tribe from taking away our private tidelands."

He whirled to the mixed booth of Indians and non-Indians and pleaded:

"If you want to understand how we feel about this, would you be willing to deed twenty-five percent of your home and property to the tribe without compensation?"

I couldn't hold back my reply.

"That twenty-five percent you talk about is the tidelands wrongfully included in your deed. Instead of ranting at the tribe, you should follow the trial judge's advice. Seek restitution from the State of Washington who erroneously included the tidelands in your deed."

He wheeled around at me, with hatred flaring in his eyes.

"Are you blind? Don't you understand where this will all end? The tribe intends to re-acquire all lands within the original boundaries of the Pt. Madison Reservation. They will if we don't stop them.

"If the tribe succeeds in acquiring all the land, thus taking it off the tax rolls, the county property tax bill is in for a hefty jolt."

Bill spun around with a wave of his arm.

"Listen up, folks! It will happen if they get that casino. They will make so much money that no one could afford not to sell out to them."

When the patrons started to get up and leave, Sonny leaped up on the table beside the front door and lifted her T-shirt to her chin exposing her perky breasts.

"Take a good look, ladies and gentlemen! There are two of them. They are separate but they are part of one body. We can, we must find ways to live together in peace."

It had been three years since his stroke and each day Bill had become more mean-spirited, sinking deeper into the slime pit of self-pity. Few people could tolerate his constant complaints.

"Where's that damn preacher? I haven't seen his ass around here for two weeks."

Pastor Jerry's visits had been growing further and further apart, and shorter.

"He's a phony, you know. He can't even tell me why God allowed this to happen to me."

Betty faithfully tended to her husband's needs and kept him company in spite of his everlasting complaints.

"It's time for your backrub," said Betty.

She turned him on his side and massaged his back with bay balm that toughened his skin against bedsores.

"Don't press so hard! Your skinny fingers cut like blades."

"Oh, I'm sorry. I'll try to be softer."

When she put on his new Pampers, fresh pajamas and bed linens he complained, "Don't be so rough! Don't you realize that living inside a frozen body is hell on earth?"

Secretly, Betty wished his mouth had been frozen with his arms and legs so that she would never have to hear his shrill voice again, an irritating voice that sent shivers up her back like screeching caulk on a blackboard.

Precisely at ten-fifteen, Betty entered his husband's bedroom.

"It's time for breakfast," she said.

"Don't be so rough," he whimpered as she rolled the Hoya harness under his rigid body.

"It's a beautiful fall morning, not a cloud in the sky."

She ignored his complaints as she pumped the hydraulic lift that lifted him out of his hospital bed then swung him into a wheelchair.

In the kitchen, she fed him his breakfast of scrambled eggs and sausage. As he chewed on his whole-wheat toast, she read the morning paper to him.

"I see Dole is after Clinton again."

"Has another bimbo come out of the closet?"

"No. Dole is opposing Clinton's invasion of Haiti."

"Damn right he should. Why should we risk a single American life for those niggers?"

Wiping the dribble from his chin, Betty wheeled her husband out onto the sundeck. Port Madison Bay was filled with fishing boats.

Betty asked, "Why do you think there are so many fishing boats out on the bay this morning?"

"Must be the fall chum run. This is the best place in Puget Sound for them."

"I understand it's because of the Indian fish hatchery at the head of Miller Bay."

Bill only grunted.

"You just can't give the Indians credit for anything, can you?"

Bill answered with a glare.

Betty picked up a book of Rudyard Kipling's poems and resumed reading "Gunga Din" where she had left off the day before. The masculine rhythmic beat soon calmed Bill's tormented soul.

With the reading of "…you're a better man than I am Gunda Din," Betty closed the book. Bill was quiet and content to gaze at the fishing boats being swept up Agate Pass on the incoming tide.

Betty picked up a thin book of poems by George Sterling, a little known American poet who lived in San Francisco around the turn of the century. She had come upon the little collection on a high dusty shelf of The Shorey Book Store in Seattle. The volume seemed to fall off the shelf and into her hands as if to say, "Read Me."

After Bill had been put into bed for his midday nap, Betty slipped out for her daily walk along Angeline Avenue.

I liked to go for long walks. On Wednesdays and Saturdays I would walk to the Longhouse Mini-Market two miles away. Often I would follow a shortcut that twisted through a stately Hemlock forest.

On each trip I couldn't help but see the piles of garbage and refuse that drew ever-increasing company along the back road. Two old refrigerators whose doors hung off their hinges joined a discarded mattress; green and black plastic bags filled with kitchen garbage had been ripped open and scattered by hungry bears. The empty milk cartons, castoff magazines, orange peelings and coffee grounds—all by-products of the rotting putridness of civilized man.

One day as I walked the cutoff, I heard a woman moaning. A red Toyota pickup, parked in the middle of the trail, was rocking side to side as if shaken by the unseen hand of a giant.

I peered through the window into the uplifted face of a young Indian woman. Her startled look at my sudden appearance quickly gave way to a coy smile signaling that everything was okay. I recognized the young woman as the Longhouse clerk who regularly sold me a Lotto ticket. I could see only the top of a blue Mariner's baseball cap and the red flannel shirt of the man who was on top of her. I quickly walked away.

I didn't know who owned the land through which the dirt trail wandered. Whoever it was, they certainly were not doing anything to stop the growing piles of stench that made the pristine forest smell like an open dump while just a few miles away the county provided a landfill to discourage just such random dumping.

"Don't you know that land is part of the Reservation?" Clara snapped disgustedly when I happened upon her a few days later.

"I can never understand why those people foul their land like that. Animals don't do such things, but then animals are supposed to be of a lower order. How's your little dog working out?"

"Just fine. I've named her Lady. She's a great dog and loves to travel in the car."

I had gotten the little Cockapoo from the Kitsap Humane Society just a day before she was to be put down.

"You were gone the other day, weren't you?"

"Yes, I made a trip over to Seattle. Why?"

"We heard her barking all day long. At first I couldn't tell where the barking was coming from so I walked up the street until I came to your cabin. She sounded so frightened."

Just then Clara's husband came out to work in their yard.

"That is my husband," said Clara, indifferently.

I replied loud enough for the man to hear, "I've walked up and down all the streets of this community and I can state, as a fact, that your yard is the most beautiful."

"It's taken years of loving care and hard work to develop," answered Clara.

"Your vegetable garden is really producing, isn't it?"

"Yes, it is," answered Clara.

Her husband snipped around a little cedar tree that stood in the corner of the yard. It had been pruned and trained into an topiary of ascending balls stacked on top of each other with a space between.

"Henry, don't cut so much off," Clara called out.

"We have lined the yard with dwarf fruit trees; apples, cherries and apricots, each with three varieties, one of which is the pollinator.

"It shows green thumbs at work."

Clara's husband was a shadow person who moved about the edges of her life unnoticed.

"I see you're all dressed up. Are you going to church?"

"Well, yes, I am. Honey and I are off to Wednesday prayer services. We're charter members of the Suquamish Bible Church, you know. We've services twice on Sunday, morning and evening, and again on Wednesday evening. Would you like to come with us sometime?"

"Well, I'm not much into church going any more."

"We've a nice young minister who is filled with the Holy Spirit. His pretty wife plays the organ for the services."

"As I said, I'm not much into church going."

"You should be. These are critical times. The Lord is coming very soon and if you're not ready, your soul will burn in hell."

She edged a few inches closer, looked to her right then to her left, and in a soft whisper said, "Do you know that Satan is gathering his forces right here in Suquamish?"

"No!" I exclaimed in a shocked voice. "I didn't realize that Suquamish was that important. I would've thought he would go after the people in Seattle first. There is much more sin over there."

"Ridicule if you must but mark my words, the battle between good and evil is taking place right here in Suquamish." She stepped closer. "Have you seen those pornographic magazines down at JC's market?"

"I'm sorry. I must've missed them. I'll be sure to look for them the next time I'm in the store."

Clara's eyes flashed with renewed intensity.

"Those magazines are filled with sin. Whores and sluts exposing their naked bodies to inflame the lust of young boys and men."

I asked innocently, "Have you actually seen what's in those magazines?"

"You don't have to wallow in mud to know that it's dirty."

"I have trouble following your analogy. Are you saying all magazines are dirty? Or just some magazines?"

"You know very well what I'm talking about. As if the dirty minds of men and young boys needed any more to stir them up to rape and abuse innocent women. Did you know that pornography caused George Bundy to rape and murder over thirty women?"

"I'm sure there was more involved than nude pictures. Twisted minds don't need nude pictures to stir them to action. It's the female they're attacking. A harmless lingerie ad can trigger the same response as a full nude."

"That's another thing. They're even advertising women's unmentionables on the TV. What do you think that does to those young boys whose hormones are already over stimulated?"

"I don't know. What does it do?"

"It increases their addiction to pornography. As Dr. Hanson's studies have shown, pornography is as addictive as alcohol or drugs."

"Oh, that's interesting. The Presidential Commission on Pornography concluded there was no causal link between pornography and criminal behavior."

"I don't believe that," snapped Clara.

"Tell me, how far should we go in covering the female body? How much of the female body could be exposed without inflaming the male's lustful passions? Should everything be covered except their heads, maybe even hands and ankles? How about the face? Shouldn't a veil be put over the woman's face? Perhaps you think that all women and girls who go out in public should wear nuns' habits or maybe those black things worn by Muslin women? Do you advocate that the vote should be taken from women so that they can return to the protected status of chattel?"

She snapped back, "Pastor Jerry discussed that very thing in his sermon last Sunday morning. You should've heard him. Since our protest demanding that the owners of JC's Market clean that trash off their shelves has been ignored, he thinks stronger measures are needed."

Clara edged nearer. I leaned back to escape her fiery breath.

"Did you know that young people can rent dirty movies down there?" She whispered, then pulled back in shocked horror.

"Yes, that's true," she continued. "They can rent that filth and spend hours soaking in the very blood of Satan. That's why there is so much adultery and fornication in this community, especially among those pagan Indians. Sex and alcohol is all they think about because they're Satan's children."

Clara had the bit in her mouth and was in full gallop.

"But the Christians of Suquamish are fighting back. Christians own the new shopping mall up on the hill. They won't permit any alcohol to be sold in either the restaurant or the grocery store. You won't find any pornography there either...."

She would've stayed in her pulpit if Honey hadn't arrived to save my ears.

"Clara, we must hurry. We don't want to make a scene coming in after services begin. Would you like to join us?"

"I can't this evening. Another time maybe."

My dog, Lady, came to my rescue by tugging furiously on her leash to be off down the road. She had spied Poco, one of Mary Wilson's cats, as it slipped across the street into the blackberry bushes.

As Clara backed her car into the street, she leaned out the window and called to me, "Remember what the Lord said, 'If you're not for me, you're against me.' There is no neutral ground in this battle."

With purring acceleration, the green Volvo carried Clara and Honey off to their Wednesday prayer meeting.

"It's not the way it looked."

I was startled by the sudden appearance of Clara's husband.

"We've never met, but I've seen you around. My name is Henry. Laverne told me you'd seen us in the pickup the other day. Laverne and I have been going together for nearly five years now.

"We don't want you to get the wrong impression about us. We hope you'll keep our confidence and maybe help us."

"I don't see that it's any of my business."

Henry dropped his voice to a soft whisper, glancing around to make sure no one was listening.

"I'm going to divorce Clara and marry Laverne."

"Why are you telling me this?"

"Because I hope you won't tell Clara. She'd go crazy if she knew I was seeing an Indian woman. You know how she feels about them."

I wanted to run away, not because of the infidelity, but at being put into this kind of situation again. I'd learned from bitter experience that, to be told a man's secret sin, was to gain an enemy.

Henry continued, "It all began soon after Clara decided to end our sexual relations and have separate bedrooms. She said, 'Sex is dirty and disgusting and that she didn't get any pleasure from it.' She decided, just like that, like it was her sole right.

"I tried everything, begging, pleading, bringing her gifts, nothing made any difference. She turned me out like a dog with its tail between its legs.

"Now, don't get me wrong. Clara is a wonderful Christian woman. She keeps a good house and is an excellent cook. She's very active in her church and neighborhood activities. Maybe she can get along without sex but I can't. Could you?"

"I could suggest you have Clara read how St. Paul counseled husbands and wives not to refuse one another their conjugal rights, but I don't think it'll change her mind."

"I did that already but she said that applied only when both the husband and wife were Christians. She intends to sleep alone until I become a born-again Christian. What do you think of that?"

"Nothing is more complex than the sexual relationship between a man and a woman. I suspect Clara is using her faith to avoid facing some sexual trauma from earlier times.

"God intended sex to be a beautiful river of energy circulating between a man and a woman throughout their time together. That's the law of nature and it's God's law. Clara's refusal violates God's laws as much as your infidelity. One sin is committed in secret; the other becomes a public scandal."

Henry squeezed my arm.

"I know that Clara will stand up in church urging prayers for her sinful husband while ignoring her sin. But, can we count on your discretion?"

"You can't make me the judge of your lives. But rest assured, I won't tell anyone. Besides, I'll be leaving soon. My work here is almost finished."

CHAPTER TEN

Normally, water is plentiful throughout the Pacific Northwest. From November to April, moisture-laden clouds sweep off the Pacific Ocean carried northeast by the steady string of low-pressure cells that spin like giant windmills. They pump rain over the low lands and pile snow on the high mountaintops bringing five months of joy to alpine and cross-country skiers.

It is expected that the huge reservoirs in the mountains will be filled. That there will be water in abundance to irrigate the Golden Delicious apple trees of Wenatchee and the Riesling grape vines of Sunnyside. That the Columbia River will be strong enough to feed the hungry irrigation pumps that lift the precious liquid up to the high plateaus where parched desert is turned into lush fields of wheat, barley and alfalfa. That there will be enough water to turn the dynamos of the Bonneville Power Dams to provide cheap electricity to the ravenous aluminum smelters, and to light homes and industries. Long before white men came to harness the water with their dams and reservoirs, the salmon, trout and sturgeon flourished in the abundant water.

It is untrue that people will grow webs between their toes if they live in the Pacific Northwest more than five years. It probably is true that Ivar Haglund once sat on a beach log shielded from the interminable downpour by a rainhat on his head, a rain slicker on his back and rubber boots on his feet, bemoaning his fate in that all he had to eat were acres of clams.

Without an abundance of water, modern life in the Pacific Northwest would not be possible. When it is in short supply, troubles abound. The lights of homes and factories grow dim, lawns dry to a brittle, sick brown, trees and vines wither and die. The crystal clear water, taken for granted to perpetually flow from the drinking taps, take on a mud taste as the drainage from the reservoirs suck up the bottom dregs. At such times, all eyes look to the Southwest seeking, hoping for rain-bearing clouds.

The year came when the winds had continued to blow out of the Northwest off the leading edge of a giant stationary high cell that fixed itself off the coast of Vancouver Island. It pumped hot dry air around the inland desert of Washington and spilled it over the Cascades and through the Columbia Gorge to blister and bake Seattle and Portland. Vancouver, BC felt the draught of that year as deeply as the others for they were all sister cities sharing the great valley that stretches from the Frazer River in the North to the Siskiyou Mountains on the Southern border of Oregon. That was the year that all shared the same great fear that a flash of lighting, a carelessly thrown match, or a neglected campfire would set ablaze the tender dry forests.

A forest fire is a terrible thing. It is violent and creative. It moans, crackles, and roars. It is a monster that is indifferent to what it consumes. Neither fawn nor doe, neither child nor mother, concern a forest fire. All are fuel for consumption. Fuel to stoke the roaring engine that swallows all in its path.

In ancient times, the fiery caldron beneath earth's crust was thought to be the realm of the Fire Goddess Hel, after whom hell was named. She was the ruler of regeneration in the underworld.

Originally, Hel's earthly caldron was not the torture chamber it became in the later Christian mythology by Dante. It was a place of purification and rebirth. All the dead went there to be purged of his or her memories of former lives and to be reconstituted in Hel's sacred fire.

The Queen of Fire was said to have fiery characteristics such as warmth, illumination, benevolence, and domestic utility. But there was always the certain danger of sudden shifts into destructiveness or cruelty. She represented the forces of hot passion, having the fire's capacity to bite the hand that feeds it unless it is treated with respect.

That year in Suquamish the dryness of summer stretched into the fall. The last soaker had been in March.

"I've never seen it this bad," said Sid Thompson as he slowly worked the backhoe controls to keep from stirring the powder that once was soil.

His foundation crew wore bandannas over their noses to filter out the gray dust that billowed up with each bucket from the footing trench.

"Tom, can you run a hose over here and spray down this dust?" Sid called to one of his men.

"Can't. The Water Department shuts off this block on even days, remember?"

"Oh Yeah, I forgot. Damn it to hell. Maybe we should shut down for today. Tomorrow, we can get some water on this dust."

Depression settled over the workmen as the motors sputtered to a stop and silence came over the jobsite. Work was hard to get, to lose a day because of the drought bit deep into their throats.

"I never thought I'd have to pray for rain, but I'll tell you true, every morning before I come to work I've been going up to the church to light a candle for rain."

Disaster struck that very night. Clouds gathered over the mountains and flowed down the valleys. But they were dry clouds, sterile clouds, bereft of life-giving moisture. The clouds bounced and jostled as they surged around the mountain peaks sending flashes of lightening crashing to the ground. Throughout the night, small fires were sparked to life throughout the mountains from Mt. Baker to Crater Lake. By daybreak, the Cascades were covered with black, billowing smoke of raging, out-of-control forest fires.

Even the forests of Port Madison Indian Reservation were not spared.

Respect was not the intention of the hands that struck the matches and held their tiny flames to the crumpled newspapers. That night, at the stroke of twelve, little fires were lit simultaneously around the four-corners of the Indian forest. No one noticed the darkened cars drive away.

The first 911 call sent the Suquamish volunteer firemen racing to the station next to the Post Office. Their trucks were waiting and ready to go, started by the full-time station attendant a few moments after the alarm.

Fifteen minutes did not lapse before the first unit arrived at the closest fire. Even then, it was too late to save the forest. Repeated alarms came in from around the forest but the concern was not for the trees but for the homes of Indians and non-Indians, the expensive waterfront homes and the cheap mobiles had to be saved.

Fire departments from Kingston and Poulsbo were called out to help the Suquamish firemen fight forest fires that surrounded Suquamish and Indianola.

During the day, a dense blanket of smoke hung over the village sucking out the last wisps of freshness, choking the lungs and smarting the eyes.

Pastor Jerry was quick to respond.

"God's hand of judgment is at work. The Bible warns that God will not be mocked. His anger is all consuming like the forest fires that are bearing down on this community at this very moment."

He went about the village pleading with everyone that he could find, man, woman, or child, to repent before it's too late.

It took three days to bring the fires under control. Only smoking stumps remained of the once pristine forest of Hemlocks, Spruce, and Aspen, the product of the reforestation that occurred after the grandfather trees were taken to the Port Madison Mills. Again the reservation was reduced to worthless stumps.

Pastor Jerry was elated to announce, "Now, we'll find the graves of those little children."

Russ Tate, the Fire Chief for District 4, was not so sure God's hand was involved.

"There were simultaneous outbreaks around the perimeter of the Reservation forests," he told me at Cafe Angeline as we savored some coffee. He raised his voice for all present to hear.

"It is obvious that God had some handymen to lighten his work. If anyone here has any information about who set those fires, I hope you will get in touch with me. There is a sizable reward being offered."

There wasn't a sound. All eyes searched the depths of coffee cups or the gray sky outside.

"Damn it," cried the Chief, slamming his fist on the table. "I know there are people in this room who know who set those fires."

There was no response.

"Think about it. A fire stick can burn at both ends. Next time it could be your homes."

The Chief threw four quarters on the table and stomped out of the Cafe in disgust.

I didn't notice Betty's handicap because she was wearing a bright yellow sweater to draw attention to her full breasts and away from her limp. A light green, ankle-length skirt masked her deformed leg but my eyes were drawn upward to her beaming face and brown hair. In her late fifties, it was obvious that she had always been an attractive woman and her later years had not been cruel. The sparkle of her bright brown eyes grew with each approaching step.

"How's your book coming today?" Betty asked.

"I'm well into it now," I answered.

"What's it about?"

"I really don't know."

She looked at me with puzzlement.

"That is true. I started out packing a lifeless thing in search of a trail, but suddenly it has taken on its own life and is carrying me off in another direction down trails of its choice.

"Each morning, as I begin writing, I am anxious to find out what will happen next. What twists will the plot take? What character will step to center stage? What revelations will that character bring? The story has taken on a life of it's own. How about you? How's your poetry coming?"

"I keep at it, but I don't think I'm very good."

"How do you know? Often we're our own worst critics. We lack perspective because we're too close to our creations, our children."

Betty's eyes sparkled.

"Would you read a few of my poems and tell me if they are any good?"

"I'd be glad to look at your work. Perhaps tomorrow you could bring a few pieces and let me give them a read."

"Oh, would you?" Betty gently squeezed my arm. "I'd like that very much."

So we parted, going in opposite directions.

I looked forward to the next day when we would pass again realizing that, with each passing, unseen ties were exchanged between our hearts.

I knew that the inevitable would happen. Was I a wiser lover or just the same blind fool who would again fall into the dismal love pool?

And what about Betty? She was married to a bedridden man who could no longer give her the love she so desperately desired. What will happen to her if she never loves again? Or if she falls in love with me what then will she do?

Each day as Dominique sorted the daily mail, she watched for the brown envelope. A week passed before she found it, as she knew she would. She slipped the envelope into her apron pocket to await inspection when she got to the quiet grove of Hemlocks next to the Catholic cemetery.

There, in quiet solitude, with the stately Hemlocks sweeping upward like cathedral walls, she carefully spread the envelope's contents on her lap. A smile crept over her lips as she studied the photographs. She squirmed a little upon feeling a familiar wetness.

She unfolded the accompanying letter.

"Jerry, I really had to beg for these shots. In addition, I had to promise to do the dishes for a week but I think they are worth it. I know you'll agree. Meg and I really enjoyed the last ones of Diane…."

The letter went on to describe the photographic techniques involved and then wondered…"Why haven't we received your latest exchange?"

Dominique pondered the situation as she glanced over at Chief Sealth's grave with its four cedar posts that held up the two Suquamish long canoes. She knew what she was doing was illegal, and if caught, she could go to jail but it was worth the risk. But what should she do with them? Then it came to her that he would know what to do. She resolved to ask him that night.

For months Morning Star's daughter had begged, "Mommy, will you give me a peyote ceremony? That would be the best present to celebrate my ninth birthday."

On the day of the ceremony, I helped Morning Star construct a sweat lodge on the beach in front of the Tribal Center. We stretched a large, blue tarp over long cedar poles that we had sunk deep into the sand.

Before the ceremony could begin, everyone—men, women and children—stripped naked and entered the tiny cave-like lodge where alderwood logs burned in a pit.

Inside, we prayed, and chanted, and sang for nearly an hour, and wept for forgiveness.

Later, after plunging into the icy waters to emerge with a happy grin, Morning Star lit a Camel cigarette and said to me, "That's what we call the cleanse and purification ceremony."

At sunset, everyone dressed again to sit down to a lavish feast of corn breads, huckleberries, shredded deer and elk meat, smoked salmon, thick chicken noodle soup and several kinds of fruit pies.

Before the meal could commence, Ed Swenson took tobacco from a tin of Bugler and rolled a giant cigarette the sixe of a Cuban cigar. After lighting and drawing four times then passed it down the table, and asked that everyone take four puffs.

"Oh, heavenly Father," he then began, "we pray to you for good things to happen in the life of this girl. We ask that you look down on us and bless this food and help us feel good in our lives and our bodies."

The birthday girl beamed as she ate as her cousin, Tom George, proud and smiling patted her on the head.

"See, we're passing our culture on to our children," he said. "White Americans have no culture other than Ice-T and McDonald hamburgers."

When the feast was finished, it was time to enter the lodge. Again everyone undressed. In the darkness of night, the lodge threw off a blue glow like an ancient lighthouse. It stood six-feet high, a plastic bubble from another time on which the dancing fire drew dark silhouettes against the tarp.

Amidst the quiet murmur of prayers and the crackling of the alderwood logs, smoke from cheap tobacco that had been rolled into paper-thin cornhusks forged a dense mist.

The old man sat next to me. He leaned over and whispered, "Many people believe that tobacco smoke will lift their prayers upward to God."

All grew silent save for the soft beat of a small drum and the gurgling of the incoming tide in Agate Pass. No cameras or tape recorders were allowed inside the sweat lodge because the peyote ceremony was sacred.

The old man said softly, speaking to all who would listen: "Many believe that peyote strengthens the spirit and fuses a oneness with nature. It's also believed that peyote embodies our deity and that eating it allows us to communicate better with the Great Spirit."

Whatever the reason, I had been told that the historic peyote ritual had fallen upon hard times. The most recent blow came when the US Supreme Court ruled that Indians lacked constitutional right to take the hallucinogenic drug as part of their religion.

The moment arrived to pass the peyote clockwise along the small unbroken circle.

After blessing themselves by waving a stalk of sage up and down their naked bodies, the thirteen people present—about half were young children—dipped into a wooden bowl and brought small scoops of peyote buttons to their mouths.

"Take as much as you want," instructed Ed Swenson who directed the ceremony.

He sprinkled cedar chips onto Grandpa Fire and added, "Take it now with a good thought for yourself."

So began the long peyote ceremony, a ritual that has remained unchanged for thousands of years. The night would be followed by a full day of fasting, prayer and peyote.

"God gave us peyote for our ceremonies. It helps us spiritually to understand ourselves," said Swenson, the revered Yakima Indian widely known widely as the roadman.

Swenson, 42, was a solemn man, shy and soft-spoken. He used only necessary words. Even his smile was serious. Long shanks of dark black hair protruded from the navy blue baseball cap he wore for the ceremony. It was speckled with red and blue beads.

Swenson was a shaman who had studied the ways of peyote and as the road man, traveled throughout Washington to conduct the peyote ceremony.

"I'm an ordinary man. I've no special powers," he said plainly. "Natives believe in one God, same as everyone. And peyote is our medicine. It makes us feel good."

Swenson said he conducted several peyote ceremonies each month. Most revolved around a family illness or to mourn a death or sometimes, like tonight, to celebrate a birthday.

"People hear of the ceremony by word of mouth," he said. "They're usually held in someone's house. Most of the ceremonies have taken place in Yakima and White Swan and here in Suquamish."

Sitting on blankets and pillows, many winced as they chewed the peyote buttons. The taste of the dark green cactus plant was bitter and toxic. No one dared leave the lodge or move between the fire and the person ingesting the peyote.

"That," continued Swenson, "would dilute the peyote's special power. The creator blessed peyote. It has its own spirit and it works for us because it was meant for us."

To wash away the peyote bite, a pail full of herbal tea accompanied the wooden bowl. The long, stringy drug, normally taken in hard brownish pellets, or buttons as they are called, was moistened and chopped so finely that it resembled a sticky, black relish.

Before the night was over, the peyote, which often induced nausea, would be passed around four different times, and slowly, the people would melt into silent reflection.

"If you feel sick, it's good to let it go. It takes all the sickness away," Morning Star confided as she chewed the peyote with a grimace. "Then the fireman, the one who brings in the wood, will come around and clean it up."

The peyote had come from the Rio Grande Valley in Texas where authorized dealers, sanctioned by the Texas government, grow and sell the mystical drug to agents of the various tribes.

Swenson said: "I pay $75 to $100 for about 1,000 peyote buttons. Back in Washington, it takes a week to ten days without rain to properly dry them out before they can be used. Peyote is only taken 'in ceremony,' like a sacrament of the church.

"It's yucky," whined a little girl as her mother fed her a small clump of the magic cactus plant.

"It's good. It's from nature," the mother told her.

The peyote had completed its circle, and the participants chewed—and chewed—and watched the fire take on many changes, transfixed, waiting, and hoping to be transfigured.

Morning Star offered a prayer.

"I've had many troubles in my life, and I want to tell Grandpa Fire the anger and mistrust I feel for the citizens of Washington, and sometimes our own people," she started, tears welling in her eyes.

"We don't want any trouble. We believe in God and we're just trying to live our own lives. We're trying to be understood but there's so much ignorance, so much racism. Grandpa Fire, please just let us live in peace."

In Washington, peyote could be used in either the home of a Native American Church member or on an Indian Reservation, but only as part of a religious ceremony. It was illegal for non-Indians to take peyote under any circumstances.

The drug never had widespread appeal, and there had been relatively little illegal trafficking of peyote. According to the US Drug Enforcement Administration, Federal authorities between 1980 and 1987, compared with more than 15 million pounds of marijuana during the same period seized only 19.4 pounds of peyote.

"It's just like the Catholics using bread and wine," said Swenson. "It's our medicine, but the white man is afraid peyote will bring us together. They don't want us to unite. They fear that."

The next morning, during a break, I looked down the beach and saw Joe Old Coyote standing in front of the blue tarp that he'd rigged over his cedar log.

When I started toward him, the old man caught my arm.

"Don't disturb him," he said.

"I was going to ask how his totem was coming."

"No. That's not a good idea. When a warrior is on a spirit quest, all his people, his wife and his children understand and support him but no one can disturb him. For if they disturb him when he is with the Great Spirit, his work will suffer and he may die."

Still later that night in another part of Suquamish as the full moon began to rise, twelve witches dressed in black gowns gathered in the

Hemlock grove. At the edge of a small clearing, they carefully and reverently pulled away the leaves that hid a pile of white rocks.

In the center of the clearing stood a large cedar stump left over from the grand logging days where on once stood a huge grandfather cedar more than two hundred feet high.

Tonight the stump was to serve another function, a sacred function, as the witches lugged the rocks to place them in a circle around the stump, by measure, exactly nine feet in diameter.

Outside the circle, a large iron kettle hung from a tripod over a bed of glowing coals. Inside the pot, something was bubbling and spitting.

A white cloth was carefully laid over the stump on which were placed candles and clay figurines. Standing around the outer stone circle, facing the altar, the witches began to softly chant an evocation:

Nema

Yrolg Dna

Rewop

Modgnik Eht Si Eniht Rof

Eno Live Eht Morf Su Reviled

Noitatpmet Otni Ton Su Dael

Srotbed Ruo Evigrof Dna

Daerb Yliad Ruo

Yad Siht Su Evig

Nevaeh Ni Si Ti Sa

Htrae No

Enod Eb Lliw Yht

Emoc Modgnik Yht

Eman Yht Eb Dewollah

Nevaeh Ni Tra Hichw

Rehtaf Ruo.

Like a phonograph playing in reverse, they chanted; they shuffled to their right, counterclockwise, around the enclosed circle. They continued to chant as the full moon rose in the star filled sky.

Nema

Yrolg Dna

Rewop

Modgnik Eht Si Eniht Rof

Around and around, they shuffled and chanted in hypnotic trance.

Nema

Yrolg Dna

Modgnik Eht Si Eniht Rof

My eyes began to droop then they snapped open at the realization! It was backwards! They were chanting the Lord's Prayer backwards! As if summoning God's other son, the son of his left hand.

When the moon reached its midheaven, a man and a woman emerged from the log house and walked, with stately carriage, across the dirt road and into the Hemlock grove.

Each wore a flower garland on their head, a long, flowing white gown, which covered their sandaled feet, a braided cord, exactly nine feet in length, wrapped around each waist. The woman carried a goblet in her upraised right hand while in her left hand, which hung limply at her side; she carried a long, twelve-inch dagger that glimmered in the moonlight. The man carried the same two things but in reverse order, the goblet point down and the dagger pointed up.

Upon their arrival at the clearing, the circle opened to accept them, then closed. From my vantage point, I could no longer see or hear the rest of the ceremony.

My eyes were heavy from lack of sleep and intending just a moment of rest, they closed only to snap open again to the bright rays of the morning sun. The old stump stood naked in the center of the empty clearing.

CHAPTER ELEVEN

It was mid-afternoon of the next day and I was again walking along Angeline Avenue. My thoughts were elsewhere. The outer world had given over to the inner world as I wallowing deep in thought about a stone wall I'd encountered in my writing.

My spirit helpers had not appeared, and the next chapter was a blank computer screen with a taunting cursor flashing its defiance, daring me to write without them and, of course, I couldn't. It was a waiting time, a time to walk, to stretch emotional muscles against the mountains, the sea and the sky.

"Gotcha," Betty giggled.

She had nearly knocked me over to get my attention. I was unaware that, as we drew closer, she had positioned herself in my path. I was startled by the sudden appearance of her smiling face with those twinkling brown eyes just like a trickster.

We stood, caressed by the warm summer sun, sharing a moment of laughter.

"I wrote a dream poem this morning," she blurted out, bursting with excitement. "Or rather I wrote down a poem I heard in a dream. It's to my son. Maybe, someday, I'll send it to him. He called last night because his son had left home. He said, 'Mom, now I know how you felt when I left home. My guts are twisted up into knots.'"

"I told him, 'our children can be the source of our greatest joys and sadness.'

"I've been reading a wonderful book by Melody Beattie entitled, *Co-Dependent No More*. Mary Wilson recommended it to me because she thought I needed to start doing things for myself, but it's hard with an invalid husband to care for."

"You still haven't brought me any of your poetry."

"I will."

"When?"

"Tomorrow afternoon," she answered. I heard a new- found determination in her voice. "Right after I put Bill down for his nap."

As we talked, a heavyset man with a large protruding stomach huffed passed, arms swinging rhythmically like a British Grenadier. He ignored my greeting.

"I can't figure that man out," I said. "Every time I've tried to exchange greetings with him he acts as if he doesn't see or hear me."

"He doesn't."

"I don't understand."

"He's blind and deaf."

"But how can he walk up and down the street like he does?"

"When Al was younger and still had his sight and hearing, he walked up and down Angeline Avenue every morning for years. He'd done it so often that he boasted he could do it blindfolded. When diabetes took his sight and his hearing failed he was proud that he could still take his morning walks.

"I thought you knew that. Everyone along the Avenue knows about Al. We drive accordingly. Do you write longhand or on the computer?"

"When I first took up serious writing, I composed in longhand on a yellow legal pad, then transcribed it into the computer. My first story, *Not All Spirits*, was written that way. My second novel was written partially by longhand and partially on the computer and went much faster. With my current novel, I'm writing it entirely on the computer, except my journal notes.

"No matter what creative method I use, the finished manuscript must be computerized."

"Why?"

"My publisher demands that I produce an error-free manuscript on a computer data disk so that the manuscript can be transferred directly into the press computer. With today's technology, a book can be on the booksellers' shelves in as little as six weeks from date of submission rather than the year-to-eighteen months by the old methods. The day of the manual typewriter was over."

"How old are you?" She asked.

"I'll be sixty in November."

"When did you learn to use a computer?"

"About twelve years ago, back in the early 80's. A friend who was a computer consultant took it upon himself to teach me. It was more by accident than choice. But the skill has proven to be a lifesaver. Why do you ask?"

"I have to write in longhand since I can't write poetry any other way. What do you enjoy most about writing?"

"It had been on my mind for many years. Professional writing is hard work. Getting published is even harder and meaningful rewards are reserved for a precious few. Yet nothing brings me greater pleasure than writing.

"There is a power that lifts me when I run aground on the rocks of rejection and am pounded by the waves of despair, a power that sets me on a new course whenever I became lost during the long and lonely nights of my soul's nadir.

"What do I enjoy the most about writing? The answer is always the same, no matter the rejections and lack of encouragement; it is the power I feel when I am in the presence of my guides, guardians and the ancient masters, when the white light of my Lord surrounds us. It is the power that flows through my body into my fingers enabling them to fly over the keyboard recording what appears before my inner eyes…people and events, past and future.

"It is always the experience of being in the presence of Holy Power that gives me the greatest pleasure. I feel that power in my garden."

"I know that's so," replied Betty thoughtfully. "Recently I've been aware of something pressing in upon my spirit, a heaviness that threatens to push me aside. It's especially heavy when I'm alone on my sundeck looking out over the waters of Puget Sound."

She was about to say more but thought better of it. Instead she said, "Well, I must get back home. Bill will be waking up from his nap. I look forward to seeing you tomorrow afternoon."

I watched Betty turn and walk home with the step and limp of an ancient mariner. I admired her courage and determination. She had a good heart. I hoped that someday she'd take up the pen and do some serious writing. I sensed she had a story to tell and it would be great therapy for her even if she never got published.

Betty was true to her promise; she arrived at my cabin at two o'clock the next afternoon.

She had just stepped inside my cabin when she blurted out her question, "Do you think it's possible to communicate with the spirits of the dead?"

Betty's eyes searched my face. I suspected that her question had come in response to my earlier comment that my writings often had settings and situations involving native Shaman and spiritualism.

"We communicate with the spirits of the dead each time we bow our heads in prayer. Christians hold the belief that we can commune with the saints. This means communion with the spirits of men and women who have died. Some fundamentalists try to weasel out by saying it means the fellowship of living Christians."

Betty handed me a newspaper clipping.

"Read what Billy Graham's column says about the subject. He urges people not to dabble or get involved in anything to do with occult practices, including communication with the spirits of the dead. In his opinion, those efforts were, at best, deceptive and fraudulent; at worst, they could involve the practitioners in matters which were Satanic in origin. Dr. Graham says the Bible is clear, such things are false and will only lead away from God and His truth."

I smiled and replied, "Yes, I understand his position. It's what he learned as a young man at Northwestern Bible College. The fundamentalists have chosen to deal with spiritualism by prohibitions reinforced by dire warnings of satanic possession. But there is a problem with their reasoning. How can you say something doesn't exist and then warn of satanic possession?

"The world of the Spirit, or the Unconscious as defined by Dr. Jung, doesn't easily fit into human conceptions. Words are porous vessels. I agree with Jack London who said, 'The only test for Truth is: Does it work and are you willing to stake your life on it?'"

"Have you actually communicated with the spirits of someone who has died?"

"Yes, of course."

She noticed the little smile that drew up the corners of my mouth and the twinkle in my eyes.

"As I told you, I communicate with the spirit of Jesus daily. The Bible says that he died, as did Moses and Elijah before him, and the Bible says that Jesus went up on the mountain and communicated with them. And because Peter, James and John were with Jesus, you could say they also communicated with spirits of the dead."

"Oh, you know what I mean."

"What are you really asking? I suspect something has happened."

"I want to communicate with Al Adams. I have to tell him how sorry we are."

"What are you talking about?"

Her story rushed forth.

"The family who recently moved into a waterfront house on Angeline have a teenage son who drives a red '88 Corvette with a vengeance. Each morning as he backs out en route to school, he stops in the middle of the street, revs the engine, then burns rubber up the street. He knows it drives the people of Angeline Avenue into frenzy. When he returns in the evening, he squeals his tires cutting around the curves.

"I remember telling Mary, 'There's going to be trouble because of that kid.'"

"Why don't you speak to his parents?" I asked.

"They're never home. His father is a big-shot Boeing executive and is traveling all the time and his mother is some kind of career woman. I never did find out what she does. They stay to themselves when they are home."

"Well, maybe a visit from the police will slow him down."

"I did call the Sheriff's Department but they said they don't have the manpower to patrol this area for traffic violations. They have their hands full with more serious crimes.

"What were we supposed to do? Wait for the kid to grow up and move away? Well, I guess we should be thankful he wasn't pushing drugs.

"Then it happened. A dull thud and bump. That's all the boy heard as he backed into the street this morning; A dull thud and a bump. He didn't even know that he had hit Al Adams until the Deputy Sheriff called him out of his morning's history class.

"The boy didn't know what the scene looked like when it happened…but I know. I saw it happen. My mind has been replaying it repeatedly, with each bloody detail moving past in slow motion…the thud, the soundless scream, the bump, and the popping eyeballs. And as the Corvette flew up the street, its exhaust floated over the whole tragic mess as if in benediction."

Betty's voice bit with frustrated anger when she said, "He didn't even know what he'd done. He just drove off, his radio blaring, his tires burning."

I dabbed the tears from Betty's cheeks as I tried to comfort her.

"The waste of a good person's life always leaves us short on words."

I wrapped my arms around her quivering body and held her tight. I knew that, for some ministers, a light goes on somewhere in their memory banks and the comfort tapes pour forth time-tested Biblical passages and religious tripe that dance around the real issue.

Betty pleaded, "What kind of God allows bad things to happen to good people?"

"If you like, we can talk with a few of my friends who are on the other side."

Betty looked up through tear-filled eyes.

"Can we? Really?"

"Yes, of course. They're quite anxious to talk with you."

Betty stopped in mid-sob.

"When?"

"I'll let you know later. For now, I'm being told that Al Adams has landed on the other side in great shape and might join us in the garden. They'll let me know when they're ready. I suspect it'll be in a week or so."

My guides nudged me to say more.

"Violent, indiscriminate death is always shocking and sad. It rips a gaping hole in our souls. Our Lord wept at the death of Lazarus though he knew that Lazarus would live again. It's right to grieve when others die. When we grieve, we grieve for our coming death."

A few minutes later, when her composure was restored, Betty glanced around the one room-cabin that was my temporary home and office.

Against the wall was a brown-plaid hide-a-bed couch covered by an orange sleeping bag, a TV on one side and on the other was a kitchen arrangement of sink, electric stove and microwave. Along the other wall was my office where I worked six-to-eight hours every day. In the center was a large fireplace built with river rocks. A cast-iron, airtight stove had been inserted in the firebox.

"My, this is a cozy little place," she said.

"It serves my needs for the present. When I finish my current novel, I'll just hook up my camping trailer and head out."

"Don't you like it here?"

"Yes, for the time being. It's quiet and the little time required to care for plants and yard leaves time for my writing."

"Won't your trailer be too cold in the winter?"

"When winter comes, I hope to be in the South, somewhere in Arizona or New Mexico. If my plans work out and I sell the manuscript I'm working on, I hope to buy a 26-foot Airstream trailer that would be self-contained and would provide year-around living."

"You travel a lot, don't you?"

"I'm always on the move. I try to follow James Mitchener's pattern of going to a locale for research and writing. It's the best way I've found to get the lay of the land and tune into the spirit of the story."

"That's what always confuses me about you. In one breath you say you're a spiritual skeptic and then with the next breath, you talk about your writing being spirit-directed."

"I've studied the writing masters. They practiced their craft in special ways, but the true masters all acknowledged a presence greater than their conscious minds.

"Take Mozart, for instance. He's quoted as saying he heard his music in the stars before writing it down. Jack London spoke of his pieces as getting away from him. H. G. Wells dreamed his science fiction pieces before he wrote them.

"The ancient Greeks referred to The Muses as the source of artistic inspiration. They were trying to explain the creativity that comes from beyond our conscious, rational mind.

"If the gift has been given, let it possess you and flow through you. Let your pen be the instrument that brings forth the music of the spheres."

Betty replied, "You said that you'd like to look at some of my poems."

"Yes, did you bring any along?"

Betty shyly handed me a small, spiral notebook that bore the inscription, *A Very Private Journal of Betty Coleman.*

I looked up momentarily, asking silent permission to enter her private world of sacred thoughts. She nodded her assent.

There is poetry that marches to the disciplined steps of academia in sterile duplication and there is poetry that flies above words and form, stirring spirits and hearts.

Betty's pieces were stillborn infants lacking publishable quality but I knew better than crush the first sprouts of the flower as it ventured into the light of day. The beauty of a flower in full bloom was a potential born of sadness. The fertile soil of poetry was watered with tears.

For the next two hours, I plowed through her pieces, the pieces that bared her soul, until I came to this one.

"Why am I not like other women,
    who are beautiful,
        Graceful and exciting?
Why am I cursed with shyness,
    a shyness that binds my lips
        so that I cannot speak
           what my heart aches to tell?
Why, oh, why can't I dance before my beloved
    as Eve danced before Adam?
Oh, if only I could dance
        naked and unencumbered,
           my dance of love,
then perhaps,
    my beloved will say,
        thou art beautiful."

When at last I looked into her anxious eyes, she said apologetically, "I know they're rough. I thought maybe you could help me polish them up a bit?"

"Betty, I'm not a poet. I have no expertise in this type of writing. Most modern poetry leaves me cold with their word play that says nothing. They're like people speaking in strange tongues, a babble of unintelligible gibberish that requires an interpreter to bring out some oblique meaning.

"But your poetry is not like that. It's clearly understood. Your style is free flowing like the feelings of your heart. You're on the right track. Just keep writing your poetry and never mind whether others think it's great or not.

"Don't be discouraged. If you keep on in spite of the discouragement, the ascended masters will say, 'Betty is serious about this poetry business. We better give her a hand.'

"Then, when you come to your poetry at the appointed hour each morning, you'll find the masters waiting to give you their daily assistance. And you'll improve and grow under their tutelage.

"Go to the library and check out all the poetry you can read. Study and absorb what you enjoy. Learn from what turns you off. For discipline, you might write a few pieces by copying a particular style. But the real stuff must be your personal style. You'll gain nothing imitating others."

Betty smiled her appreciation, then glanced around the cabin's interior. She peeked into the bathroom with its green plastic shower curtain.

At several points along her inspection, I became aware of Betty's warming smiles, the brushes of hands and body. So it came as no surprise when she shifted the conversation to my private life.

"You're not married, are you?"

"I've been married twice, but I've been single for nearly ten years now."

"I imagine you've had many opportunities to re-marry, or don't you like women?"

"I love women. I prefer women to all other sexes. Whenever I've a chance, I enjoy their company. But I'm a traveling man. My trade keeps me on the move under very austere conditions. You've seen my trailer. It's only large enough for my dog and me. A traveling companion would go nuts with that confinement."

Betty stood beside the couch studying a Wal-Mart litho of Van Gogh's summer countryside.

She spoke in a soft, sad voice, "Being married to an invalid is confining for a woman, too. I wouldn't do anything to hurt Bill but sometimes I think I'll go mad. Do you ever feel that way?"

Betty slowly raised her hands to my shoulders. Her brown eyes were searching, fearful, anxiously pleading, for acceptance as she tenderly inched her body against mine. I slipped my arms around her waist and waited with the stillness of a hunter at the approach of a doe, avoiding the slightest movement that might panic her into flight.

CHAPTER TWELVE

Betty's voice was filled with warmth and affection when we met on Angeline Avenue the next afternoon.

"Do you like it?" She asked, swirling with outstretched arms as her black pleated skirt ballooned around her.

"Aren't these mirrors and swirls cute?" She asked, pointing to the multicolored embroidery on her ivory sweater vest.

"I went shopping this morning. I wanted something new and exciting."

"Did you get those black leather boots and dangling earrings at the same time?"

"I felt like going Spanish."

"It's truly stunning," I said.

"I call it my magic outfit."

"How come?"

"I feel transformed…It makes me feel alive."

"What's brought this on?"

"You," she said with a loving smile. "I want to thank you for your kindness yesterday. You were just marvelous. I'd forgotten what being a woman feels like. When I got home and thought of how badly things could've turned out, I was horrified. I'm so deeply grateful that it was you."

"You're a beautiful woman…and very desirable and…perhaps…."

Betty reached over and squeezed my arm.

"I didn't realize how gracefully you had refused me until I got home and could look Bill straight in the eyes and with a clear conscience, tell him what I had been doing."

"What did you tell him?"

"I told him that I showed you some of my poems."

Betty stretched her arms above her head and drew a deep breath, filling her lungs with clear, fresh air.

"Oh, God, it's great to be free!" She shouted.

I smiled softly—like the smile that comes to the hunter as he watches the beautiful doe bound gracefully away through the trees, unaware of death's nearness.

"Could you come to my cabin tomorrow afternoon, say about three?"

"I think so. What's up?"

"There are some friends I think you'd like to meet."

"Are we going to talk to spirits of dead people?"

"They refer to themselves as being on the other side. Yes. We're to meet in my garden."

"Oh, I didn't know you had a garden."

"Oh, yes, it's a very special garden that can only be entered by way of a secret door."

"It sounds marvelous but…it's January, it's winter."

"Yes, out here it's winter but in my garden, it's always summer."

"I'll be there unless something happens to Bill."

I invited Betty to sit beside me on the floor, our backs against the couch, facing to the east.

"Close your eyes and relax. Let the tension flow out of your body. Visualize coffee beans flowing out of a torn bag. Count the beans as they slip away. Beginning at 100 count slowly backwards…99…98…97…96. By 95 all the beans will have slipped away and you are totally relaxed. So relaxed you can't lift your eyelids. Try as you can, you can't open your eyes.

"Feel your body began to lift and float, up through the ceiling, up into the clouds…Now, you are floating high above the clouds. It's a beautiful clear day; so clear you can look down and see the sailboats on the Sound; their sails billowing in the gentle winds.

"Now we have reached the snowcapped mountain peaks. Down we slide on a giant sheet until we land on the ground.

"We are on a rock ledge high above the valley below. In front of us is a thick door of ancient oak with a rough iron latch and hinges like the kind used in medieval castles.

"You lift the latch and open the door. We enter.

"The door swings shut behind us, unaided by human hands. We bow our thanks by placing the palms of our hands together and bringing them up to our faces in the manner of Buddhist monks.

"Welcome to my garden."

"Oh, it's unbelievable," Betty responded in the soft hushed voice one would use upon entering a grand arboretum.

The moist air was heavy with the fragrances of flowers and plants. A bubbling brook contributed its special sound to the heavenly symphony that stirred our senses.

"We've entered what the old man calls the real world. Here miracles are commonplace; here earthly limitations are suspended. This garden leads to the kingdom of God. Do you remember? Jesus said the kingdom is within us.

"In a vision to John, Jesus showed how he found the kingdom. John recorded the vision in the book of Revelation."

"I thought Revelation was a book of prophecy."

"No, it's a book in which Jesus describes the way to the Kingdom of God. The opening sentence makes it clear—the book is 'The Revelation of Jesus Christ which God gave him.'

"As I meditate in this garden, I discover that its symbols are like two-way mirrors. In one direction, I see the reflection of myself with all my imperfections. From another direction, I see beyond myself to the kingdom that words are inadequate to describe, that can only be experienced."

Betty was silent as we strolled leisurely along a redbrick path that wound through finely groomed rose beds.

Slipping her arm into mine, she said, "What a luscious green! I've never seen a green rose before."

I didn't explain how they came to be. I'd said enough that day. I just smiled and motioned to the bench beside the oval fishpond where we watched the goldfish swim among the lily pads and the passing clouds reflecting off the dark blue water.

"When I was a young boy, my grandfather would take me to church. Occasionally I was asked to sing a solo. There was one hymn that was especially dear to the my grandfather."

"I didn't know you were a singer."

"I'm not, but in a small church any voice was appreciated. Besides, there were only six or seven people who attended regularly. Maybe, you've heard the hymn *In The Garden*?"

"Oh, yes, my grandmother loved that old hymn and would sing it while she worked in her flower garden."

"Listen to it carefully and you'll discover why this garden is so important to everyone.

> I come to the garden alone,
> While the dew is still on the roses,
> And the voice I hear,
> Falling on my ear,
> The Son of God discloses.
> He speaks, and the sound of His voice
> Is so sweet the birds hush their singing,
> And the melody
> That He gave to me,
> Within my heart is ringing.
> And He walks with me,
> And He talks with me,
> And He tells me I am His own;

"Then others join in like a Greek chorus."

And the joy we share
As we tarry there,
None other has ever known.

"It's time for you to meet my spirit guides."

Betty squeezed my arm in excitement as we walked up the knoll strewn with blue violets and sat beneath the mighty Oak.

"Are they here now?" She asked, looking around the garden.

"Yes, they greeted you at the gate. I'd like to introduce my grandfather, Kayourak and here is my friend of many lifetimes. My friend has been my guide in several recent lifetimes. Grandpa came to me in this life time when I was forty-seven."

"Where are they? I don't see them."

"My grandfather is sitting on your left, and my friend is on my right."

Betty twisted nervously, uncertain how to greet what she couldn't see. She leaned over to whisper, "What do I do?"

"Just nod your head in both directions. They understand."

Betty nodded as instructed.

"What do they look like?" She asked.

"I see them as they were when they were alive.

"My grandfather is a short man about five-foot-five, black eyes which twinkle with life, sea-weathered skin, a strong jaw set with determination, a full head of white hair. He talks with me in the Inupiat language

"My friend was known to me most recently in the American Civil War as a young man in his early twenties, blue eyes, sandy blonde hair, bowl-cut as was the custom of those times. His strong shoulders and arms served him well in his trade as a harness maker. The most impressive thing about him is that he's always smiling—a very happy fellow to have around."

Betty nodded, but her eyes had the unbelieving look of someone listening to a mentally disturbed person describing people that others couldn't see.

"That's how they appear to me, but others would see them as they knew them in their experiences."

"Why is that?"

"Because we're bursts of energy that trigger memory projections in the people we encounter. When we concentrate on the physical, we see our projections. When we look beyond, we see their souls."

Betty's face twisted with confusion, an overload was threatening.

"What now?" She asked.

"I want to introduce my guardian angel. You probably won't be able to see him either."

"Can you see them?"

"Only if he thinks it's necessary. It's very difficult for him to slow his vibration enough to be seen by human eyes. More importantly, I feel his presence and see his power...like when he closed the gate behind you."

"Who did that?"

"Nifi, one of my lesser angels, who is presently in the branches above your head."

Betty searched the still branches.

"Nifi, could you let Betty know you're here?"

Betty bounced with joy, "I see him, there," pointing at a branch that wiggled gently.

"Hello, Nifi," she called out.

"He's over there," I replied, pointing to another branch.

"Oh...What did I see?"

"Just a breeze."

"Where are the others?"

"To your left, Nifi is sitting on that branch."

"But, I thought you said Nifi was over there."

"Yes, Nifi is over there, and Nifi is here."

"I'm confused."

"Well, it's just their way. Two of my angels have the same name. Names are not important to them. They know when I'm addressing them. But mainly, they relate to my soul."

"Which of these angels finds parking spots for you?"

"Oh, that's my guardian angel. Finding parking places is a minor sport for him who has been assigned to protect me until the appointed time for my death. Some other time I'll tell you about a few of the scrapes he's gotten me out of."

"Where is he now?"

"Just above our heads. He's always very close to me."

"Even when you're in bed with a woman?"

"Yes."

"Oh, no," she giggled.

"Yes, it is a bit disturbing to realize that we're always surrounded by spirits even when we're making love; something most people think they're doing in secret, under the cover of darkness, but for spirits there is no darkness and we're never alone."

"Will I be able to see your spirit companions someday?"

I listened while my grandfather gave me the answer. When he urged me to tell Betty, I resisted because I thought it might confuse her and scare her away. But he insisted.

"My grandfather asks me to tell you that your inner eyes and ears will be opened when we become one."

"What does he mean by that?"

"He asks that you meditate for the answer."

Betty moved into the lotus position and closed her eyes.

"Not today," I said, gently shaking her arm. "There is something else we're to experience."

"What's that?"

"Didn't you want to talk with Al Adams?"

"Is he here?"

"Yes. He's down by the yellow roses, the one with the two statues that face in opposite directions, the majestic lion, and Mars, the god of war."

When Betty hurried to greet her old friend, I called after her, "Don't try to touch him."

She was obedient to my instruction as they talked and walked. I couldn't hear what they said to each other, but when Betty returned her bright eyes flashed with tears of joy.

"It was so wonderful to hear him speak and know that he could hear me. He wants everyone to know how happy he is. I can't wait to tell the girls."

"And if they don't believe you?"

"I don't care whether they believe me or not. I'm grateful to have talked with Al and to know that he's all right."

"My grandfather wants to know if you have any other questions?"

Betty closed her eyes to deepen her thoughts and formulate her question. Several moments passed.

She opened her eyes and asked, "Can they tell me why I feel like a stranger in this body?"

I listened to their discussion. Some said yes, others urged caution, but in the end, they agreed and Kurt, my friend, told me what to say.

"They say because of the accident, you're a walk-in soul."

"What does that mean?"

"That means, when Betty Coleman had her accident, her soul decided to leave her body because she had become so discouraged and depressed with her life. The doctors pronounced her dead but before the body started to disintegrate, another soul was given the opportunity to take that physical body that was you. You're still assimilating the other Betty's body memories."

"Can they tell me who I am?"

"You're a soul who has lived many lifetimes and has been known by many names. The life that has the greatest influence is the most recent, when you were in another female body."

"Can they tell me something about that woman?"

"She was born near Los Angeles. The time was a few years after the Civil War."

"When did she die?"

"She died at a ranch near Glen Ellen, California, eighty years later."

"Oh, how exciting! What else can you tell me?"

"Many things, but more importantly, there is much you can discover through research. Many historical records have been preserved. For now, let me tell you this much. You and I were acquainted in that life time."

"Oh, my! Who were you?"

CHAPTER THIRTEEN

When Pastor Jerry opened his mailbox the next Tuesday, he found catalogues from *Victoria's Secret* and *Land's End*, mid-week ads from Albertson's, PayLess and Safeway, bills for electricity and telephone but not the long-expected envelope.

Returning home, Pastor Jerry threw the day's mail on the kitchen table and called out to his wife, "I think I'll give Jim a call. We haven't heard from him in over a month. I hope nothing is wrong."

"I'm sure everything is all right. They've just been too busy remodeling the sanctuary of their new church," Diane, his wife, answered from the next room, keeping her head down to her sewing machine.

Pastor Jerry completed his call and put the phone down. His face was flushed.

"See. There was nothing to worry about, was there?" Asked Diane.

"Jim said he'd mailed his envelope several weeks ago."

"When did you mail ours?"

"Several weeks ago…."

Fury rose in Diane's face, flushing it with red, as she slammed her fist on the table.

"That's it! No more pictures. It's too risky. What if someone here finds out like they did in Minneapolis? We'll be out on our ears. Then what'll we do?"

"No one will find out."

Pastor Jerry cuddled his wife in his arms, brushing back her hair as he leaned her head on his shoulder.

"Besides, how often have you told me how much you enjoy the exchange?"

Diane's expression softened.

Pastor Jerry drew her lovingly onto his lap and with his arm around her small waist squeezed reassuringly. She returned her head to his shoulder.

His eyes floated over to the bookshelves and ran down the stack of photo albums.

"Do you have your album?"

"No, isn't it there?"

His face twitched as he searched the shelves.

"It's gone. So is Meg's and Judy's. Lord Jesus! What's going on?"

Late that evening when the people of Suquamish had settled down for the night, the rapid CLICK! CLICK! CLICK! Echoed in the dark sanctuary as a light switch was flipped repeatedly.

"Galdarnit," Pastor Jerry blurted out in frustration. He was forced to grope his way through the darkness from pew to pew, down the side aisle, toward the electrical panel in the far corner of the room.

Midway he stopped, sensing another presence, a cold dark presence, somewhere in the room. He tried to shake it off but it was too real, too close.

"Who's there?" He called.

Receiving no answer, he continued inching his way toward the electrical panel, feeling along the wall for its reassuring metal cover. Momentary relief surged through him at the touch of the cool, smooth, steel surface. Pulling the cover open, his fingers felt their way up the row of circuit breakers, feeling for the thrown switch but he didn't find one; every switch was on. Looking out a side window, he saw lights in the houses across the street and down the block.

'Just a local outage,' he accepted as he moved on to more pressing business. He shuffled cautiously along the front pew until he reached the center aisle, then slowly lowered his body into the pew.

Clasping his hands together, thumb knuckles to his lips, and head bowed, Pastor Jerry prayed:

"My Lord, I come before Thee this evening with a heavy heart. The harder I fight for your cause, the greater are the forces of evil that rise up against me. Without Thee, I'm lost and defeated.

"My Lord, I don't know which way I should turn. Thy word teaches me that when you give the bread of adversity, you also send a teacher who will say 'This is the way, walk in it.' Please send me such a teacher now."

Pastor Jerry waited silently in the dark, cold sanctuary, sweat beads forming on his forehead, hands growing damp and clammy. Minutes merged into hours and still he remained in the pew, head bowed, waiting for God's response.

Then a response came, there was movement in the shadows on the far side of the room as a dark shape rose up and floated toward him.

Pastor Jerry called out, "Who's there?"

A whispered answer floated through the darkness, "A friend...who has come to help you."

Pastor Jerry and the dark one talked long into the morning hours. Great things were discussed.

"Ever since I won the homiletic prize in my senior year of college, I've hoped that one day I'd have a big church like Falwell's with a network of TV and radio stations carrying my services featuring a large choir with professional soloists, and of course, my sermons. At long last, the true faith would be spread across the country and around the world.

"But, these are only dreams. As you know, this is a very small congregation. And we're fighting for our very existence."

"What's going on?" Asked the dark one innocently.

"Are you a stranger to our village that you don't know about our troubles? Haven't you heard that this village is filled with Satan worshipers?"

"No...I didn't know that. What are you going to do about them?"

"Oh, I've got plans, plenty of plans. Satan is not going to win this battle if I have anything to say about it."

"I'd sure like to help you. What do you need the most?"

Pastor Jerry's answer was quick and to the point.

"Money. These days it takes a lot of money to fight Satan."

"How much money?"

"Three, four…maybe even five million dollars to build a church and equip it for radio and TV broadcasting. Then we'd need a staff to operate the church, and professional music people need to be hired not to mention buying time on the Christian TV and radio networks. All this would be upfront money before we could expect sustaining contributions to come in."

As he spoke, Pastor Jerry's face took on a glow as the vision began to materialize in front of his eyes.

At last his father would be proud of him, a father who glowered at him from the pulpit of Riverside Church, the largest and grandest church in Dallas, a father who told him that he didn't have what it takes to be a successful minister.

"But, that's dream talk," said Pastor Jerry bringing himself back to the moment. "We're a mere handful of people."

"It seems to me that God prefers to work with small groups of people. Didn't he require Gideon to send away the thousands after selecting three hundred good men? And didn't Jesus choose only twelve disciples to convert the world? Since you seem to be a man after my own heart I'll tell you what I'll do. I'll get you the money you need. In return, you could help me with a few things."

"What things?"

"Oh…minor things, to protect my interests. You understand, don't you? I mean five million dollars is a lot of money, no matter how you count it."

"Of course, that's understandable. What minor things?" Pastor Jerry's enthusiastic voice was tinged with caution.

"We'll talk about them later after you get the five million."

"When will that be?"

"Saturday night."

A shadowed hand slithered out of the darkness pushing a Washington Lotto ticket across the pew.

Sunday evening Pastor Jerry was again at prayer in his church. A celebration was going on in the adjoining fellowship hall. He had informed his congregation at the morning services that God had armed him with five million dollars with which to fight Satan. He had invited them to join in celebrating his good fortune.

"Are you here?" Pastor Jerry whispered.

"Yes," came the soft answer.

"I got the money as you promised. Should I go ahead with my plans?"

"Of course. If that's not enough, I'll get you more."

Pastor Jerry looked troubled.

"What's the matter?" The voice asked.

"You said there were some conditions. I'd like to know what they are."

"Oh, yes, that. As I told you, they're just minor things. Nothing like your grand plans. All I ask is for you to tone down your attacks on the Satanists."

"I can't do that."

"Be realistic. It's not a good time to stir up trouble. You need all the goodwill you can get to buy that property you have your eye on and secure the building permits. All I ask is just cool it for a couple of months. There'll be plenty of time to attack the Satanists after you've got your building and programs solidly in place."

"That's all?"

"That's all...(and in a soft voice Pastor Jerry didn't hear)...for now."

Pastor Jerry had trouble convincing Clara that God had shown his priorities by providing the money for a new church.

"We'll be in a stronger position to take on the hoards of Satan," he told her. "Everyone is looking forward to the first Sunday when we can worship in a new sanctuary and hear a grand choir sing the great hymns. Such a church is certain to draw huge crowds."

So, Clara softened with this explanation.

Several months later, Pastor Jerry told his congregation, "It's as if a guardian angel with a flaming sword is going before us to part the waters and vanquish all opposition."

Soon concrete was being poured, bricks, stones, lumber and nails were delivered to the site, and Christian workmen were busy constructing the grandest church in Kitsap County.

I was standing at the corner of First and South Streets. Behind me was the hovering Totem and in front of me, covered with brush and hidden in the tall grass, was a huge boulder with a flat top.

The old man had told me, "It's the power rock of the Suquamish tribe. When a warrior has passed his spirit test, he sits on it as a full moon rises and receives a vision."

I could not see any signs or marks that anyone had been near the boulder in a long time, certainly not that summer. As I was getting a feel of the place, Clara Goodwill slipped up beside me.

"Can I talk with you?" She asked, her eyes red from crying. "Somewhere private where we won't be disturbed."

"Sure. My cabin is close. Would that be all right?"

We'd just stepped through the door when she unloaded.

"Have you heard the rumor? The Suquamish Indians are infested with a sex ring of incestuous pedophiles engaging in kidswapping."

"You mean like what went on in Wenatchee?"

"Exactly! Dozens of these filthy creatures have been swapping their children at orgies that take place in their homes on the Reservation. At these gatherings, men and women take children, six at a time, to a room with six single beds. The little boys and girls undress and lay down on a bed; one child on each bed. Then the adults undress and get in a line to take turns with everybody, including each other. It's just a wild, disgraceful orgy."

"Sex rumors fly faster than e-mail on the Internet. Without authorship, each teller is convinced they are true. No rumor is as convincing as sexual molestation of children."

Clara had the bit in her teeth. There was no restraining her. Like a runaway horse, I had to let her run herself into exhaustion.

"I heard that one 14-year old girl was taken into a room. There, four men took turns raping her on a shag-carpet. When they were finished, they told her that, if she told anyone, they would kill her or hurt her family and friends. Then they told her to put on her panties and go."

"Are these rumors or fact?"

"Because it's happening on Reservation land, only the Tribal Police can investigate. Naturally, they are covering it up."

"Then, as far as you know, it's all rumors. Such rumors quickly burst into witch hunts."

"I know where your sympathies lie. But I heard it from a friend who has seen it with her own eyes."

"If she saw it, then she must have been a participant."

Clara drew a deep breath before continuing.

"Did you know that Henry has left me for an Indian whore?"

"No. Have you talked to Pastor Jerry?"

"That pig? I won't give him the time of day."

"What's happened? What did he do?"

"Did you know that he didn't ask our permission to build that new church?

"And he didn't tell us that it would be his personal church which he calls The-Church-Of-The-True-Faith, or that the deeds to the land and buildings were to be held by a new non-profit corporation, and that he had the final say who could be members.

"When I asked him why he didn't consult with the church board, he laughed at me and said that he didn't have to pander to a small group of stupid laymen anymore. Then he laughed at me again. Can you imagine the gall of that man to laugh at me?"

The silent Clara stood defiantly in the middle of the room like Liberty-on-the-battlements, muscles set and face determined. Then gradually a change crept over her body. An almost imperceptible flicker in her taut jaw muscles betrayed her resolution. Her rigid body began to quiver and shake. Suddenly she collapsed in a sobbing pile on the couch.

Between crying jags she sputtered, "You can't trust men."

Drawing back a sniffle, she sat up straight.

"I hope that black animal sucks him dry. Do you know that Indian whores are insatiable animals without morals?"

"I don't agree that…."

"The Lord knows I tried. If a woman wants any peace, she has to suck her man dry. I learned that from my father."

"Why are you telling me these things?"

"Because I have nowhere else to turn."

"I don't understand."

"No, I guess you don't," said Clara. She looked out the window as she gathered her nerve.

"Frankly, I'm glad to be rid of Henry. He wasn't happy and neither was I. When two people make each other miserable, they should get divorced. And the Suquamish Bible Church will get along just fine without Jerry Hanson.

"The beauty of our church has been that it's a small, closely knit congregation committed to the Lord."

I moved to sit next to her on the couch as I replied, "That can be beautiful, and it can be dangerous. A coterie can delude its members into believing they live in a special atmosphere in which they see things more clearly than others do—see them differently—are responsive to the superior demands of their faith, the only true faith.

"Down through the ages that has been the attraction of men like Jim Jones and David Koresh and thousands of other self-appointed prophets and messiahs, Christian *and* non-Christian. The results are always the same: death, violence, destruction and disillusionment.

"But you didn't come to talk about church polity. What's really troubling you?"

"I want you to cure my breast cancer."

"What did you say?"

"I said, I want you to cure my breast cancer."

"I'm sorry to hear that you have cancer. But what makes you think I can cure it? There are doctors for that."

"The doctors say it's progressed too far. There's nothing more they can do," Clara said softly. Then reaching over, she clasped my arm, "Betty tells me you can heal."

"Only you can heal your body. The very most I can do is to help you heal yourself."

"Would you? Would you help me?"

My spirit guides were urging me to agree, telling me they would help. It was something they'd been urging me to do for several years. 'A gift from God. The gift of healing is in your hands,' they had said.

So I said to Clara, "Please understand that I don't do faith healing like the charlatans on TV and at tent meetings. Whether you live or die is your soul's decision, not my decision, not yours, but your soul's decision."

"I'm confused. My soul? Are not my soul and I the same thing?"

"No. Your ego came into existence at your birth and will pass away when you die. But your soul is that immortal energy created to be a companion with God. It passes in and out of the earthly plain through the revolving doors of birth and death, birth and death."

I caught sight of a red balloon floating in an upper corner of the room. I had brought it home from a friend's birthday party. I pulled the balloon down to hold it in my hands.

"Let me illustrate with this balloon. Inside the balloon are the atmosphere and dimension of earth. When I press a finger into it, the rubber covering my finger is like my ego personality in life. It's the impression made by my soul. At death, my soul withdraws like my finger from the balloon.

"Paul understood this mystery when in the eighth chapter of Romans he wrote. 'Neither death, nor life, nor angels, nor principalities, nor things present, nor things to come, nor powers, nor height, nor depth, nor anything else in all creation, will be able to separate us from the love of God in Christ Jesus our Lord.'

"I know you believe that, Clara, so the most important questions for you are: Does your soul want you to live longer? What would your soul want you to do with any extra time?"

Clara's face went blank with confusion; her mouth dropped open as with sightless eyes, she considered my words. It's not easy to accept the Christ dilemma: To live you must die…Not my will but Thy will be done.

"Oh, no, you don't," she shouted, jumping up and bolting toward the door like an aged virgin on the brink of seduction.

"You're not going to seduce me with your New Age Teachings."

She was out the door before I could draw a breath to reply.

During the weeks that followed, whenever we were in danger of meeting at the Post Office, she'd cross the street and wait until I'd returned home. But I noticed that in her continued avoidance, she never failed to watch me from a distance.

She was like a moth beating its wings to flee but finds itself drawn closer and closer to the lightbulb. The day came when, answering a soft knock on my door, I opened it to find Clara with down-turned eyes.

"May I come in?" She asked in a near whisper.

"Of course."

She stood in the center of the room wringing her hands, waiting for an invitation to sit. Her body was beginning to show cancer's ravages, sunken eyes, thinning of face, arms and legs. I quickly motioned for her to sit in my brown leather recliner. She accepted.

"Can I get you something to drink?" I asked.

"A glass of water would be nice."

Sipping from her glass, her eyes fixed on a portrait hanging over my computer that had been done years earlier when I was a different man.

"When was that painted?"

"Nearly fifteen years ago when I was in my entrepreneur period."

"What do you mean?"

"In many ways it was one of my most exciting periods. I owned a company in Anchorage that did great until it was washed away in the undertow of the 1980 recession. Close behind came my bankruptcy and divorce."

"Oh, my, that must have been terrible."

"The process of being born again is usually a very painful experience."

"There you go again, twisting the Bible."

"I died in every sense but biological. When I woke up, I was a new creature, living a radically different life. Looking back, this new life has been the most meaningful."

Clara shifted her attention back to the portrait.

"You looked good in a beard. Why did you give it up?"

"Male vanity, I guess. One day I looked into a mirror and saw an old man with a graybeard. I wasn't ready to be an old man then, so I cut my beard off."

The man in the portrait held a pipe in his hand in thoughtful reflection. Clara glanced over my rolltop desk.

"Don't you smoke a pipe anymore?"

"No. And again, on an impulse, I stopped, just like that."

"I always like the aroma of pipe smoke, especially in the evening. Don't you miss your pipe?"

"Sometimes, when I'm sitting outside on a summer evening, I feel the desire for my pipe. Perhaps, I'll take it up again…someday maybe."

I knew Clara's small talk would eventually give way to serious discussion. Like the spring breakup of river ice, it'd have to occur at Clara's comfort time, which came after several minutes of silence.

"Can we start again?" She asked in a pensive voice.

"Of course, Clara, I want to help you all I can. If you're willing to do your part, I'll do mine."

"Oh, yes, I will," she said. "What do you want me to do?"

"For starters, you can go into the bathroom and take off your clothes."

"Not on your life!" Clara responded firmly.

Holding out a sheet to ease her shock, I added, "Wrap this around you before you come out."

"What are you going to do?"

"Today we're going to start by helping you to relax; a deep-muscle massage should help. Then I'm going to teach you how to meditate."

"Isn't that what Eastern religions do? I'm not sure I'm up to that sort of thing."

"Meditation is Eastern, Western, Northern and Southern. It's the ancient healing method found among all peoples, races, and religions. All I'm asking is for you to give it a chance. What have you to lose?"

Clara blinked back a tear.

"Nothing," she said. "And if it helps, I could gain a lot."

"That's the spirit. Did you know that you're a beautiful woman when you smile like that?"

Soft flute music was floating through the air when Clara emerged from the bathroom, embarrassingly clutching the white sheet under her arms.

"Would you climb up on the table, please?"

I turned my back while she eased her thin body onto the massage table and tucked the sheet around her.

"Face down, please."

Turning on her stomach, she rested her face in an oval hole that was padded for comfort, with her arms along her sides. She nervously tugged at the sheet to reassure herself that everything was covered.

"Now, I want you to relax. Go to sleep if you feel like it."

I rubbed a mixture of olive and peanut oil in my hands.

Zamfir's pan flute wrapped a musical blanket around us as I gently eased the sheet from her neck and shoulders. At first, her muscles were taut like coiled steel. But gradually, ever so gradually, I could feel the tension ease away as she drifted off to sleep, the sleep of the gods.

"Will I see you again?" I asked at the doorway.

"Yes, of course," she said, her smile bursting with sunlight. "Same time tomorrow?"

The healing process began by gently peeling away the fears and inhibitions, leaf by leaf. When she was relaxed and accepting of her body, we added sessions in the hottub.

During one of these hottub sessions as she relaxed in the massaging jets, her dark secrets began to bubble to the surface, the ones she had buried deep inside, the festering sores that infected her body and her mind.

Like the stillness preceding a storm, Clara had been silent and pensive for nearly an hour. She appeared to be floating away, mentally.

With the suddenness of a ship's keel hitting a deadhead she began:

"Did you know that my father got into me when I was just five-years old and he kept it up until I was sixteen? For eleven years...."

I started to reply but remained silent when I realized that Clara wasn't with me any longer. She was floating back to another time.

"...My mother helped him. 'Now there sweetheart,' she'd say while stroking my hair, 'Daddy will be finished in a few minutes.' But he wasn't finished in a few minutes. He kept it up night after night, and year after year. My mother told me that if I sucked him dry, he'd give me presents. Do you know what it does to a little girl to have that big thing shoved into her, stretching her until she bleeds?"

"No, but I...."

"At first I cried but my mother put her hand over my mouth so the neighbors wouldn't hear. My mother said I'd get used to it, that God created women to suck men dry. But I never got used to it, and I hated it because it took my sweet father away and replaced him with a dirty lusting animal.

"But I made that disgusting animal buy me many, many presents. When my girlfriends asked me why I had so many nice dresses, I told them it was because my daddy loved me so very much."

Clara fell silent, allowing the hot water to bubble and swirl around her body, before continuing her catharsis.

"I'll tell you why I hate pornography so much. My father collected dirty pictures. That's why. He'd stir up his lust by studying them for hours. When his pajamas burst, he'd slipped into my bed and…well, you know what he did. I thought Henry wasn't like that, but I was wrong. All men are lusting animals."

"Even me?"

Her eyes snapped open. Remembering that she was naked, she scrambled out of the hottub and grabbed a terrycloth bathrobe for cover. Clutching its whiteness around her body, she glared down at me, her eyes darting to my limp manhood then away like a hummingbird at a feeder.

"Men are always trying to trick women out of their clothes."

"Why do you think they do that?"

"So they can rape them with their eyes."

"Do you think nudes by the great artists like Michelangelo and Rubens are demeaning of women? Don't you realize that God, who created the human body, thought his creation was good to look upon? That nakedness was God's intended state for mankind?"

Clara's eyes flashed with emotion and her jaw was set with determination as she spit out her reply,

"Sin changed all that. Would you cover yourself? This discussion has gone far enough. I don't want to hear any more about nudity and art."

Clara whirled about and stomped into the house. Dressing quickly, she was out the door in a flash leaving me to soak in the hot water and recall the second half of the riddle, the part that asked: When is a woman her father's son?

I felt sad knowing that Clara's healing could not begin until she raised her father's son to the surface. Also, I remembered that my seventh Vail was yet to fall.

CHAPTER FOURTEEN

"Can you tell me about my previous life? What kind of woman was I? Was I beautiful? Was I talented?"

Questions were bubbling up faster than the jets of the hottub that pummeled our bodies. The evening had been wonderful.

My daylong bouillabaisse project had been inspired by the gifts of butter clams and mussels from Joe Old Coyote. Tom Proudfoot had brought over a fresh salmon with a Dungeness crab. Betty contributed carrots and new potatoes from her garden, and I added the seasonings.

After eight hours of slow simmering, I ladled the stew into hallowed-out sourdough loaves I'd baked that morning.

"Here's to life," Joe said, raising his glass filled with Glen Ellen Chardonnay.

With the clink of our glasses, we echoed the toast.

We retired to the hottub to finish off the festive evening with the soft and easy conversation between friends. Facades dissolved, inhibitions gave way to open honesty as our naked bodies soaked in the hot bubbling water.

At Betty's questions, I switched off the jets and allowed the bubbles to settle, leaving our four heads to bob serenely on the placid surface of steaming quietude.

I replied, "You provided the answers to most of your questions in your diaries and personal correspondence. I've copies of both. You can take them home with you if you'd like."

"I'd like that. But can't you tell me something now?"

I searched the faces of Joe and Tom for some direction. When they nodded their encouragement, I closed my eyes as if to collect my thoughts but in truth, I was floating back to another time and place. There was a slight shift in my voice as I picked up the description of Betty in her prior life.

"You came into my life rather imperceptibly. You were just another young woman who came to my Wednesday afternoon gatherings, another accessory of a blooming author.

"Had I been asked any time during the first months you were in our group, I would have been unable to tell anyone the color of your eyes. The fact that your hair was brown resided dimly in my subconscious.

"Likewise I had an idea that you were not thin, but there was an absence in my mind of any idea that you were fat. As to how you dressed, I had no ideas at all. I had no trained eye in such matters nor was I interested. In the lack of any impression to the contrary, I took it for granted that you were dressed in some acceptable fashion. I knew you as one of my secretaries, and that was all, though I was aware that you were said to be a quick and accurate stenographer.

"That impression, however, was quite vague for I was more interested in other women and had had no experience with stenographers. I naturally believed that they were all quick and accurate.

"One morning, you came over to help with some typing. While checking over a few of your pages, I came upon an 'I shall.' Glancing quickly over the page for similar constructions, I found a number of 'I wills.' The 'I shall' was alone. It stood out conspicuously. I called you over.

"'Did I say that?' I asked, extending the letter to you and pointing out the criminal phrase.

"A shade of annoyance crossed your face. You stood convicted.

"'My mistake,' you said. 'I'm sorry. But it's not a mistake, you know,' you added quickly.

"'How do you make that out?' I challenged. 'It sure don't sound right in my way of thinking.'

"You had reached your desk by this time and now turned with the offending letter in your hand.

"'It's right just the same.'

"'But that would make all those 'I wills' wrong, then,' I argued.

"'It does,' was your audacious answer. 'Shall I change them?'

"'I shall be over to look that affair up on Monday.'

"I repeated the sentence from the page aloud. I did it with a grave, serious air, listening intently to the sound of my own voice. I shook my head. 'It don't sound right,   It just don't sound right. Why, nobody writes to me that way. They all say 'I will'—educated men, too, some of them. Ain't that so?'

"'Yes,' you acknowledged, and returned to the machine to make the correction.

"On my way back after lunch, I dropped into the bookstore and bought a grammar. And for a solid hour, my feet up on the desk, I toiled through its pages.

"'Knock off my head with little apples if the girl ain't right,' I communed aloud at the end of the session. For the first time, it struck me that there was something about you. I'd accepted you up to then as a female creature and a bit of office furnishing. But now, having demonstrated that you knew more grammar than businessmen and college graduates, you became an individual. You seemed to stand out in my consciousness as conspicuously as the 'I shall' had stood out in the typed page, and I began to take notice.

"I managed to watch you leaving that afternoon, and I was aware, for the first time, that you were well-formed, and that your manner of dress was satisfying. I knew none of the details of women's dress, and I saw none of the details of your neat shirtwaist and well-cut tailored suit. I saw only the effect in a general, sketchy way. You looked right. This was in the absence of anything wrong or out of the way.

"'She's a trim, little goodlooker,' was my verdict when the door closed on you.

"The next afternoon, dictating, I concluded that I liked the way you did your hair though, for the life of me, I could have given no description of it. The impression was pleasing, that was all. You sat with the window at your back, and I noted that your hair was light brown with hints of golden bronze. A pale sun shining in set the golden bronze into smoldering fires that were very pleasing to behold. Funny, I thought, that I'd never observed that phenomenon before.

"In the midst of the letter, I came to the construction which had caused the trouble the day before. I remembered my wrestle with the grammar and dictated:

"'I shall meet you halfway in this proposition.'

"You gave me a quick look. The action was purely involuntary and in fact, had been half a startle of surprise. The next instant your eyes had dropped again, and you sat waiting for me to go on with the dictation. But in that moment of your glance, I'd noted that your eyes were brown. I was later to learn that, at times, there were golden lights in those same brown eyes. But I'd seen enough, as it was, to surprise me for I became suddenly aware that I'd always taken you for a brunette with brown eyes as a matter of course.

"I discovered that in the intervals, when you had nothing to do, you read books and magazines, or worked on some sort of feminine fancy work.

"Passing your desk once, I picked up a volume of Kipling's poems and glanced quizzically through the pages.

"'You like reading?' I asked, laying the book down.

"'Oh, yes,' was your answer. 'Very much.'

"Another time it was a book of Wells', *The Wheels of Chance.*

"'What's it all about?' I asked.

"'Oh, it's just a novel, a love story.'

"You stopped but I still stood waiting, and you felt it incumbent to go on.

"'It's about a little Cockney draper's assistant who takes a vacation on his bicycle and falls in with a young girl very much above him. Her mother is a popular writer and all that. And the situation is very curious, sad, too, and tragic. Would you care to read it?'

"'Does he get her?' I demanded.

"'No. That's the point of it. He wasn't....'

"'He doesn't get her, and you've read all them pages, hundreds of them, to find that out?' I muttered in amazement.

"You was nettled as well as amused.

"'But you read the mining and financial news by the hour,' you retorted.

"'But I sure get something out of that. It's business, and it's different. I get money out of it. What do you get out of the books?'

"'Points of view, new ideas, life.'

"'Not worth a cent cash.'

"'But life's worth more than cash,' you argued.

"'Oh, well,' I said, with easy masculine tolerance, 'so long as you enjoy it. That's what counts, I suppose, and there's no accounting for taste.'

"I asked around and found out that you came from Los Angeles and was very nice to work with in the office, of course; but you were rather stuck on yourself—exclusive, you know.

"Well, you thought too much of yourself to associate with those you work with in the office, for instance. You wouldn't have anything to do with a fellow, you see. You had many fellows asking you out repeatedly to the theater and the chutes and such things. But nothing doing. It was said that you liked plenty of sleep, and couldn't stay up late, and had to go all the way to Berkeley—that's where you lived.

"That report gave me a distinct satisfaction. You were a bit above the ordinary, and no doubt about it. But the report's next words carried a hurt.

"But that was all hot air. You ran with the University boys; that's what you did. You needed lots of sleep, and couldn't go to the theater, but you could dance all hours with them. I'd heard it pretty straight that you went to all their hops and such things. Rather stylish and high-toned for a stenographer, I'd say. And you kept a horse, too. You road astride all over those hills out there. I saw you one Sunday myself. Oh, you were a high-flyer, and I wondered how you did it. Sixty-five a month don't go far.

"You didn't live with your people; didn't have any. While they were alive, your parents had been well to do, I'd heard. They must have been because your father had a large hotel after he got out of the Army, got to speculating and went broke before he died. Your mother died long before that. You were raised by an aunt who practiced free love."

At that point Joe broke in.

"We're sorry but we must go. Tom has night duty at the fire station and I have to get back to my carving."

"How's it coming along?" I asked.

"Just fine now. I had some things I had to work through but now its going great."

"What are you going to do with it when you get it finished?" Betty asked.

"I don't know. I thought of asking the Tribal Council for permission to put it up next to the downtown pad."

"Let me know if I can help in any way," I said, "Would you mind if I dropped by your worksite one of these days?"

"Why?"

"I've never seen a carver at work and with you being a master carver, who could better show me the craft?"

"I don't allow anyone to see my work until it's finished. Not even a friend like you."

"I can understand that. I've the same attitude about my work in progress. But remember, if you need any help, I'm your man."

"I'll be sure to take you up on that," said Joe as they toweled themselves off. "Thanks for the great meal and evening. See ya around."

Betty stayed to help me clean up. When we were finished, we relaxed by finishing off the Chardonnay out on the deck to watch the moon rise.

"What time does Bill expect you home?"

"Once he takes his sleeping pill, he's down until morning," Betty replied. Her thoughts went deeper.

"Most of the time I feel like I'm nursing a stranger; I hardly know him. I've tried to remember our earlier years together but I've no emotional memories. It's as if I'm reading the story of other people."

A searching look came over Betty's face. Her eyes plumbed my eyes for reassurance as she gathered her strength prior to her question.

"I need to ask you something very personal."

"Go ahead."

"Did you know that some men take pictures of their wives and sweethearts posing in the nude?"

"Yes, what of it?"

"Can you imagine any woman doing that? I'd be afraid that someone would get a hold of my picture and try to blackmail me."

I didn't respond.

After a long silence, she asked reflectively, "Do you think my other self ever posed in the nude?"

"Yes, I know you did and thought nothing of it. In fact, I was shown a collection of your nudes taken by one of your boyfriends who was a photographer. I have a copy of the one you gave your lover in June of 1903 just as he was leaving for a month's writing cruise on the Sacramento River Delta. It was a close-up frontal photo."

"Can I see it?" Betty asked.

I dug down in my files and after flipping through a stack of pictures, I came up with the one she wanted to see. Betty studied it intently.

I said, "He was a good photographer and had a home processing lab."

"What do men do with such pictures? Do they show them off to their buddies?"

"Some clods do, but most keep them as personal treasures to be appreciated in private. He told her that her boo'ful bosom captivated him so much, he spent hours studying them. Her picture served to increase his ardor for the time when they'd be back together."

"I just don't get it. Women don't get turned on by looking at photos of nude men, do they?"

"You'd be a better judge of that; but as a rule men are aroused by sight."

"Thank goodness for that. A women relies on catching her man's eye in order to capture his heart."

"The degree of dress or undress is a fashion matter, not a moral issue. Climate permitting, if all women walked around naked, there would be so little interest that they'd have to start wearing clothes to attract attention."

Betty drew herself up straight and with a brave, tentative voice asked, "Would you take my picture? You wouldn't get to keep them, of course."

"Why?"

"I want to experience what it's like to pose in the nude, to fantasize I had such a beautiful body that I could be a *Playboy* centerfold. I want to fantasize a man making love to me with his eyes."

When I didn't answer immediately, she pressed further as her cheeks blushed pink.

"Would you? Please. I wouldn't dare ask any other man."

"Why me?"

"Because I trust you. I trust you because you're a nice man."

There it was again, being perceived as a nice man, a harmless man, a comfortable man, a neuter man, but not as a real man.

"Okay. When do you want to do it?"

"Right now…While I still have the nerve."

"But I don't have a Polaroid…."

"I brought mine along just in case you'd agree."

"So that's what's in the bag you brought?"

"Yes, and the outfit I want to wear to start with."

While Betty was in the bathroom, I shifted the furniture to make room for the photo session and checked the camera for film, all the time visualizing the different poses I'd like her to take.

I wasn't prepared for the beautiful sight that materialized out of my bathroom. She was wearing a magical turquoise silk chemise beautifully finished with French seaming, low-scooped front that teased her full figure, slim straps crossed in the deep back, side slit on one side that drew attention to her graceful good leg and away from her crippled leg. Flipping her hair over her ears, her eyes dancing with seduction, she wet her ruby lips with quick sweeps of her darting tongue.

"Where do you want me to stand?" She asked.

"Let's start over here," I answered, motioning toward the French doors that opened onto the deck.

I took several photos of her in the open doorway. Then using the lace-covered doors as background, she lifted first one strap and then the other and let the chemise slowly, teasingly, slip to the floor. All the time the camera flashed capturing Venus as she dropped her seventh veil.

CHAPTER FIFTEEN

The saffron Queen of the Night nodded her greeting to Cygnus the Swan and curtsied her respect to Cassiopeia, the upside-down Queen, and Perseus, her consort while the mighty steed, Pegasus, raced to join the heavenly host assembled for the annual celebration of Halloween.

Across the highway of fishes, Seattle cringed beneath a blanket of low-hanging clouds, a city of Perpetual Mist where, when the bright sun climbed the sky and put the stars to flight, none of its rays penetrated to its streets nor could any of the sun's rays be seen as it dropped from heaven and sank again in the West. For dreadful night had spread her mantle perpetually over that unhappy folk.

But on the western shore, Suquamish was the land of the sun and the moon, the land of happy folk who lived in the land of Perpetual Halloween, where spirits lived and the beast laired in spite of the sour, hilltop people who frowned on such things.

Halloween was the time when the northwind blew little sheet-covered ghosts, florescent goblins, black witches and white princesses down my jack-o-lantern-lined River of Fire to where the River of Lamentation joined to form the River Styx.

There I waited beside my pool of dark red blood like the hooded ferryman to collect the tolls required to enter Persephone's Grove. All around, the souls of the dead and departed floated and shrieked such ungodly wailings and moans that Hades herself cupped her ears.

Over that ghastly scene of blood and gore, the moon in her fullness, dressed in her benevolent orange, beamed down her pleasure at the bounty of that dreadful night's harvest.

It was on such evenings that the moon reached with silver fingers into the beast's lair, stirring him to rise and to prowl the shadowed rain forests he loved to haunt. Halloween was the night of the beast.

Sleep was impossible. Whether in a dream or not, I can't tell, but I found myself walking the beach without direction. Yet I must've been led by unseen hands for I entered the sacred cove at the head of which grew a grandmother cedar, an old cedar with long branches that modestly covered a cave in which medicine people wove their marvelous blankets that made the wearers invisible so they could walk with the ancient ones and receive wisdom. The cave had a spring, whose waters never failed, and it had two entrances, the north entrance was for humans while the spirits used the south entrance.

I entered by the north entrance and stood to allow my eyes to grow accustomed to the placement of things. Much of the cave was shadowed in darkness. A broad cone of silver moonlight filtered in through the south opening on which the little dancing people from the sea entered to swirl around in the darkness like scintilla. I watched spellbound as the chaotic furies came together to concentrate a ghostly gray light on a bed against the far wall and upon her who lay sleeping in it. Her mounded fullness beckoned from beneath a thin sheet.

Should I leave? No! I knew she would want me to take possession of what had drawn me there. But looking down at her beautiful, sleeping, high-cheeked face, I was afraid to violate her dreaming for dreams were the only place of true privacy.

I didn't leave; the beast wouldn't let me. He, who had been sleeping in his lair, now stirred to life and pressed against the restraints to rise into the rain forest of my love and probe for the inner cave, to force his way into the cave of wetness and warmth.

But not yet, I commanded; Not so fast to the prize; be not like the animals that strike without preparation, who by brute strength force submission.

It was in the quest that true love was discovered. And what was courtship but a tenuous stretching out of searching fingertips, to touch; and in the touching, the knowing; with the knowing, the acceptance of kindred souls. But love? What of love? Where was that found?

Love, like God, was not something to be found; but it is a power that takes possession of us. It slides into our bed of intimacy, like I into hers, and, gently, slowly, sensitively, reaches out and around to ease her curved body against mine.

In the presence of love, the beast was transformed from a ravenous thing single-mindedly set upon satisfying itself into an umbilical cord by which two bodies became one in love's holy mystery of oneness.

My firmness shocked my body. The sudden jolt of it shifted her into accommodation. She felt it and was aroused. I was glad when she articulated to provide me the position I needed to thrust my passion as deep as I convinced her I would…and, to myself, that I could. She purred. I giggled. An affirmation each was happy I was there.

As quickly as a chilling sensation could grasp one's breath, she had taken the beast into possession. As it entered her rainforest I felt a warm and moist safety. The humidity in her forest sucked my breath away. She was awake now, her body expecting the positioning to receive me in the way a violin awaits the bow, the creator of its music. She lullabied with me from side to side.

At the perfect moment, she suffocated my flame and extinguished all insecurities with which I'd entered her bed. I thanked Jesus for having brought me to her and for her domestication of the beast.

I appreciated the passing of time as she snuggled in my arms. For it was Halloween, a time for mystery, mischief, fantasy and disguise! For as long as there was Halloween and sensitivity, there would be love and a place for the beast to cave.

On the way home, I found a beached log to sit upon where, in the setting light of the moon, I meditated on one of life's great mysteries, the mystery of the beast. The beast had fascinated humankind since Adam and Eve discovered its power.

Like all mysteries, the beast had become an object of worship and adoration as the dispenser of life's seed, the primogenitor of humankind, the wand of life.

The beast was the center point of Michelanglo's man with all other dimensions radiating out from that point. The beast was important but how did a man view it? And how did a woman view it?

I'd come to manhood without instruction beyond the physical facts. What could my mother tell me that would've enlightened me about the strange power that resided in my loins? My father was no help either for, in those days men never spoke of such things to their sons. That left me to discover, by exploration, the magical power of the beast. In some ways I suppose I was lucky for I came to know the beast and made it my friend while other men have been possessed by its power and became its slave.

When I came to maturity and thought about my beast and its function I realized that I viewed it in many ways: as the source of my masculine power, as a place of great pleasure, as an organ of penetration, as a pleasurable connection with a woman, and a tube of elimination. What would I be without my beast? Would I be a man?

Angels don't have one nor do spirits of the departed, I'm told. But Jesus, the man, had a beast. How did Jesus view his beast? Did he feel the pleasure of its arousal? Did he pleasure himself? Did he become one with Mary Magdalene as some ancient texts suggest?

It is suggested by some that centuries before, when Mary Magdalene as Potiphar's wife, tried to seduce Jesus, then Joseph, was she not seeking her perfect lover, her perfect mate? Was she not condemned by her acts to appear centuries later at Christ's feet, first as supplicant, then as a lover who washed his feet with her tears? Had she finally found her one true love only to watch as he was sacrificed on the mother-tree?

The Church Fathers avoided these questions by making Jesus into an androgynous being without sexual desires. But was their Jesus a real man?

I thought not. The Jesus of the Church Fathers was a creation of their theology. Just as they modestly hid Jesus' genitals beneath a loincloth, when, in fact, Jesus, like all victims of Roman crucifixion, was hung naked on the cross with genitals exposed in ultimate humiliation. God used that ultimate humiliation to define all dimensions of mankind.

Beast adoration and beast fear bowed down to the same King who, with scepter or sword, could bless or destroy.

In popular mythology, beast size and potency were attributes of the gods and all men favored by them. Did such worship spring from the primeval need for the warrior to survive? The gods were not without humor. The mystery deepened with the non-relationship of the beast's size-potency factor to the physique-beauty factor though macho myths abounded leaving the "nice man," less endowed and confused about his manhood, to be defined by woman.

And that led me to consider the greatest beast mystery; The three definitions of man by woman: Circe, Venus, and the Temple Virgin.

Sara, and others like her, was my Circe, that ubiquitous castration figure ever apparent in men's dreams and myths, the *vagina dentata* (toothed vagina). She had lured my beast into her mysterious rainforest, where like a mongoose, she'd teased the dumb beast to rise and enter her cave of wetness and then overwhelmed it. Then she laughed triumphantly as the vanquished beast withdrew into its lair to await her call to service.

For Sara, it was power, the bigger the beast the greater the power; by luring it into her cave, she sought to take power from the beast and make that power her own. But sadly, no victory won her the ultimate prize. For every beast she vanquished was proof it was inferior. The greatest beast remained unconquered. Who was the greatest beast of all? Was it a fantasy or a memory that drove her quest? The morning-after would inevitably arrive when she'd awake to find herself defeated by another goddess who helped the beast to be triumphant.

Who was the goddess that could defeat Circe? It could be none other than Venus who saw the beast as a part of me, not my entirety. Beast's size and dexterity were of secondary importance to her who valued reciprocal love above all else. Her love did not seek to rob me of my power, but to enhance my power as I enhanced hers. Such reciprocal love was desired by all, but found by few.

The game of life was waged on a battlefield of treachery and deception. Many withdraw like defeated lions and lionesses who limp back into their lairs to lick their wounds that sometimes fester into bitterness and hatred and give birth to Mars and Circe.

The Temple Virgin held herself above the game of life, retreating from the beast in righteous horror, encouraged by the Church Fathers who equated virginity without sexual desire with sainthood.

Origen, the third-century church father, castrated himself in his quest for spirituality. Saint Tressia sealed her vagina with a white-hot iron to bar the entrance of the beast and to burn away all fleshly desires.

Such accounts of self-mutilation served only to enhance the voyeuristic ecstasies of the dysfunctional. The passion of the beast was enflamed by the thought of a Temple Virgin waiting just for him.

Suppression of the sexual energies was like damming a surging river; the blocked waters only went underground to break out in another place and in another form, unexpectedly and violently.

The closest that a woman could come to feeling what the beast felt, what it was like to be wrapped in a warm wetness which contracted and pulsated, was when she nursed a sucking baby that drew nourishment and life from her nipple.

The Church Fathers were right to focus their attention on sexual desires, but went astray when they called them "sin" and made woman the source thereof. By ignoring the beast, they set it free to ravage the earth in the name of God.

Will that mystery ever be resolved?

I pondered these thoughts long into the night. Still whether dreaming or awake I cannot say.

Just as I can't say whether or not it was an apparition that appeared in my open doorway. Was it a goddess wearing a long robe of silvery gauze, light in fabric and charming to the eye, her face hidden beneath a veil? Around her waist she'd fashioned a splendid golden belt. The figure silhouetted against the moonlight was familiar. The goddess spoke not a word as I rose from my bed.

When she lifted her wand to enchant me, I lunged toward her with a knife in my upraised hand as if to strike her dead. She fell at my feet and clasped her arms around my knees; her eyes, those sparkling green eyes, pleaded for life. And then she was gone.

Dawn's rosy lips were kissing the eastern mountains when I woke to find Sara beside me in my bed. Her long, red hair, tussled and mussed about her head, hung over the closed lids behind which I knew lurked those enchanting eyes.

As I looked upon the sleeping beauty, her form and face were like the goddess; and like Odysseus, I knew that I'd again been required to enter Circe's world to be free of her. Would her sensuous beauty still be the powerful drug that would take me to the land of forgetfulness where, without self-respect, I'd wallow at her feet like a swine forgetting everything dear and precious, forgetting even Betty? Was the old man's antidote strong enough to ward off her poison?

These thoughts I pondered as I sat in my leather chair waiting for her awakening, studying her beauty from toe to head, when my eyes fixed upon the long red scar on her neck. My wonderment of the who and the why of its occurrence was cut short with the opening of her eyes.

"Where have you been?" She demanded as one who was accustomed to being obeyed.

"Out walking on the beach."

"All night?"

"Most of the night."

She rose up in the bed with the grace of a sea nymph; a broad loving smile crept over her lips.

"I've missed you terribly," she said. "Why didn't you visit me at the hospital?"

"If you will recall, your departure was hardly any encouragement for me to follow you."

"Oh, you silly man, you take everything so seriously. You know I love you and I always will."

She slipped into the bathroom. When she emerged, the scar was gone; perfection restored.

"While I was recovering in the hospital, I had time to think. I realized that you're a wonderful man and that I'm lucky to have you in my life."

"There's something you must know...."

"Please, let me finish," she whispered, holding a finger to my lips. "It's very difficult for me to say this. But I've been a stupid fool not to realize how much you mean to me."

She slid onto my lap, her soft body stirring up the coals of erotic memories; lifting her arms around my neck she kissed me fully and firmly and deeply.

I could feel the jerking beast coming to life, expanding and lifting. She reached down and lifted my hand to her full, firm breast. I could feel her poison entering my body, bringing me to the verge of defeat, of forgetting, when a vision appeared before my eyes, the vision of Betty as she posed so gracefully, and the remembrance of her in the moonlit bed, of our togetherness filled with reciprocal love and passion.

I eased Sara from my lap and walked out on the deck to breathe deeply the clean morning air. Sara followed.

"What's the matter?" She asked, cuddling to my side. "Don't you want to make love with me?"

"Of course I do, but I won't."

"Why not?"

"Many things have happened since our last morning together. You were almost killed. And I died."

"What do you mean, you died?"

"It's a long story and difficult to tell but the result is that I've been born again."

"Oh, no, you haven't got religion, have you?"

"I've always been a religious man. What I'm talking about is that the man you knew died in a grave up on Spirit Point. The man who stands here is a stranger to you. And that man is in love with another woman. A few minutes ago I realized that I no longer love you. The beast, which you ridiculed as too insignificant, is my true love's joy and satisfaction. It has roared about in her rainforest like a mighty lion. But when you invited it into your forest, it remained in its lair."

With the suddenness of flashing lightning, Sara transformed herself into an avenging Fury.

"God damn you! How can you do this to me? You know how much I need you. How can you forget what we meant to each other? I didn't forget."

Sara stomped around the deck with clenched fists shaking the air. Then, with equal suddenness, she changed back to a seductive Siren whose purring voice was honey sweet.

"When I was in the hospital, I remembered the times we walked on the beach with the morning fog heavy about us, your arm around my waist, my head on your shoulder

and…."

"Sara, it's over between us. I've a new life, and you have to go back to your husband."

Sara's green eyes flashed with anger as her fists shook like a twin-tailed rattlesnake preparing to strike.

"I can't believe it…You're dumping me! Oh, no, you're not. If you think you can pull that shit on me you've another thought coming. Who is she?"

"A figment of my imagination. What difference does it make? Who I love is no longer any of your business."

"You're not going to get away with this. I won't let you."

"Sara, wake up. It's over between us. Go back to Seattle and get on with your life without me."

"It's not over. Just you wait. You won't get away with humiliating me like this."

"Sara...."

She didn't let me finish. The last thing I saw was the trailing edges of her white gown disappearing into the house. A few moments later I heard her white Mercedes roar out of my driveway with tires squealing up the street toward Angeline Avenue.

CHAPTER SIXTEEN

I recognized her soft knock and hurried to the door, anxious to learn whether the events of the previous night had been real or a dream. Instead of the joyous reunion of lovers hugging and kissing, Betty's face was tear-stained and drawn; her bloodshot eyes told of deep sorrow. She slipped past and dropped onto the couch, burying her face into a white-lace handkerchief. I sat at her side with my arm around her shoulders waiting for her sobbing to ease.

"What's the matter?" I asked.

Between sobs, the answered dribbled forth.

"Bill died last night. I found him this morning when I got up to give him his water. He'd thrown off his blanket. His bare back was toward me. I thought he was asleep. When I touched his shoulder it was cold and rigid. When I turned him on his back, his eyes were open and his tongue stuck out at me. The coroner said he probably choked to death on some phlegm he was trying to cough out. It was my fault. I didn't hear him because…we were…"

"Hush, my darling. You don't know for sure."

"I feel so guilty. When he needed me, I was betraying him If only we'd waited."

I could give her no answer that she wanted to hear. She was right, of course. Had I restrained the beast for another night, we'd have been free to come together, openly, without quilt or shame. Even now, no one knew but us. At least, so I thought.

"The Deputy Sheriff asked about us. He wanted to know if we were lovers."

"What did you say?"

Betty lifted her chin, bravely.

"I told him we were."

"What did he say about that?"

"Nothing. He just made a note and went on to ask more questions about my morning routine with Bill. How did he know about us?"

"The houses of this village have eyes that see all things, and tongues that tell all things. Nothing is a secret unless it wears the blanket of invisibility."

Suddenly, breaking off her story, Betty turned to me and asked, "Should we feel guilty about making love while Bill was choking to death?"

Guilt! What was it? We all suffer from its malaise, but what do we do with it? Transfer it to others? Suppress it in hopes it will go away? What if it doesn't go away, but hovers in our unconscious like a shadow figure haunting our nightmares, the black stranger that leaps out of the darkness and sends us scrambling for the safety of the streetlight? When the woman cringes in her bed, are the night sounds that of a prowling rapist or desires from the past that refuse to be forgotten?

Will the sound of Bill's choking haunt our bed? Will our ecstasy be interrupted by the cough, cough, cough from the other room? Will he be like Poe's Raven crying out, "Never More, Never More?"

That is what guilt would have us believe. For it is the nature of guilt to be self-punishing, thereby, usurping God's role in our lives. Who knows but God's compassionate hand might have rested on us all last night? Then who are we to render judgment on God's will?

If Bill could be conjured up from Hade's realm, what would he say now that he has solved the puzzle? I listened for his answer as I waited beneath the Oak tree in my garden. And when he didn't come, I asked my grandfather, Why?

My grandfather replied, "How cluttered and distracting life would be if all from beyond the grave could cry out their pain and misery! It's enough for the living to duel with their ghosts, and leave the dead to theirs."

During the week following Bill Coleman's death, the living of Suquamish quickly forgot even his name as they returned to their own tasks of surviving.

The sharp knock sent Lady barking to the door. The Deputy Sheriff looked past me to Betty, who sat on the brown couch.

"I thought I might find you here," said Deputy Johnson.

Without invitation, he entered my cabin and dropped into my leather easy chair.

"It seems that you keep popping up in my investigations. I've just come from the Duggan residence. Sara Duggan was found drowned in her hottub this morning."

"Oh, my God," I said. "What a horrible thing!"

"Yep," replied the Deputy in a voice hinging between indifference and exhaustion. "When Clara saw a red thing bobbing on the surface of the hottub this morning, she thought it was one of those inflatable dolls sold by sex shops. Yep. Sara was cooked like a lobster."

"How did it happen?"

"The Coroner thinks she drank too much wine, fell into a drunken stupor, then slipped under the water and drowned. All evidence points to her being alone, an empty wine bottle and one empty glass but...."

"But what?" I asked.

"The thermostat was turned as high as it would go. The water was 146 degrees this morning. Now, she might have hit the thermostat with her arm as she slipped under.

"Then again, Clara claims she saw another person visiting with Sara late last night. It was dark and when I pressed, Clara wasn't sure what she saw. Clara has a history of seeing things that aren't there like that second man who entered the Duggan house before the murder. But I still need to ask some questions of both of you."

"Fire away," I said.

"Perhaps we should step out on the deck so I can ask you some questions in private."

"I've nothing to hide from Betty."

"Okay then. Were you and Sara Duggan lovers?"

"Yes, we were…A long time ago."

"When was the last time you saw her alive?"

"A week ago, the morning after Halloween. She came by to talk over some things."

"What things?"

"Her ordeal had caused her to re-think her life. She'd come to the conclusion that she really loved me and wanted us to get back together."

"Did you get back together?"

"No. I told her it was over between us."

I turned toward Betty and looked deep into her searching eyes.

"I told her that I was in love with Betty."

"How'd she take that?"

"She got angry…Cursed me…And stomped out. The last I heard was the squealing of her tires."

"And you, Mrs. Coleman, did you know Sara Duggan?"

Betty's eyes were clear and steady, as was her answer.

"I've heard about her, but I never met the woman."

"That jives with Clara's opinion. Clara didn't think you two had met, you being tied down taking care of your husband and all that."

The Deputy flipped his notebook closed and turned to leave.

"Well, that's all the questions I have…for now. Thank you for your cooperation."

"You look exhausted. Can I get you something, a cup of coffee, a cinnamon roll, perhaps?"

"Thank you. I'd like that."

We drank our coffee and munched on the large frosted rolls that I had made that morning.

The Deputy spoke in a rambling fashion, "Things are getting crazy around here. Do you recall how, over in Wenatchee, two 12-year old boys came across a migrant worker who was camping beside the railroad tracks? When the drifter threw a rock at the boys, they shot him eighteen times with stolen pistols."

"Yes. Wenatchee has been a star-crossed community."

"Well, Suquamish must have its stars crossed, too. Two kids caught an Indian digging clams on what they claim is their private mud flats. When they threw rocks at him and shouted at him to get off their beach he chased them home. They got their 22 rifles and started shooting at him."

"Oh, my God, no!"

"What made it worse is they made it into a sport. First, they shot him in the right leg, then chased him along the beach like a wild animal dragging its wounded leg. They took sport in killing him a little bit at a time. It was a contest to see how slightly they could wound and still keep the man alive as he struggled to escape.

"When we found the man, there were wounds in both arms and legs, a gaping hole in his buttocks, all inflicted before the fatal shot between the eyes as he laid on the ground pleading for his life.

"It makes you sick to think 14-year-old boys could be so cruel. When confronted, they confessed, without emotion. They said the Indian was trespassing, and they were only protecting their private property. They come from good church-going families, too."

"Who was the Indian?"

"His name was Tom Proudfoot."

My heart exploded.

"Oh, no. Tom was a good friend of mine. No man deserves to die like that. He was the firekeeper for the tribe. This going to lead to serious trouble. Everyone has guns."

"That's what I'm afraid of."

It didn't surprise me. Such hateful things were as ancient as Cain's murder of Abel. It has always been easy to kill an underperson, a savage, a worthless person, a sinner who is not like us, not as good as we are. Such actions do not drop out of the sky, but they sprout in ground carefully prepared.

The steady cultivation of attitudes in the home and the church and on the streets, innocent comments that degrade another human being, watered by sermons, talk shows and neighborhood gossip, all may lay festering within until the hate filled one, the unstable one, can kill an underperson, and actually believe it is a service to God.

I listened for the Deputy's car to drive away before I began to explain my relationship with Sara to Betty.

"I was going to tell you of Sara's visit; but with Bill's death and funeral, I decided to wait until things settled down."

Betty's brown eyes searched my eyes as if expecting more revelations before the tears began.

"Is that true, what you told the deputy?" She asked.

"Yes."

Betty dropped her eyes to her hands, which began to twist of their own volition.

"I saw Sara drive away that morning," she said softly. "I thought…."

"I can understand. But, it was over."

Betty's facial expression began to change, taking on a faraway look as if she was moving back into another time and place.

"Oh, I wasn't angry with you," she said in a soft, disconnected, lilting voice. "I was angry with Sara. I knew she was the kind of woman you couldn't resist. It was so easy for her. She needed only to catch your eye, smile sweetly and coyly, lift her chest and show a little leg, and you would've followed her like a lamb to slaughter. I didn't want that to happen to you again, so I…."

"Yes?…What did you do?"

"Last night Clara mentioned to me that Sara was in her hottub. So I decided to pay Sara a visit."

Betty reached out for an unseen pill bottle and in pantomime, re-enacted that evening's events.

"I took three Zantac pills that Bill had used for his stomach trouble and ground them into a powder. Then I mixed the powder into a half-bottle of Chardonnay wine. I packed the bottle into a beach bag with two wineglasses.

"I could hear her soaking in the tub as she listened to soft, romantic music. When I slipped up onto the deck, she wasn't surprised to see me.

"'I thought you might come,' she said.

"I hated the way she lounged in her hottub, her arms stretched out on the edges, her breasts bobbing in the water, her smile warm and friendly. She was so confident.

"I said to her, 'I just came by to introduce myself and share a glass of wine. My name is Betty Coleman and I live at the end of the block.'

"'I know who you are. Yes, I'd love a glass of wine. Did you bring any with you?'

"I patted my beach bag as I set it down on the table. I had carefully washed and wrapped the wine bottle and glasses in white towels to remove any fingerprints. When I handed Sara a glass wrapped with a towel, she took it without question, then handed the towel back.

"'This is such a beautiful setting,' I said to her. 'A clear fall evening with the Seattle skyline all lit up and the strobe lights of airplanes floating silently across the night sky like giant fireflies.'

"'Would you like to join me?' Sara asked sweetly.

"'In the hottub?'

"'Yes, it's a wonderful experience to feel the warm bubbles between your legs.'

"Sara allowed the bubbling jets to lift her naked body to the surface, exposing herself to me. When she saw me look away, she smiled and licked her lips. Her green eyes twinkled seductively. Can you imagine, that bitch was actually trying to seduce me?

"'Not tonight,' I told her. 'But perhaps I will another time. How about a refill?'

"She held up her glass."

I interrupted to ask, "Why Zantac powder?"

"It accelerates the effect of alcohol on the body; one glass has the potency of three. Soon Sara was deep into lullaby land; but before she drifted off, when the wine and drug had stripped away all restraints, she took her pleasure in telling me all the details of how she made love to you in the cabin.

"She told me, 'I would get his little pony to rear up, then I'd climb on and ride it with fury driving him crazy with delight.'

"Then she threw her head back and laughed her fiendish laugh, her laugh of victory…. At me. She was laughing at me.

"I couldn't reply. I just sat there like a whipped dog tied to a stake, numbly listening as she lashed out at me delightfully sharing the details of how she made love to you.

"'Do you think a flat-chested mouse like you could keep a man like him?' She asked me, continually lifting her chest to taunt me further. Then, throwing her head back, she laughed into the sky.

"But I didn't care anymore because I knew her time on earth was coming to an end. She became maudlin, crying and laughing at the same time going from sentimental and silly, flipping in and out of different personalities; One moment she was warm and friendly, the next, a taunting shrew.

"When she dropped off to sleep, I reached over and gently placed my hand on her head; the weight of my hand eased her under the water. She didn't struggle much, only for a brief moment; she even laughed, a laugh of bubbles, her green eyes thanking me for her release."

I had sat in stunned silence during Betty's confession, struggling to put words to my question.

"Why did you do it?"

"Because…I knew you could not."

"But it was over between Sara and me."

"For her, nothing was over until she said so."

"Oh, my God, my God…I kept repeating, holding my head in my hands. "What are we to do?"

"About what?" Asked Betty in a clear controlled voice.

"Sara's death!"

"When did she die?"

"The Deputy Sheriff was just here to tell us that she drowned in her hottub last night."

"I don't remember that. I must have been in the bathroom."

"Yes…Perhaps you were. It was a terrible accident. Apparently, she drank too much wine and fell asleep and drowned."

"I never met Sara but I heard a lot about her. Weren't you good friends awhile back?"

"Yes, we were…a long time ago."

CHAPTER SEVENTEEN

I asked the Old Man, "Was Sara Duggan an evil woman?"

With a grunt, the Old Man eased his ancient frame onto a beached log. Bending over, he silently wrote in the soft sand with the point of his walking stick. After a long pause, he answered in a voice that was gentle and wise.

"There are evil people in this world, but Sara Duggan was not one of them. Her father determined her destiny.

"A person's unconscious world is like a cave. When you enter another person's cave, without a light to show the way, you'll fall into bottomless pits to be swept into underground streams or be attacked by strange cave creatures.

"Wherever there is light, there is equal darkness. I saw this on television. The spacecraft going to the moon was bright and hot on the side facing the sun while the other side of the spacecraft was dark and cold."

I replied, "There are those who say that proves there is no such thing as evil. There is only light and the absence of light."

"Humph," nodded the Old Man. "Perhaps. But don't we live in a world of opposites? We could make long lists of opposites: cold—hot, up—down, light—dark, good—evil and so on."

I asked, "How do you know what is good and what is evil?"

"It's not difficult for my people. We have the trickster to remind us that, where there is good there is also evil."

"Tell me about the trickster."

"The trickster is a master of disguises who can be a demon or a god, a fish or a bird, a man or a woman. The most amazing thing about the trickster is that he doesn't know what he's doing.

"The trickster is so unaware that his two hands even fight each other. He takes his ass off and blows it like a horn. Even his sex is optional. He can turn himself into a woman and bear children, and from his penis he can make all kinds of useful plants.

"The trickster does the most atrocious things out of sheer ignorance and indifference.

"He's not as smart as the animals and gets into one ridiculous situation after another. This dullness is shown by the story where he gets his head caught inside the skull of an elk and overcomes this condition by imprisoning the head of a hawk inside his ass.

"He immediately forgets and falls under the ice. He's outwitted time after time by the animals. But in the end, he succeeds in tricking the cunning coyote; therefore this hints at his potential to be a savior.

"This is a comforting hope because the trickster creates such a terrible mess that nobody but a savior can undo the tangled web of fate."

I asked, "Would there be a Savior if there was no Satan?"

"The two are always found together because they are the two sons of God. In the Bible Cain slays Able; Satan tempts Jesus, and the prodigal's brother waits for his return just as the dark one now waits for you in his cabin."

I followed the twisting path that led from the street into a grove of tall hemlocks to a small A-frame cabin with a majestic high-bank view of the sound. It was nearly eight-thirty in the evening, time for the full moon to lift her face.

My knock went unanswered, but the sliding glass door was open. I paused as I stepped into the dark interior. A row of dancing candles beckoned toward the backroom where I knew the dark one waited.

At a recent meeting of the local writer's club, the dark one had arrived dressed completely in black, black sweatpants and black turtleneck sweater. Beneath his pointed Mephistopheles beard, a gaudy, gold pentagram pendant hung from a gold chain necklace.

His manner was outgoing, an intimate glad-hand, as if seeking alliances. He loved the center stage in discussions and meetings. He would arrive before other guests and stay after others departed to continue his campaign.

That evening he read a piece he called his autobiography, a pathetic tale of his dissipation and failures since early childhood written in a cynical dark-humor style filled with glib self-serving cliches.

When he finished, he looked up expecting acclamation. But Dave, also a member of the group, responded with, "That's pure bullshit."

Paul, always the one for the positive response, said, "Well, you surely have a way with words."

But the dark one was not content as he whirled at me, "I haven't heard a word from his excellency. What do you think?"

I began in a quiet, tentative voice, "I've been silent because I'm embarrassed for you. This autobiographical sketch would be great reading for your psychiatrist but not for the public. It's an often-told tale of one man's slide into self-destruction; a tale you've told in your paintings as well. Strip away the thin veneer of cynical dark humor, and you find…nothing."

"Nothing?" The dark one spit out. "That's exactly what your opinion is worth since you've published nothing."

I didn't respond because I realized that his quick mind would accept nothing less than the last word. I'd been a fool to let him suck me into responding in the first place. It was obvious that the dark one viewed my presence in the writer's group as a personal threat to his Hollywood ego.

We bantered like fighting gamecocks as the discussion moved on to agents and publishers.

When he weaved his hands up and down in front of his face like a snake charmer and said, "I'm seeking a local agent who will be in perfect sync with me, fully compatible," I countered with, "Well, you'll have to go to New York since 90 percent of book publication is controlled there. Local agents can only help you with small, regional presses."

He ignored me and charged aggressively ahead.

"I'm planning to send my manuscript to a friend who is a successful writer and ask her to submit it to her publisher. I helped her get into movies so she owes me a big favor."

I countered with, "Established writers shun reading other writer's manuscripts because of the danger demonstrated by the recent Art Buckwald affair. If successful writers read unpublished manuscripts, they expose themselves to the danger of cryptomnesia."

The final eruption occurred when Dave asked me, "What character in your writings do you relate to?"

I replied, "I seek to let each character develop as a full person, loving them all, the good, the bad and the ugly."

The dark one suddenly jumped up and pointing his long finger at me, shouted, "All your characters are nothing but boring two-dimensional projections of yourself."

A shouting match erupted, as everyone became involved. Paul and Madelene sought to defuse the confrontation. Dave objected to personal attacks in the group. And the rest sat in stunned silence.

I shouted, "You know nothing about writing, much less my writing."

The dark one retorted, "I most certainly do. I've waded through eight hundred and seventy-five pages of your boring crap."

"And I've mucked my way through fifteen hundred pages of your contrived conversations with Satan."

His black eyes flashed red with hatred at my indiscretion. During a weak moment, he had allowed me to read the manuscript that he claimed was the product of five years living with Satan in a Bainbridge Island cabin.

Paul suggested it was time for a coffee break.

When the dark one went outside for a smoke, Dave came over to me and said, "You're right and he is totally wrong. He's got his head up his ass; that's why all he can see is shit."

Paul, who held a doctorate in psychology, came over, stirring his coffee.

"Perhaps it's good to get it out into the open. You know he has a hidden agenda. Arguing with a mentally disturbed person is like associating with an alcoholic. They are constantly trying to draw you into their madness."

"Do you think he is mentally ill?" Dave asked.

"If he is, the steady fragmentation of his personality will continue. So far he has shared only pieces written fifteen years ago, nothing current. Haven't you wondered why?"

Dave responded, "He says he is having a hard time jump starting the writing process. He finds himself needing to sleep 18-to-20 hours a day. He can hardly drag himself out of bed."

Then I shared a recent experience.

"Several weeks ago he let me peek at a novel he was trying to resurrect. It, too, had been written ten-to-fifteen-years ago. It was a dark novel along the lines of Hemingway's *Night of the Iguana*. The hero, in the throes of alcohol and drugs, flees to a Caribbean setting where he continues his self-destructive slide by plunging into round after round of orgies, drunken brawls and eventually, commits suicide by drug overdose."

Paul suggested, "That's a self-fulfilling prophecy, isn't it?"

"That's what I thought when I read it. What really shock me are his more recent paintings that now hang in his cabin. They are loaded with dark colors, contorted faces, blocked within heavy circles and squares."

"The cry of a trapped soul," said Madelene. "He needs help not criticism."

Paul replied, "I'm not sure anyone can help him."

I went on to say, "Women who have reached out to him have found themselves quickly bedded, then cast aside. When it comes to women, he possesses the powers of a Svengali. He doesn't have to seek them; they come running to him.

"I remember the time of my first amazement. We were spending the evening discussing methods of past-life recall when a beautiful, dark-haired woman with a gorgeous figure came to his door. She was evidently a friend from Seattle, an extremely intelligent and gifted businesswoman listed in the Real Estate Who's Who of top brokers in the country.

"I could see that she had not expected him to have company when she whispered something into his ear. Then he asked me to step outside. 'The lady has the hots tonight,' he said in a soft, macho voice. 'She's brought along her ditty bag filled with frilly things and toys. She says she'll go mad if I don't help her.' Then he gave me the wink that told volumes. 'She says only my hose is big enough to put out her fire. I'm sure you'll understand if we put off our conversation to another time.'

"I recalled his earlier comparison of women to playing cards. They are temporary playthings to be cast aside when the game was over."

Dave said, "I can't believe a mature woman couldn't see through a man like that."

Madelene dropped her eyes.

I continued, "Neither could I but there she was in the flesh. How could I deny that? What further amazes me, he has proudly played the libertine wherever he has lived, be that London or Hollywood or Tokyo or Suquamish. According to him, we're talking about hundreds of women. Somewhere along the way, the HIV virus must have been waiting."

"But won't it have shown up by now?" Asked Madelene, her voice tinged with concern.

Paul said, "Incubation period of some strains can be fifteen years. Besides, you must understand the suicidal mindset. It doesn't matter what happens to other people; the moment is the only thing that matters."

Then Madelene said, "Oh, I'm sure you've overblown the danger."

"I hope I have," said Paul. "But when I look into his dark eyes, I see more than Svengali."

Paul's words echoed in my mind as I stepped through the glass bead curtain. The scent of jasmine filled the darkened room.

"Hello, my friend," the dark one hissed.

His white teeth smiled at me from the shadows. Above the white teeth, two red orbs glowed. He didn't move.

"It's time for us to have our little talk, isn't it?" He asked, inviting me to sit on a cushion against the opposite wall.

We sat silently in the soft candle light like two Bengal Tigers inside a cave, each cautiously sizing up their opponent and knowing that any mistake would be fatal.

The dark one was the first to speak:

"What do you think of the preacher's new church?"

"It's a beautiful building."

"He'll begin services soon. Did you know he plans to broadcast his services nationwide over the Christian TV and radio networks? It's amazing that such great things are happening in little Suquamish."

"What are you up to?"

"Me? What makes you think I'd have anything to do with such things?"

"I know you too well. I smell the sulfur of your handiwork all over the preacher."

The dark one roared in laughter, a primeval laughter, and a bestial laughter that echoed up from the smoky depths of Hades' realm.

"You're always the clever one, aren't you? Everyone has been impressed by the shining whiteness of the preacher, truly a servant of God, they say. But not you! What gave him away?"

"It's easy. Anyone who follows the yellow brick road that leads to the land of fame and power, will fall under the influence of the great Oz of deception, who especially loves to hide behind clerical robes."

"You're guessing. You don't know for sure."

"Did you give him the winning lottery ticket?"

"Of course not. That was pure luck."

"You answer according to your nature. You'd rather lie than tell the truth. But what difference does it make? The money was the spark that merely ignited existing kindling. You don't have the power to capture anyone's soul."

"You don't think so?"

"No, I know you for what you are. You're a fraud."

"A fraud! A fraud!" The dark one shrieked. "I'll show you who's the fraud. Just watch me as I destroy the preacher and his church. I'll spread a madness over Suquamish just like I did over Wenatchee."

"You're crazy. Your only power is what people give you. Take away their fear and you evaporate into nothingness."

"Nothingness! Evaporate into nothingness! You're not as smart as I thought you were. For every fear conquered, seven new fears take its place."

"You're nothing but a hack actor strutting on an empty stage in front of a nonexistent audience."

"I'll show you…." The dark one paused in mid-sentence, "I know what you're up to," he continued as he wagged his finger at me. "You're trying to provoke me into attacking you. But it's not going to work. You'll have to try and destroy me."

"If I don't want to play by your rules, what happens?"

"How about a contest for the preacher's soul? If you can save him, then I'll go away. If not…Well, you know what happens to losers."

"Why would I want to play your crazy game?"

"I really don't care if you play or not because either way, I'll destroy the preacher with these."

The dark one slid a stack of photo albums across the floor. I opened the top one labeled *Diane.*

The dark one snickered, "I'm sure you recognize the lady, a bit saggy in the chest but not bad."

"Where did you get these?"

"I borrowed them from Pastor Jerry. All preachers have their dirty little secrets, so high and mighty in the pulpit but behind close doors…I never cease to be amazed what big hypocrites they are.

"I only give them what they desire: money, power, fame, flashy cars, big mansions, little boys, little girls, dirty women, whores…They want them all, and they're entitled to them as servants of the most high God."

"They're only human, as you're so quick to whisper into their ears. What are you going to do with these albums?"

"I've majestic plans for them. Just as Pastor Jerry reaches the top, pictures of his wife, naked as God created her, will begin to flutter down around the village."

The dark one threw his head back and roared in fiendish laughter.

"Can you imagine how the good Christian women who follow him so faithfully will react? Can you imagine their horror when they discover that their good preacher is a pornographer and that his sweet wife is his erotic model?"

The laughter of the dark one sent chills up my spine.

"Enough!" I shouted. "I don't know how I'm going to do it but I'm going to beat you. You'll not get the preacher's soul."

"Wonderful! Wonderful!" Exclaimed the dark one gleefully, noticing how I continued to glance through the photo albums.

He knew that my love of the female form would draw me to those who so willingly posed in erotic ways. No matter whether they had long hair or short, were blonde or brunette, had blue eyes or brown nor did it matter if their breasts were large or petite, pendulous or perky, the variety of shapes and sizes cast a spell over me and pulled my eyes to every detail of their bodies.

Each woman's God-given body was different and beautiful in its own way. For the Lord God who created them said it was good to look upon them.

As I looked upon Diane and beheld her beauty, words from the *Song of Solomon* flowed into my mind:

O Diane, behold, you are beautiful!
When I look upon your face

I can hear your voice,
  for your voice is sweet,
  and your face is lovely.
Your blue eyes are as innocent as doves.
Your flowing blonde hair
    is like a flock of goats
      moving down the slopes of Gilead.
Your white teeth are like a flock of shorn ewes
    that have come up from the washing.
Your thin ruby lips are like a scarlet thread.
Your mouth is as lovely as a ripe tangerine.
Your cheeks are like halves of a pomegranate.
Your neck is like the tower of David
    built for an arsenal.
Your breasts are like two melons, full and ripe.
Lovely is your mound of myrrh,
    and your black glen
    that smells of frankincense.
Diane! How fair and pleasant you are,
O loved and delectable maiden!
Let us go early to the vineyards,
    and see whether the vines have budded,
    whether the grape blossoms have opened,
    and the pomegranates are in bloom.
There I will give you my love.
Come to my garden,
    that I may gather your myrrh with your spice,
    That I may eat your honeycomb with your honey,
    That I may drink your wine and your milk.
  Carefully, I searched Diane's smiling face for any trace of reluctance,
but found only excitement. I tried to put myself into her body and

mind, seeking to become one with her as Jesus said we should. I wanted to experience what she thought and felt.

I tried to visualize myself as a woman posing before the camera knowing that with each flash, my body would be fixed on a Polaroid print to be appreciated by the eyes of men and women whom I could trust to keep me from harm. At long last, I could rejoice in being free from the fear that kept me bound within my Victorian corset.

My brown eyes twinkled with excitement as I coyly flipped my long black hair over my right ear while dropping the left side of my hair teasingly over my breast.

I felt eye-energy fixing upon my breasts, studying every detail of my pink nipples. I took a deep breath to lift my chest. I felt my nipples stiffen and extend.

Then the beam shifted to my loins with its thick black hair. I felt the tingle, the moist excitement.

I had long been aware that, what women said in public and how they acted in private rarely agreed. I was especially excited by the realization that here was the vestal virgin of Suquamish posing unashamedly in the nude. And she was Diane, Pastor Jerry's wife.

Her natural beauty had so captivated me that I had not noticed the dark one slip away into the night.

CHAPTER EIGHTEEN

Pastor Jerry sat in his tall pulpit chair surveying his huge new sanctuary with seating for 2,000 people. Moonlight poured through the wall of stained glass behind him, filling the row upon row of empty pews with ghostly worshipers shrouded in variegated shades of the rainbow.

Slowly, Pastor Jerry stood up and walked to the pulpit. The pulpit itself was elaborately decorated with biblical scenes, hand carved from kiln-dried North Carolina oak and stained to a rich, dark luster. He increased the volume of the amplifier system until his voice boomed throughout the sanctuary. Clearing his throat, he began:

"Welcome to the Church of the True Faith. Today we come to dedicate these new facilities to our Lord."

When Pastor Jerry had finished rehearsing his inaugural sermon and the echo of his voice had faded away, he returned to his chair, his face beaming with pleasure as he looked around the beautiful vaulted structure.

The sharp CLAP, CLAP, interrupted his revelry, CLAP that rebounded off the walls like pistol shots.

"It has turned out nicely, hasn't it?" Came the whispered voice from behind the chancel curtain.

Pastor Jerry whirled around but saw no one. Settling back in recognition, he replied, "Yes, it has. And we've God to thank for this blessing."

"No, I'm afraid you have me to thank."

"Yes, of course, I meant God working through you."

"No, he didn't. I did it alone. But never mind; we've got much work still to do."

"What do you mean?"

"Don't you realize it yet? You're working for me now."

"What makes you think I'm yours to command?"

"This," whispered the dark one as Diane's Polaroid slipped out from under the chancel curtain.

Pastor Jerry slowly leaned over, picked it up, and turned it to the moonlight. He caught his breath then let the picture slip from his fingers. He slumped into his chair.

"There's more where that came from," whispered the voice.

"So it was you who stole my albums?"

"Yes, and a very fine collection they are. But don't worry. I have them in a safe place along with the ones you never received.

"They make for wonderful viewing. I spend hours pouring over their details with a magnifying glass, studying all their features. As you know, they're from all over the country. Are they all preachers' wives? Who'd believe so many good pastors would be into photography?"

Pastor Jerry gripped the chair arms, fighting to control his trembling hands:

"What do you want from me?"

"I have what I want. But, since you asked, there are a few little things you could do for me."

"And if I don't?"

"Oh, can you just imagine the trouble that might cause? What would the community say if tomorrow morning, they were to find flyers featuring Diane in all her natural glory, stuck in their doors?

"I'd hate to think what the news reporters would do with such a revelation. Surely, you haven't forgotten what they did to poor Jimmy Swaggert? They were so cruel. It didn't have to go that way. Jimmy just forgot who made him successful. You're not going to forget, are you?"

Pastor Jerry, with a voice resigned to his fate, asked again, "What do you want me to do?"

"There is much talk that the end of the world is close at hand. Preachers have been playing on that fear for thousands of years, even before that misguided fool, Jesus, was born.

"I want you to build on that fear by featuring the Second Coming in your sermons, emphasize that the battle of Armageddon is about to take place but don't forget to hang out the hope of escape for the select few. That's my favorite. Fear without hope of escape just doesn't work; it doesn't bring in the money.

"Also, you have to narrow down the number who will be saved by emphasizing that obedience to God's will is the key to their salvation and that you're the true prophet through whom God makes his will known."

Pastor Jerry snapped, "And, no doubt, you'll tell me what is God's will?"

"But of course. Who better knows God's will than one of his sons? Your sermon for tomorrow just won't do. I want you to give this one."

Sheets of white paper began to wiggle out from beneath the chancel curtain like snakes leaving their den.

Ruby dawn found Pastor Jerry still laboring in his study, the more he went over the sermon, the more excited he became; he even ignored Diane's call to breakfast. He went over it repeatedly, fixing it in his memory.

"Genius. Pure genius," he mumbled to himself as he stood up to stretch his aching limbs.

"What's that, dear?" Asked Diane as she entered carrying a tray with two cups of coffee and freshly baked cinnamon rolls.

"My sermon for today. I've been at it all night. I was caught in the grip of the Holy Spirit and this divinely inspired sermon appeared on paper."

"I'm sure it did, dear. I'm so proud of what has been accomplished for the Lord. I know your father is, too. He called last night to wish us well and said he will set his VCR to record the service."

"I wish he had come."

"You know he couldn't be away from his congregation at this time of year."

"Yes, I know. But just once I'd like to have my father see that I've accomplished something, too."

"Well, he'll see that when he replays the service on his VCR. By the way, the radio and TV crews are over at the church getting everything hooked up."

A fanfare of trumpets and the roll of drums opened the service. The choir, one hundred strong, processed into the sanctuary dressed in sky-blue robes trimmed with white silk, singing the anthem:
Stand up, stand up for Jesus,
Ye soldiers of the cross;
Lift high His royal banner,
It must not suffer loss;
From victory unto victory
His army shall He lead,
Till every foe is vanquished,
And Christ is Lord indeed.
Following in the choir's wake strolled a confident Pastor Jerry, wearing a royal-blue clerical robe with three doctrinal stripes of black velvet on each sleeve; down his back hung a blazing scarlet hood trimmed in white silk with a royal-blue lining. His smiling face beamed showing off perfect, white teeth, recently capped. His long blonde shoulder length hair had been fluffed and swept back like the mane of a lion, then fixed in place with a heavy dose of hair spray. The makeup artist had finished with a touch of powder to prevent a shine under the glare of the TV lights. He clasped a red leather Bible to his chest. With his free arm, he encouraged the congregation to sing with gusto.

The well-orchestrated service flowed smoothly from the very beginning. First the choir director led the congregation in several anthems. Followed by Diane's reading of a scriptural passage. That was followed by a choral presentation to the featured climax. Pastor Jerry stepped to the pulpit, an open Bible in his hand, and took his position in front of the cameras and microphones, the upraised faces of two thousand-plus expectant worshipers, and an estimated eight million more in the TV and radio audiences.

Lifting the Bible above his head, he began in a soft voice that rose to a shout, then fell back, to rise again like waves of an approaching storm.

"My friends in Christ, the prophecy of the last days are now being fulfilled. I'm here to tell you that the Anti-Christ is on the prowl seeking to devour innocent souls and destroy our great country.

"At this very moment Satan's disciples are stalking new victims. Right here in Suquamish, Washington, devil worshipers practice their dark arts under the guise of native culture.

"You can find Satan's tools everywhere:drugs, alcohol, sex orgies, and gambling. Witch covens proliferate like dandelion; satanic rites flourish. Around every corner there are pornographers, drug peddlers, and murdering abortionists.

"What are we going to do about it?

"Are we going to forsake our Lord at this critical moment in history?

"Soldiers of Christ, let us lift up our banners and swords and march into battle.

"Let us hunt down the filthy sodomizers who lick asses and violate little boys.

"Let us surround the drug dens and burn them to the ground; let us destroy the potheads, the sniffers, and shooters.

"Let us cut short the murderers of the unborn, the ones who hook and tear those little bodies out of their mother's womb then chop them up as if they were laboratory animals, dissecting their little brains, their tiny feet and hands.

"Oh, My Sweet Lord Jesus, give us the strength to stamp out these evil people, to grind them under Thy righteous heel.

"Send forth Thy servants to purge our holy land of all abomination and wash our holy mountains with the blood of Thy enemies.

"Rise up, ye men and women of God!

Have done with lesser things;
  Give heart and soul and mind and strength
To serve the King of Kings.
"And all God's people said, Amen.
"What do you say?
"Let me hear your answer, loud and clear."
The choir director prompted the congregation to shout in unison, "Amen!"
Pastor Jerry strolled around the chancel shaking the red Bible over his head:
"God's word condemns those who practice homosexuality.
I know there are innocents among us who speak of civil rights and say that homosexuality is a matter of nature, not choice.
"I'm here to tell you that the founding fathers didn't intend civil rights to cover the licking of another man's anus or the sticking of a penis up another man's rectum. Even animals don't do such filthy things. But Satan has convinced many in this country that it's natural. It's okay. It's not natural. And it's not okay.
"How can we ask our young men to share a foxhole with someone they can't turn their backsides to?
"It's time for Christians to stand up for their faith and purge our country of these servants of debauchery.
"The time is short.
"If God's soldiers don't take the field, the victory will be won by Satan.
"When the Lord appears with his avenging Angels, where will you be found?
"Will you be in His army or in Satan's army?
There is no neutral ground."
With a dramatic pause Pastor Jerry swept over the congregation with his fiery eyes, left to right, then straight into the camera.

"My dear friends in Christ, I'm here to tell you that an angel of the Lord appeared to me last night. He told me that in a few days he'd return with a message from the Lord.

"Next Sunday morning, God willing, I'll bring that message to the world. Will you be listening and watching?

"We pray that you will support this vital ministry by sending your contributions to:

The
Church Of The True Faith
P.O. Box 801
Suquamish, WA, 98392
"Until next Sunday,
     May God bless you, real good."

That night when her majesty, the moon, stirred from her bed and lifted her face above the eastern curtains, she found the Old Man and I sitting on my deck. Her silver, light brought forth thoughts and conversation kept hidden during the day.

I was the first to break her enchantment:

"The preacher gave quite a sermon this morning."

"Yes. I was watching on a friend's TV."

"What did you think?"

"Terrible things happen when a man raises his fist against his neighbor. I'm sad for everyone."

"There was a meeting at his church this evening for everyone who wants to fight Satan."

"Why didn't you attend?" The Old Man asked.

Before I could answer, Betty and a young native woman in her late teens came around the corner of the cabin.

"Hi there. May we join you?" Asked Betty.

"Of course, come and sit," I replied, pulling the deck chairs into a semi-circle facing the moon.

"What brings two beautiful women to my house this evening?"

Betty nodded toward the Old Man, "I'm glad you're here. We came to ask both of you for your advice."

"What's the problem?" The Old Man asked.

Betty reached over and touched the young woman's arm, "Angeline, why don't you tell them?"

"I…can't," said Angeline in a soft, barely perceptible voice. "You tell them."

Betty began the story, "Pastor Jerry asked Angeline to help in the church office, stuffing envelopes, answering the phone, and other such things. When they'd work late into the night he'd drive her home. That's when it started."

Angeline picked up her story, "We'd sit in his car and talk. He'd listen to me. No one ever listened to me before. I could tell him anything, and he'd listen."

"Tell them what happened when his wife was out of town," urged Betty.

"We were working in his new house up on the bluff when he took out a Polaroid camera. He told me I was pretty and wanted to take my picture to add to the album he called *The Lord's Helpers*. He kept taking pictures of me. I was so pleased he thought I was pretty, that I did whatever he asked."

I could not help but ask, "Then he asked you to take off your clothes?"

"How did you know?" Asked Betty.

"Just a wild guess. But that wasn't all, was it?"

"No," whispered Angeline, hanging her head.

Betty picked up the story. "On the way home he didn't say a word to her. But when he reached over to open the door, he kissed her."

"I…I wanted him to…I wanted to thank him for the wonderful experience."

"Did it happen again?" I asked.

"Oh, yes, often. Every time his wife was away, he'd get out the camera, and we'd make love."

"So, what's the problem?" The Old Man asked.

"She's pregnant," answered Betty. "And Pastor Jerry wants her to have an abortion…at the new Women's Clinic down at the Tribal Center."

"To avoid an embarrassment for Pastor Jerry, I'm sure. How do you feel about it, Angeline?" I asked.

"That's why we came to you," said Betty. "She's confused. One minute Pastor Jerry says abortion is murder. The next he's telling Angeline that she'll be serving the Lord if she gets an abortion."

The Old Man raised his hand for quiet.

"Don't get worked up about the Preacher. He has his destiny to keep. Angeline, what do you want to do?"

"I don't know. Sometimes, I want to get an abortion. But isn't that murder?"

The Old Man cupped his chin in his hand as he thought long and hard before answering.

"The Master said, 'Do not fear those who kill the body but cannot kill the soul.' When did the immortal soul of Jesus enter his mortal body? I will tell you. It entered at the moment of birth. Just as it did for me and for you and for all human beings. It's not murder to terminate an unwanted fetus; it's an act of stewardship. Murder is when an unwanted child is brought into the world to be unloved and uncared-for. That kills both the soul and the body.

"My advice to you is to search your heart. If you can't bring this child into the world to be loved and cared for, then have your abortion quickly, as soon as possible, and get on with your life, remembering the lessons you've learned.

"But if you can bring this child into a world filled with love and caring, then that would be the best thing to do. It's your decision. It's not our place to judge you. I have nothing more to say."

Angeline nodded her head in appreciation for the old man's wisdom.

Betty and Angeline exchanged searching looks.

"What?" I asked. "Is there more?"

Betty eyes flared in anger.

"Angeline, you've got to tell them."

"I can't. He said he would kill me if I told."

The Old Man reached over and squeezed Angeline's hand.

"He is killing you now by forcing you to bottle up this terrible secret. Speak, for the Great Spirit is watching over us all."

"It happened two weeks ago during the Sunday evening youth fellowship. After scripture reading, I was asked to lead the young people in songs. As we were singing, I saw Pastor Jerry and his wife pick out six of the youngest boys and girls, escort them into a back room, and close the door. I thought they had a special program for them. Then, two men and two women came into the fellowship hall and slipped into the back room, too.

"When the fellowship hour was over and the young people had gone home, I went to the back room to tell Pastor Jerry I was leaving. The door was locked. When I knocked, Pastor Jerry asked who was there. I told him that I was leaving. He just said, That's fine, thank you for your help.

"I could hear people moving around inside so I peeked through the keyhole. Everyone was naked, the little boys and girls, the men and women.

"I saw Pastor Jerry laying on a bed with a little girl sitting on top of him. Diane was in another bed with a little boy. I couldn't see what else was going on but I heard everyone laughing and having a good time. I was about to slip away when Pastor Jerry caught me."

Angeline's eyes widened as she said, "He threatened to kill me if I told anyone what I saw."

Betty put a comforting arm around Angeline's shoulder. "That man is the biggest hypocrite I've ever known. What do you think we should do?"

The old man looked at me then said, "I think Angeline should go to the police. Let them investigate the situation."

When the two women had gone, I asked the Old Man, "What do you really think? Is Angeline telling the truth?""

"The truth in such matters is difficult to know. Angeline is a little girl in a woman's body. She has been starved for love and affection all her life. Pastor Jerry may have taken advantage of her and done everything she says. Then again, he might have shown her a little harmless attention and her imagination has done the rest."

I replied, "Tensions have been building in the village. All we need is for sexual hysteria to kick-in. If Angeline's story goes public, Suquamish will experience its own version of the Wenatchee hysteria. There will be plenty of accusations but little truth."

"People will take sides."

"No matter what happens, Pastor Jerry and his wife's reputations will be destroyed. How can we know the truth?"

"Young girls like Angeline may start out telling the truth then, because of the attention they receive, begin to embellish.

"And the more incredible the allegations, the more likely they are not to be true."

The Old Man closed his eyes in concentration. Then he said, "I see the hand of the trickster in this. The chaos of a witch hunt fueled by sexual hysteria is just what he would orchestrate."

The landing lights of airplanes on approach to SeaTac Airport were like moving stars among the fixed stars that filled the sky. After a long period of silence, I said, "It seems that Calvin's Convergence is bearing down upon Suquamish."

"What's Calvin's Convergence?" Asked the Old Man.

"It comes from the comic strip, *Calvin And Hobbes* by Bill Watterson. Little three-year old Calvin and Hobbes, his stuffed Tiger, are constantly caught up in imaginary, converging catastrophes.

"Like when at 35,000 feet, the engines of Flight 430 exploded for no reason! With plumes of dense smoke trailing from the wings, the giant aircraft plummeted out of control! Meanwhile, a 50-car freight train hit a penny on the rail at 80 miles an hour and jumped the tracks dragging half a million tons of metal into the air behind it!

"In a freak coincidence, both the jet and the train converged on one spot…Where tectonic plates in the earth's crust had just begun to shift! That spot was the house of Farmer Brown who, at that moment, was unaware of a gas leak as he attempted to light his stove! As he struck the match, he casually glanced out the kitchen window; his eye twitched involuntarily at the sight of the converging plane, train and splitting earth.

"That's an example of a Calvin's Convergence."

"And you think that's what's about to happen to Suquamish?"

"All it'll take is for someone to strike a match."

CHAPTER NINETEEN

Joe Old Coyote was not a member of the Suquamish Tribe. He was a mysterious native who floated in and out of the village. Shortly after Joe arrived, he rented a mobile home in an isolated part of the Reservation. Rumors raced like wildfire, jumping from mouth-to-mouth of natives and whites alike. But he was a friendly man with skin tones of a perpetual tan, neither completely white nor red. His brown eyes had the depths of a dark pool in the mystic forests of ancient times where the fairies and gnomes would come to dance and play.

The staff of the Suquamish Tribal Museum was the first to notice of Joe. He had come to stand daily in front of the large exhibits of cedar canoes and totems. He sought out Old Running Bear, the last of the old wood carvers.

"May I become your apprentice?" He asked.

Old Running Bear scrutinized him through the gray mists of his cataract eyes for a long time before answering,

"No," said Old Running Bear.

"Why not?"

"You are not Suquamish."

And that was that. But Joe would not give up. Daily, at the first light of day when Old Running Bear sat in front of his house to welcome the new day with a clap of his hands and a prayer to the great spirit, Joe would appear to ask again, "May I become your apprentice?"

And repeatedly, he received Old Running Bear's answered "No."

After a month of petitions, the day arrived when Old Running Bear was not in his morning chair. Joe entered the old man's house to find him still in bed.

"Are you all right?" Asked Joe.

Old Running Bear nodded that he was.

"I've been thinking about my dream," Old Running Bear said. "I stood at the end of a long trail. I was about to leap into the great darkness when you appeared and pulled me back. You said, 'I'll not let you go until you teach me.' I struggled to get away but you were too strong. So I agreed to teach you."

Joe's face broke into a broad smile.

Old Running Bear, eyes wet with joy, had finally found an apprentice who would take the time to be taught the ancient ways.

Old Running Bear said, "Most young people are too distracted by the white civilization to take the time. It takes much time to learn how to become one with the tree spirit before the first blade of the adz bites into wood."

Old Running Bear told Joe, "Listen to the spirit of the cedar tree. It'll tell you about the canoe or totem that sleeps within."

One year passed since Joe and Tom had brought the cedar log up from its watery hiding place. He had worked hard on his totem. Nothing could deter him from his evening trips to the tarp shed on the beach, not the onset of the fall rains nor the cold winds of winter. The whole tribe knew he was on a vision quest, and they left him to do what he had to do. His wife and family were proud of him and supported him in every way they could. But even they were not permitted to see what he was carving.

July's full moon arrived and Joe's totem was finished. During the early morning hours while the village slept with the help of a few friends, Joe set the huge totem into the hole they'd prepared beside the concrete pad in the center of town. It faced the rising sun. A blue tarp shrouded the pole in secrecy. When the blue tarp came alive with the sun's golden rays, Joe planned to pull the tarp away and reveal his totem not only to the sun's rays but also to the searching eyes of those who would come to the ceremony.

Throughout the previous day and evening, Joe's family and friends had been posting notices on community bulletin boards and tucking them into every door in the village.

When the unveiling time arrived, a huge crowd had gathered. Joe sang the sun from its bed to the accompaniment of his drum. It was a beautiful, cloudless morning. The morning stars of Venus and Mars in conjunction were bright and glowing as if they knew what great thing Joe was about to reveal. The village elders were escorted to the waiting chairs of honor. Old Running Bear came, as did Bigjim, walking proudly beside Sun Dog and Morning Star. Bill Eagle went before them carrying the leather pouch with the sacred pipe. Joe's wife and two teenage sons stood close by, beaming with pride.

When Joe had sung his song and drummed his drum and danced his dance, he stepped to the foot of his totem, grasped the rope that held the tarp, and gave it a sharp tug. Like a woman dropping her vale, the tarp dropped to the ground to gasps of Oh's and Ah's from the crowd. Then the crowd fell silent.

Old Running Bear stood up and slowly walked around the totem, carefully studying its every feature.

Everyone waited for Old Running Bear's opinion.

Finally Old Running Bear spoke:

"It's very interesting. But where are the traditional symbols? How can we understand its story if there are no traditional symbols?

"Where is Raven? Where is our spirit helper and main guide on our journey? Raven teaches our people how to build a canoe and how to fish.

"Where is Salmon? Why have you not honored the one who feeds our people?

"Where is Sis/luth, the Double Headed Serpent, who is guardian to the underworld, the world of the ancestors?

"You've used none of our traditional symbols so I can't read your totem.

"I don't even find Lightning Snake, the symbol of this place, this land and the power of the Suquamish Tribe."

Old Running Bear was obviously disappointed with his last apprentice for whom he had such high hopes to carry on the old traditions. His disappointment showed with the sagging of his head and shoulders as he shuffled back to his chair of honor.

The crowd silently melted away, uncertain what they had seen and heard. Joe's wife held her quivering chin high in respect for her husband, but the tears edging their way down her cheeks registered her disappointment and shame.

The people turned away leaving only the four elders, Joe's wife and two sons, the Old Man, and me. Joe, anger spitting from every pore, rushed to his pickup, and grabbing an ax, ran at the totem intent on cutting it to the ground and reducing it to chips.

Just as Joe raised the ax to strike the first blow, I stepped forward and grabbed his arm, blocking the swing. My action startled him into submission and he weakly let me take the ax from his hands.

"Why do you stop me?" Asked Joe, with tears flowing.

I rested my hand on his shoulder and said, "It's a beautiful totem, a work of art that brings a great message for today. Most will not understand it, but the few who will take the time to learn its language will receive a great insight into themselves and into the nature of God.

"Some of the ancient Christians understood that, in the end, we must all become as you've depicted. According to the Apostle Thomas, Jesus said:

'When you make the two into one,
　When you make the inner life like the outer
　　　And the outer like the inner,
　　　And the upper like the lower,
　When you make male and female
　　　into a single one,
　　　so that the male will not be male
　　　and the female will not be female,
　　　then you will enter the kingdom.'

"To me, the outstretched arms and smiling face of your Jesus say, 'Come unto me and I'll nurture you and make you fruitful.'"

Old Running Bear's eyes snapped open with excitement as he exclaimed, "Now I understand your totem! It's a great story. All my life I've struggled with the traditional symbols to tell such a story. But now I see the old symbols can't tell such a story."

Old Running Bear's eyes were bright and sparkling, his back was straight, and his head was high.

The people gathered around Joe's totem took on a new spirit.

The Old Man asked to speak: "My people, listen to my words. Raven comes to speak to us."

When he looked at me, I was startled. I didn't know what he wanted of me. Then my vision blurred. When I heard a voice inside my head, I opened my mouth and the words flowed out.

"He-Who-Walks-Upon-The-Earth said, 'When you can be like little children and undress without being ashamed and let your clothing fall at your feet, you will see the Son of the Living One, and you will not be afraid to enter his Kingdom.'"

"What does this mean?" Asked Joe's wife.

The Old Man answered, "It means that the time has come for us to become naked and dance the dance of freedom."

The small group was slow to respond as they looked at each other, searching for guidance. The thought of undressing in the center of town before strangers and non-natives was too much. It took the leadership of the Old Man and myself to show the way. One by one, shirts came off, pants were dropped, dresses slipped over heads and underclothes shed.

Joe took up his drum and began to sing the Suquamish song of freedom, a song previously sung in quiet hope but now was sung for the entire world to hear.

We didn't dance the old way with men and women apart and doing their traditional warrior and maiden dances. The Old Man reached out his hand and took Joe's wife's hand, and she took mine, and so we all joined hands to dance around the totem in the dress that God had made for us to be worn without shame.

Of course, not everyone shared our joy. Clara and Honey sat in their car parked in front of Cafe Angeline. They'd come to witness the great unveiling, but now they sat in shock.

"On my life, I never expected to see such a sight as this in our village," said Honey.

"Remember, it's prophesied in the book of Revelations that in the last days a great abomination, a blasphemous creature, will appear and men and women will worship it."

"Oh, dear," said Honey. "What are we to do?"

Clara spit out her invective through clenched teeth.

"This thing must not, it will not, remain in our village."

Throughout the day, passing cars slowed to a crawl as the occupants gawked and clicked their tongues at Joe's totem. Coming down the hill, they saw what appeared to be a statue of the risen Christ like the statue, which hovers over Rio de Janeiro. But as the curving road opened a frontal view, the face was indeed of the Christ, but the upper body was that of a full-breasted woman and the lower body was that of a man with a huge, erect phallus.

To many, Joe's totem was an obscenity.

"Only a perverted mind, a demonic mind, could conceive of Christ having breasts and an erection."

"Isn't an erection the result of sinful desires?"

"Jesus was without sin therefore he couldn't have had an erection."

"And breasts? Aren't they the devil's creation that mocks the Christ?"

The soft, amber streetlight flowed through the big stained-glass windows of The Church of the True Faith casting glowing multicolored bands across the dark sanctuary. Pastor Jerry knelt on the chancel steps, head bowed against clasped hands. His soft voice floated on the quiet night air.

"My Lord Jesus. I come to Thee this evening with a heavy heart. An evil, blasphemous thing has been raised in our village."

His clasped hands tightened in anguish as he beat his forehead.

"Thou knowest our struggles against the evil one. How I've wrestled with Satan himself. You know how we've been viciously attacked by the evil one's disciples. They're everywhere. Now they've raised this obscene monstrosity to mock our precious Lord before our eyes."

Pastor Jerry's voice rose as he shouted to God.

"Strengthen my arm, Dear Lord. Help me to lay the axe to the root of that barren tree and deliver it to the flames with its unfruitful branches so that they who speak filth might hold their tongues. Strengthen me like you did Sampson so that I may tear your adversaries to pieces. Amen."

Pastor Jerry rose and joined the men waiting in the cars outside. Soon the muffled chainsaws were biting into the tender, cedar skin.

"Look out!" One of the men shouted.

The extended phallus of the crashing totem struck Pastor Jerry a glancing blow to his head, knocking him down. Stunned but alert, Pastor Jerry called out: "I'm all right. Finish the Lord's work we've come to do."

The dissectors finished in a few minutes what had taken twelve months for Joe Old Coyote to lovingly carve. Chainsaws and axes quickly reduced the totem to kindling wood that was doused with diesel fuel. As the men climbed into their cars and drove away, Pastor Jerry tossed a burning Molotov cocktail, setting the pyre ablaze.

The light from the fire lit up Chief Sealth's totem; its eagle screamed its protest against the fire that burned in the hearts and minds of Christ's soldiers. On a large rock across the street, the dark one laughed himself to tears.

The Volunteer Fire Department raced to put out the totem fire as Christ's soldiers marched against other bastions of evil.

I had been invited to a sweat lodge ceremony that was taking place on the beach in front of the Tribal Center. Old Running Bear introduced young Chris George, a twelve-year old lad to the council of old men.

"Chris has been my student for the past five years. I've taught him the ways of the ancient ones. I gave him a task. I asked him to find a fox's kitten and bring it to me. This he did, after a long journey. Then I told him to return the kitten unharmed to its mother and thank the mother for the loan of her child. This he did. Then I took him up to Spirit Point where he remained for four days and four nights without food or water. While there he had a vision."

Young Chris began to speak, "I saw…."

But Old Running Bear held up his hand for silence.

"Do not tell any one your vision. You must keep it to yourself and think upon it often."

The other old men nodded in agreement.

Old Running Bear dipped water out of the bucket and poured it over the white-hot rocks; plumes of steam filled the sweat lodge.

Bill Eagle was the next to speak, "What does the young Chris want?"

"I want to be accepted as a man," Chris answered in a strong, firm voice.

When the four old men nodded their agreement, the initiation rite began with the shaking of a sage smudge over and around the young boy now becoming a man as the old men sang the ancient song of manhood.

Old Running Bear nodded his head toward the door indicating it was time for me to leave. He'd told me earlier that the balance of the ceremony was only for the elders and the young boy, now becoming a man. Joy filled the lodge as I disappeared down the beach.

The firekeeper saw them coming, the torches in the night, but before he could call out, a Molotov cocktail crashed at his feet turning him into a living torch. In rapid succession, six more flaming cocktails rained down onto the sweat lodge like blazing meteors. The Night of Fires had begun.

The flaming gasoline spread over the sweat lodge, dripped down onto the four old men and the boy as they struggled desperately to escape the inferno, but it was too late for them. Soon their bodies became fuel for the Fire God. On their way out of the Tribal Center, Christ's soldiers torched the Women's Clinic and the Museum. The last offering to the Fire God was the new Tribal Casino and Bingo Hall. They were set ablaze as the fire trucks raced past en route to the Tribal Center. The crews from

Kingston and Poulsbo arrived too late. All they could do was keep the fires from spreading into the surrounding homes.

The large rock, hidden beneath brush and trees across the street from Chief Sealth's Totem, was known to the Suquamish medicine people as an ancient power rock. Few people knew of its existence. But the dark one knew. He sat upon it watching the futile efforts of the firemen rushing through the night chasing fires that were beyond control. With upraised arms, he sang his victory song.

The next morning a shocked village stumbled around the streets. Inside Cafe Angeline, the words were hot and furious.

"Who would have done these things?" Asked Sunny.

"I bet it was some of Pastor Jerry's followers," came the reply.

"Did anyone see them do it?" Asked Sergeant Lewis.

When no one spoke up, he continued, "Unless you saw who it was, you better keep your suspicions to yourself. We don't need anymore vigilantes. The police will get those who did these things."

"Yeah, like they didn't catch the murderers of those three kids over on Bainbridge Island."

"There's no connection," insisted Sergeant Lewis.

"What about the Duggan murders? They didn't solve those either. I think the Sheriff and his department are a bunch of incompetent idiots."

"But this time the FBI is in charge," said Lewis.

"How come they're involved?"

"The fire bombings appear to be a conspiracy to violate the Tribe's civil rights."

"Thank God, someone with intelligence is in charge this time."

"If they can't solve the problem, I know there are others who will."

"Hey, did anyone else find a flyer in their doors this morning?"

"Did you get one, too?"

"Yeah, as far as I can tell everyone got one. What do you make of it?"

"Pastor Jerry has a lot of explaining to do. Has anyone seen him today?"

"Haven't you heard? He was rushed over to Harborview Hospital early this morning. He suffered some kind of head injury. They say he fell in the sanctuary last night and struck his head."

No one planned it. It just happened by consensus. Molotov cocktails flew in the night. The fire volunteers, scattered between the casino area and the Tribal Center knocking down hot spots from the previous night's fires, were slow to respond. The flames leaped so high into the sky that the blaze was clearly visible from Seattle. The freshly varnished beams and timbers flared like presto logs as the flames danced their death dance behind the stained glass windows before crashing to the ground.

The huge crowd gathered in the streets all agreed. The Church of the True Faith was the grandest fire anyone had ever seen.

The Old Man and I stood in the crowd watching and listening with heavy hearts.

The Old Man asked, "Did you know that the soldiers burned my house down? Oh, yes. They, too, came with torches. They thought by destroying an old man's house, they were destroying me."

"Why did they want to destroy you?"

"They thought by destroying me, my people wouldn't stop them from cutting down the grandfather cedars for their sawmills at Port Madison."

"They got their cedars."

"Yes, but I'm still here."

"So is the dark one who was sitting on the large rock down by your totem. When I passed a while ago, he pointed his finger at me and laughed."

The Old Man looked straight into my eyes and said, "Ah, yes, this is the time of the trickster. People have died, and our village has been reduced to ashes. What will be next?"

CHAPTER TWENTY

Diane's frantic phone call brought me rushing to Pastor Jerry's house. The door opened before I could knock.

"Thanks for coming," Diane said, her eyes red and her voice breaking. "I'm so scared. He sits, day after day, in his study and broods. He won't talk to anyone. He hardly answers my questions. He just sits with his head down like one of those poor souls at Martha and Mary Nursing Home. Can I get you a cup of coffee?"

"Yes, I'd like that."

We sat at the kitchen table cradling coffee cups in our hands, their warmth bringing a bit of comfort to a cold and desperate situation.

"How are you doing?" I asked.

"I'm not handling it very well. I rarely go out in public. I put a mailbox on the street so I don't have to go down to the post office."

"What do you do about groceries?"

"I drive to Tacoma so I don't have to meet anyone that would recognize me."

"Oh, that's a shame."

"I'm even afraid to answer the phone. I've had men with heavy breathing tell me in graphic detail what they liked about my body. Just last night a woman who I thought was my friend asked me if I would party with her and her husband."

"People are amazing, aren't they?"

"Why are they like that?"

"It's stupid, isn't it? If we're ashamed to do something openly, we shouldn't do it in private. As Jesus said, whatever is done in secret will be shouted from the housetops."

"And how right he was. Everyone in this village has seen my picture. Who could have done such a terrible thing?"

"So what? You did nothing wrong. People get excited about nudity because something within them, something they don't want to acknowledge, lifts its ugly head. They seek to suppress and control in others what they fear within themselves."

"What did you think when you saw my picture?"

Pastor Jerry called from the study, "Diane, who are you talking to?"

We walked into the study.

"Do you remember me?" I asked. Pastor Jerry ignored my extended hand.

"So, you've come to gloat, have you?"

"It may surprise you, but no, I haven't come to gloat. I've come as a friend."

"I don't need your friendship," he snapped. "What I need is a new pair of eyes, or didn't you know I'm blind?"

"Yes, I know. Diane told me when she called this morning. I know what you're going through."

"How could you?"

"I was blind ten years ago."

Pastor Jerry was so withdrawn he ignored what I'd said.

"It's all over...I'm ruined...I'm blind, my church is in ashes and my congregation has turned against me."

"Can't the building be rebuilt with the insurance money?"

"There is no insurance money. I was too busy to buy insurance. Now, ashes are all I have. Satan is testing me like he did Job."

Pastor Jerry stretched out his left hand, feeling the air. "Where are you?" When he found my arm he grabbed it with the steel grip of anger.

"You burned my church down, didn't you?"

I patted his hand.

"No, I didn't have anything to do with it. Nor do I know who did it. I'm surprised that you seem more concerned about a building than the deaths of seven men and a boy."

"I didn't have anything to do with that," he snapped. "Naturally, I don't approve. But, it didn't surprise me. Something like that was bound to happen after Joe Old Coyote put up that totem pole. God will not be mocked."

"Why is it that religious fanatics always justify their violence under the mantle of God's wrath?"

"Don't you believe that in the last days the Anti-Christ will appear?"

"The Anti-Christ has been around since creation or did you forget Satan in the Garden of Eden?"

Pastor Jerry waved his hand in dismissal.

"Don't waste my time. Just leave me alone."

Pastor Jerry's words were sharp and true like a hara-kiri knife, they plunged through my solar plexus into my heart.

Years before, I was President of my native corporation, a builder of buildings, of companies, and of a large family of seven children.

After the disillusionment, I entered a cynical period in which I wandered in a dark void. I was still in that dark void when I was led to Suquamish. I would've remained under that dark influence if not for two helping hands that appeared out of the fog, the ancient, wise hand of the Old Man and the soft, healing hand of Betty. As I received, so I extended my hand of friendship.

"I'd like to show you something I've been working on that I think has great value for you."

"What's that?" Pastor Jerry asked.

"My garden."

"Why bother? I couldn't see it."

"But you could smell and remember. It would do you good to get out into the fresh air."

The heavy, oak gate swung open and the three of us, Pastor Jerry, Diane and I, started down the red brick path.

Getting Pastor Jerry to relax and begin to meditate proved to be more difficult than if I asked him to physically fly. His mind shut out the very process of meditation as being New Age and Eastern. But when we searched the scriptures for instances of prayer and meditation, the overwhelming evidence softened his opposition. Even visualization, which he was conditioned to believe was Satanic, was tentatively accepted.

"The Psalmist commands us, 'Be still and know the Lord.'

"Ezekiel was by the River Chebar when the heavens were opened, and he saw visions of God...He saw the four living creatures...He saw the valley filled with dry bones.

"The book of Isaiah begins with the statement, 'The vision of Isaiah, which he saw....'

"The Bible is filled with men and women meditating, but the most graphic account is Revelation.

"John says, 'I was in the Spirit on the Lord's day, and I heard behind me a loud voice like a trumpet saying, "Write what you see in a book and send it to the seven churches. So Pastor Jerry consented, with resignation, "What have I got to lose?"

Once inside the inner garden, Pastor Jerry experienced its beauty.

After a few steps I said, "Let's stop here for a moment and take a deep breath."

Three sets of lungs drew deeply.

"The garden contains a potpourri of fragrances, floral and herbal. Like God, fragrances must be experienced to be known."

When we came to the first bench, I asked, "Why don't we sit on this bench and you tell me what you experience?"

Diane and I guided Pastor Jerry to the wood bench. A black marble statue of a raging bull standing over a vanquished lion began to materialize in the midst of the dark red 'Mister Lincoln' roses. He took another deep breath and the statue faded away.

"I smell roses."

"Yes, they're close by. Now wait for the shifting breezes to bring some other fragrances."

A moment or two passed.

"I smell something strangely sweet but not unpleasant."

"That would be valerian. It has small, pink-tinged, white flower clusters."

Diane added, "That piney scent has to be rosemary."

We moved on to the next bench beside the bed of coral-orange 'Tropicana' roses. In the midst of these a white marble, half-sized replica of Michelangelo's victorious David standing over a fallen Goliath, materialized then faded away.

Behind us, lovely, rounded shrubs of English lavender interspersed the apple and pear trees. Their spiky leaves and deep purple blossoms added their fragrance to the garden.

"This area is flooded with the scent of English lavender," said Pastor Jerry.

We moved on to the bench beside the bed of lemon yellow 'Sun Flare' roses. A roaring African lion, its foot on a fallen gazelle, materialized then faded.

It wasn't long before Pastor Jerry recognized the pungent scent of thyme.

"I just caught a whiff of the warm, spicy fragrance of sweet basil," said Diane.

Within the bed of dark green roses, the statue of a large bald eagle, lifting from the water with a salmon in its talons, floated into our vision, then disappeared.

Diane was amazed.

"I didn't know there were green roses. Where did they come from?"

"I really don't know. Pure white 'Honor' roses were planted but green roses appeared."

"What do you call them?"

"I've named them 'The Rose of Healing.'

Pastor Jerry said, "I smell spearmint gum."

"Behind you is a bed of mint, spearmint and peppermint."

Silvery artemisias, blue-green rue, deep-green parsley, and the shaggy red flowers of bergamot and cherry orange calendulas bordered the oval fishpond.

I guided Pastor Jerry's hands among other plants.

"What's this one that feels soft, like velvet?"

"That's lamb's ears."

"Ouch!" Cried Pastor Jerry pulling his hand back. "And that prickly, stinging plant must be a nettle."

"Yes."

"How about this one with pebbly leaves?"

"That's sage, which is used by our native friends in their services as smudges."

Diane whirled slowly around.

"This garden is breathtaking."

"It's a celebration of senses that enhances all aspects of our lives."

"What's that pungent smell?" Asked Pastor Jerry.

"That's coriander."

"What's that licorice smell?" Asked Pastor Jerry.

"That's fennel."

Pastor reflected out loud, "When our Lord was dying on the cross and was thirsty, the soldiers held up hyssop that had been soaked in vinegar. Is there any hyssop?"

"Yes. It's that bushy plant in the far corner."

"Why do you think the soldiers used hyssop?"

"Perhaps because it was growing nearby and was a handy sop."

"Could you bring me a sprig?"

"Of course."

When I returned, Pastor Jerry carefully smelled it and felt it with his fingers. Then he pulled off a leaf and put it into his mouth.

"That's bitter," he said, spitting out the leaf.

We paused to savor again the potpourri of smells and sights that were wafted about by the summer breezes.

Pastor Jerry asked, "Would you mind if I sat here by myself for awhile? This place is very comforting."

Diane and I nodded our mutual agreement and left Pastor Jerry sitting beside the fishpond with its bubbling brook and splashing carp. Crows, perching in the overhead trees, cried their protection, and the sun warmed his back.

He was unaware of the large goldfish that rose from its dark hiding place to pause just below the mirrored surface, its fins gracefully fanning the water as its large eyes studied the human who sat on the other side.

"It's getting dark," said Diane. "He's been sitting there all afternoon, hardly moving a muscle. Shouldn't we bring him in?"

"Yes," I said. "It's time. I'll go and get him while you set out our supper on the deck table."

As I guided Pastor Jerry back from his meditative visit to the inner garden, I felt a new energy in his steps, the bounce of enthusiasm. During the meal, he bubbled as he told us of his afternoon in the garden.

As we sat back from our plates, I said, "I'm glad you came. But no visit to the garden would be complete without a session in the hottub."

"We didn't bring our suits," Diane protested.

"According to house rules, suits are optional."

"What do you think, dear?"

"It makes no different to me. I couldn't peek if I wanted to."

Diane hesitated, then said, "Oh, well. The entire world has seen me naked so why not? Yes, I'd love to try your hottub. I've never been in one before."

Soon we were soaking in the hot water as the jets massaged our backs and legs with swirling bubbles. When we were thoroughly relaxed, I switched off the jets, allowing the hot water to become calm. A stillness eased over the surface. We soaked silently for nearly thirty minutes with just our heads bobbing on the surface as we listened to the distant calling of loons in the fading twilight.

Then Pastor Jerry said, "Today, I was reminded of the time I was deer hunting back in Wisconsin."

"How so, dear?" Asked Diane.

"I'd gone into the woods during the dark morning hours, using a flashlight to guide the way to my stand. I thought I had entered quietly; but after settling in the darkness, I could hear other hunters going to their stands. The woods shook with their stealth. I leaned back against the tree and became so quiet I could hear my heart beat.

"Then a marvelous thing happened. The woods gradually came alive; little gray squirrels, frozen by my onslaught, crept from their cover to resume their early morning pursuit of nuts, chattering at the jays and crows, which filtered through the trees as dawn's light seeped into the swamps. The damp, crisp, fall air was heavy with the pungent scent of freshly fallen oak leaves.

"Then it came, the soft rustling of a leaf as a deer approached cautiously through the brush. I held my breath in fear my breathing would reach its ears. Adrenaline pumped; eyes dilated as I focused on the spot where my ears said the deer would appear. My sweaty hands gripped the rifle as I waited.

"I didn't have to kill that beautiful creature. I had a freezer full of beefsteaks and roasts, chicken thighs and pork chops. Yet I lifted the gun to my shoulder and swung on a majestic stag, which appeared in the brush, its grand rack held proudly, challenging all comers.

"Suddenly, a hawk flashed to the ground, a cottontail screamed once, the forest animals froze in silence, then the hawk silently rose into the air with a rabbit in its talons, and disappeared over the treetops. With the hawk's departure, the forest came back to life as if nothing had happened.

"Then it struck me. The hawk had acted in harmony with nature; it had taken only what it needed to survive, a weak or stupid cottontail, and left the stronger and smarter cottontails to carry on the species. But

I was about to act out of harmony with nature by killing the strongest and the best of a species for no good reason other than to satisfy my blood lust.

"I had the most wonderful experience just watching that glorious animal slowly browse for acorns beneath the oak trees under a warm fall sun. Frozen against the tree, I watched him for hours. Occasionally he would lift his head, perk his ears, keenly alert to any approaching danger.

"During the day the stag would lift its head and look directly at me, deep into my eyes, as if to affirm my existence and let me know he understood why I was there and gave me permission to take his life if I needed his flesh to live. That was the last time I went hunting with a gun.

"That day I learned the importance of being still and listening. When I left the woods that afternoon as the sun was setting, it hit me. I felt at peace with the whole world.

"This afternoon I had that experience again. Thank you for inviting us into your garden."

I reached over and patted his arm.

"I would like you to come back in a few days. There are some friends I'd like you to meet."

CHAPTER TWENTY-ONE

The second full moon of August appeared on the 30th, dressed in her blue gown. She modeled and beamed as I lounged alone in my hot tub. My head floated on the quiet water as mists of steam lifted arms of adoration to the goddess.

With my body relaxed, my mind still, my soul rose out of the water and was about to join the heavenly hosts in a joyful dance of celebration when the snake hissed his presence.

"I've been watching you," he hissed. "You think I've gone away but I'm always here, so close you can't see me unless I want you to."

I knew who it was. The dark one slithered up to the tub and rose to hover over me like a giant Cobra. He held something behind his back.

"What do you want?" I demanded.

"I've won, the contest is over. I've come to collect my winnings," hissed the dark one.

"You're wrong, as usual. The contest has just begun."

Emitting a whistling, breathy sound like a leaking inner tube, the dark one weaved from side to side. With tongue darting, he wheezed, "I know what you're trying to do. But it won't work. You're only delaying the inevitable. In the end, Pastor Jerry will come crawling back to me. This little garden of your is ridiculous. I can destroy it with the snap of my fingers."

"Then why don't you?"

"No, No, No," hissed the dark one, shaking a finger at me.

"You can't trick me into that old trap."

"What's it about my garden that makes you afraid?"

"Afraid? Me? Afraid? I'm not afraid of anything, much less flowers and herbs."

"You're a liar. My garden is much more than flowers and herbs, and you know it."

The dark one threw back his head and laughed.

He replied, "The world is filled with liars and cowards. That's what makes it so exciting, don't you think? The world would be a boring place if there were only truth tellers and selfless heroes. It's much more exciting when people lie to themselves and to others. You're afraid of me, aren't you?"

"Yes, I'm afraid of you. But fear is a gift from God. All living creatures possess it. Nothing could survive without it. Without fear, there would be no civilization, only a chaotic jungle where the final Scene of the human drama would be of the last two human beasts chopping each other to bits with AK-47s.

"Oh, won't that be a wonderful sight?" Hissed the
Dark one.

"There's something you haven't thought about."

"What's that?"

"What will happen to you when the last man dies?"

The dark one, pondered and pondered, shifting his
weight from one foot to the other. Like the trickster,
he couldn't, or wouldn't answer.

Then I asked, "What are you holding behind your back?"

"Light," hissed the dark one. In his right hand
he held out a trouble light whose cord stretched across the deck and plugged into an electrical outlet at the far corner of the cabin.

"I thought I'd bring a little light into your life."

He snapped the light on and off slowly.

"On…Off…On…Off. I'm a light bearer or didn't you know?"

I fell silent with the cold realization of why he'd come, as he kept switching the light on and off.

"On…Off…On…Off. I bring light and darkness, life and death. Did you know that if I were to drop this light into your tub you could solve the great puzzle? Wouldn't that be wonderful?"

"I don't think you have the courage to drop it."

"Oh! Don't I?"

"I know what will happen to you if I were to die."

"What do you mean?"

"Without me you wouldn't exist."

The dark one froze, his face began to twist as a demented smile crept over his mouth.

"You think I'm bluffing, don't you? Do you think you're another Job? Do you think that God has given me power to torment you but I'm forbidden to destroy you?

Well, I'll show you my power."

The dark one smashed the trouble light against the edge of the hot tub. Glass shards pebbled the water as the globe was shattered. Holding the broken bulb over the tub he let the cord slowly slip through his hand.

The gapping socket descended. Like the fangs of an open mouth adder the broken filaments were ready to strike their lethal blow. Down, down, it slithered, slowly, inexorably.

Then the dark one closed his fingers, stopping the socket an inch above the water. His twinkling red eyes searched my face for fear. When I smiled up at him he screamed his fury to the universe and dropped the gaping socket into the water.

The dark one was shocked into silence. He looked around in confusion.

"Are you looking for this?" Said the Old Man, casually leaning against the cabin corner, as he nonchalantly swung the plug end from his hand.

The dark one's body began to shake. First his hands and legs, then sweeping up his torso, until he bounced and twitched around the deck like a Mexican jumping bean. Screaming his curses at the universe, at me, then disappeared into the night.

Stepping out of the tub and wrapping myself into a white terry cloth robe, I asked, "Where did you come from?"

"I was walking in the village when I saw him creeping up the street in this direction. So I followed him."

"Thank God you did or I'd be one blown circuit by now. What'll happen to him?"

The Old Man answered, "Oh, he'll disappear for a while to lick his wounds. Defeating the dark one is only a temporary victory."

"Yes, even Jesus couldn't destroy the dark one."

"What began in heaven must end in heaven."

"But, if I can't destroy him, what can I do?"

"Like the way we deal with the trickster, it's better to keep him before your eyes, where you can see what he is doing, than to have him behind your back where you don't know what he's doing."

Diane and Pastor Jerry appeared at my cabin door the next afternoon.

"When I called you this morning," said Diane, "I had hoped to spend the afternoon with you in the garden, but a strange thing happened. When I hung up the phone rang again. I answered it thinking that you were calling back. But, it was Dominique from the post office. She invited me to her house for coffee.

So, if you don't mind, I'll just leave Jerry with you and pick him up around five. Okay?"

"It's okay with me but...."

She turned and was gone before I could caution her about Dominique. Taking Pastor Jerry's arm, I guided him into the cabin.

"Would you care for something to drink?" I asked.

"Thank you, I'd like some white wine."

As we sat at the deck table sipping our wine, I was uncertain where to begin. Pastor Jerry shifted nervously in his chair. I understood. Newly sightless, he was struggling to adjust to his remaining four senses.

Pastor Jerry asked, "Yesterday, you said that you had been blind, what happened to you?"

"Ten years ago, I lost my sight through a hemorrhage in one eye and a cataract in the other.

There was nothing that could be done about my right eye, except to wait. An operation on my left eye to replace the cataract with a plastic lens had to wait until I could get eight thousand dollars, because I didn't have any insurance. That took four months.

"Those four months of blindness turned out to be a great blessing. It took the loss of physical sight to open my spiritual eyes."

Pastor Jerry didn't respond. He sat quietly sipping his wine. The warm afternoon sun felt good. Overhead, the black crows who had chosen the three tall hemlocks beside my cabin as their base of operations, cawed out their departures and arrivals like airport dispatchers. Several monarch butterflies quietly fluttered among the marigolds that bordered the deck.

"Would you like to go into the garden?" I asked.

"Yes, please. Perhaps, you could tell me about the statues. Diane said that they are very impressive."

As I guided Pastor Jerry into the garden I told him that, "We're approaching the bed of red 'Mister Lincoln' Roses. Why don't we stop here for awhile?"

When we had settled onto the bench Pastor Jerry said, "Diane told me that the statue in the red roses was of a raging bull standing over a slain lion. Could you tell me what it means?"

"I could, but it'll mean more if you could sit quietly and let them tell their story. I'll be nearby if you need anything."

I waited quietly beneath the grandfather Oak tree with my guides and guardians.

Each visitor to the garden had a different experience. Strolling its paths, they'd be attracted to different things. Sometimes to the roses, other times to the statues still other times the herbs or the fruit trees would be their point of interest.

Whether it was the pond with its fish or the hill with the oak tree, they were always aware of being in the presence of spirits, sometimes angels would walk and talk with them.

For many years, I'd prayed for the healing of my inner eyes that I might see Christ's face, and for the healing of my inner ears that I might hear his voice.

Why? I had to struggle a lifetime to know enough about myself to give an honest answer.

"But that is your path, what is Pastor Jerry's path?" Asked the Old Man, who strolled up the hill to join me under the Oak tree.

"Welcome, my friend," I said. "What have you been up to today?"

"I've been walking about the village, looking at all the beautiful houses. I told you that the village is about to change, didn't I?"

"Yes, in a general way. Is something more imminent?"

"What does imminent mean to you?"

"It means, about to happen any time now."

"Yes, it's imminent. Grandfather is about to speak. If you listen with your heart you'll hear his voice stirring deep within his throat.

"We all live in a different houses, not one is identical, some by choice, some by circumstance. There are those who say that everyone should live in the same house. They get angry when people don't agree with them.

"When they pass laws that would force everyone to live like them they offend the Father. The Father created many different people. The master taught that we're to love and respect our neighbors as ourselves."

I asked, "Did you see that program on TV about Egyptian mummies?"

"No."

"Well, a group of French scientists were unwrapping a four thousand year old mummy to learn what they could from the corpse."

"Archeologists disturbed our ancestors' bones in the same way. They would never let strangers dig up the bones of their mothers and fathers, why do they disturb ours?"

"To learn about their lives."

"Can petrified bones and skin tell them about the soul that once inhabited that body?"

"While I watched the archeologists unwrap that mummy another thought came to mind. It reminded me of the Christ experience that has been mummified by doctrines, ancient traditions and structures that have no life in them.

"The human mind always weaves complex patterns from the simplest yarn. We wrap our minds like mummies within layers upon layers of doctrinal winding cloths while the Christ experience remains hidden to us. This is so, though the doctrines of men are logical and systematic, buttressed by holy writ, and confirmed by powerful charismatic leaders."

"What are you saying?" The Old Man asked.

"I'm saying, doctrinal winding cloths, old or new, can never hold the Risen Christ. Like herbal tastes and floral fragrances the Risen Christ must be experienced to be known. He makes his presence known in the garden."

The old Man motioned toward Pastor Jerry, "What has he been experiencing today? Let's go find out."

I set coffee and cookies on the deck table as we anxiously waited for Pastor Jerry to tell us about his day beside the red 'Mister Lincoln' roses.

"I sat quietly," he said. "Like I did on the deer stand. I heard the crows coming and going, the bees buzzing about the flowers, even a hummingbird whirled by. I sat in a sea of herbal and floral fragrances that stirred up a host of memories."

"Tell us about some of them," I said.

"After awhile I started to think about the statue, about the scene of a raging bull standing over a fallen lion. The next moment, I saw an ancient Roman arena.

I was part of the crowd packed into the seats. Below, the arena was empty, its sand floor raked smooth.

"Then I heard the blaring of trumpets and gates were opened at opposite ends of the arena. The crowd roared to life as a terrified lion was driven into the arena. It charged the attendants as they scrambled over the walls. Then a huge black bull, with long sharp horns, eyes red with terror, came snorting out of the opposite gate.

"I shouted as the blood fever surged through the crowd at the gory spectacle unfolding before our eyes. The terrified beasts fought for nearly an hour before a horn hooked the lion into defeat. It ended just as Diane had described your statue.

"Then a gladiator entered carrying a long spear and   riding a white horse. He cautiously approached the exhausted, panting bull. When he was almost upon the beast the gladiator drove the spear through the bull's heart.

"The last thing I remember was the attendants dragging out the slain beasts with draft horses. The defeated lion was taken to a burial pit, the victorious bull was taken to a barbecue pit.

"What do you think my vision means, Old Man?" asked Pastor Jerry.

The Old Man pondered for a few moments than said,

"Your vision tells you that when desire and fear fight, desire wins, but love conquers both."

"Hi, fellas," called Diane, as she bounded onto the deck. Her cheeks had a blush on them and she was carrying two grocery bags brimming with food.

"I decided to fix supper here this evening. Is that okay with you?"

"Of course it is," I replied. "Did you bring enough for five? I'm expecting Betty this evening."

"Oh, that'd be wonderful," Diane called back as she disappeared into the cabin. "Yes, I bought a big rack of ribs. We'll have a real southern cookout, with baked beans and cornbread."

Pastor Jerry called out, "How was your visit with Dominique?"

Diane's head popped out of the kitchen window.

"Marvelous, simply marvelous. But I want to wait until after dinner to tell you all about it."

Diane's head popped back inside the kitchen.

I phoned Betty to alert her to the cookout.

"Diane, Betty wants to know if she can bring anything."

"Ask her if she can bring some red wine, I can't find any around here."

"Would you mind stopping by JC's and picking up a large bottle of red table wine?…Fine, I'll see you soon then."

When the final bones had been tossed to Lady, my dog,

we settled back, with our wine, to await Diane's account of her visit with Dominique.

"How come you didn't tell me that she was a witch?"

I replied, "I was about to when you rushed off."

"I'd never met a witch before. So when she said that she was one I didn't know what to do or say. But her warmth and friendship quickly put me at ease."

Diane's afternoon visit had begun in a sunroom filled with plants. Flowers and herbs grew lustily to the ceiling like in an arboretum.

Diane related Dominique's story as she had been told that afternoon.

"Dominique had been caught up by the Rev. Jimmy Jones and just barely missed the Kool-Aid party down in Guyana. I was surprised when she told me that. She is a very intelligent woman."

I said, "She has an I.Q. in excess of 145."

"Why the Jones' cult?" Betty asked.

Diane answered, "She said it was a vulnerable time in her life. Jimmy was such a warm, loving man, who worked in the most run down part of Oakland. Dominique had never attended a church before so everything was exciting, the choir, the office work, the special attention Jimmy paid to her.

"The next thing she realized, she was pregnant and

Jimmy was moving his followers to Guyana. Fortunately, her advanced pregnancy prevented her from going with them right away.

"The shock of those hundreds of men, women and children laid out on the ground was too much. She was disillusioned with churches. When her baby died she moved to Suquamish to start a new life."

Pastor Jerry asked, "When did she get caught up in witchcraft?"

"About five years ago, she said. "There's a coven that meets in her house every month at the full moon. She's invited me to attend next month's meeting."

Pastor Jerry sat up, grasping the edge of the table, he asked, "You're not going to, are you?"

"Yes, I am," Diane replied with a lift of her chin. "Except for the people around this table, the women of this village don't even say hello to me anymore and all the men leer at me. Only Dominique has extended her kiss of friendship."

CHAPTER TWENTY-TWO

As his royal majesty wearily tucked himself beneath his western blanket, his queen lazily lifted a pale face from her eastern pillow for one last time before a fortnight of sleep.

Betty and I sat, side by side, on the edge of the deck. The September evening was comfortably warm. The sky was clear. The evening stars of Venus and Mars reigned in the eastern sky. Betty snuggled close as our thoughts turned toward the matters of the heart. Eventually I asked the question.

"Now that you've read the diaries and correspondence, what have you learned about her and about yourself?"

Betty looked intently at her hands, slender hands with long, strong fingers, the hands of a pianist, a typist, and a gardener, the hands of a lover and a poet.

"I had a dream the other night," Betty said thoughtfully. "What I can recall is but a fragment.

"Hands. I was looking down at a pair of hands, like I'm doing now. They were familiar hands that floated in front of me, turning again and again, as if they were telling me something."

I smiled and said, "Her husband was forever marveling about her hands. Her hands told her story. Hands that took down flying dictation using Uncle Roscoe's unorthodox shorthand method. Strong hands that pecked away at the Remington No. 7 typewriter. Firm hands that could hold a magnificent horse like Belle, nimble hands that could caress the keys of her Steinway, confident hands that were unhesitant when taking her turn at the *Snark's* wheel, and healing hands that caressed his temples and ran tippling fingers through his hair.

"He put his thoughts about her in a book. Subsitute the names and you have his thoughts about her.

"In that connection, using his man's judgment and putting his man's foot down, he refused to allow her hands to be burdened with the entertaining of guests. For guests they had, especially in the warm, long California summers, and usually they were friends from San Francisco and Oakland, who were put to camp in tents and care for themselves, and where, like true campers, they had also to cook for themselves.

His steadfast contention was that her hands shouldn't become the hands of a cook, a waitress, or a chambermaid.

"Chafing dish suppers prepared by his stepsister, and served by his manservant, in the big living room for their camping guests were a common meal.

"After a patient struggle, she taught him poetry. In the end he might've often been seen, sitting slack in the saddle and dropping down the mountain trails through the sun-flecked woods, chanting aloud Kipling's 'Tomlinson,' or, when sharpening his ax, singing to the whirling grindstone Henley's 'Song of the Sword.'

"He never became a skilled poet in the way his teacher was. Beyond 'Fra Lippo Lippi' and 'Caliban

and Setebos' he found nothing in Browning, while George Meredith was ever his despair.

"So all went well with that well-mated pair. Time never dragged. There were always new wonderful mornings, and still cool twilights at the end of the day, and ever a thousand interests about the ranch claimed him, and his interests were shared by her. More thoroughly than he knew, He came to a comprehension of the relativity of things.

"In the game of agriculture, he found in little things all the intensities of gratification and desire

that held found in frenzied big things. With head and hand, at risk of life and limb, to bit and break a wild colt and win it to the service of man, was to him no less of an achievement than a new Klondike novel or a short story set in the South Seas.

"And so she and her husband were content to watch the procession of the days and seasons from the steps of their cabin perched on the hill, to ride through crisp frosty mornings or under burning summer suns and to shelter in the big room where blazed the logs in the fireplace, while outside the world shuddered and struggled in the storm-clasp of a southeaster.

"Once she asked her husband if he ever regretted and his answer was to crush her in his arms and smother her lips with his. His answer, a minute later, took speech.

"'Little woman, even if you were to cost thirty million, you'd be the cheapest necessity of life I ever indulged in.' And then he added, 'Yes, I do have one regret, and a monstrous big one, too. I'd sure like to have the winning of you all over again. I'd like to go sneaking around the Piedmont hills looking for you. I'd like to meander into those rooms of yours at Berkeley again for the first time, with its poetry books and Steinway piano and the little crouching Venus. And there's no use talking, I'm plumb soaking with regret that I can't put my arms around you again like that time you leaned your head on my chest and cried in the wind and rain.'"

We nestled quietly, my arm around Betty's waist, her head on my shoulder. It was a loving time, a time when kindred spirits intertwined and the knowing was without words. The calling of the loon to its mate echoed from below the bluff and all was well with the world. Still, it had to be spoken, words had to give voice to the heart of the matter, Betty had to be told.

I held her away so I could look into her brown eyes and gauge her reaction.

"I've a confession to make," I began slowly. "Women scare me. All my life, women have torn me apart. The women I loved rejected me. And women who wanted to smother me repulsed me. That's especially true with older women.

"When I was younger, when I was but a lad of seven, older women wanted to hug and kiss me and fondle me. But I wasn't able to accept what I never received from my mother. So I've run away from smothering women, fearing the apron strings.

"Then you revealed another side of woman, the side I didn't know was there and couldn't have dreamed how important it could be to me. Yet, I doubted. Maybe it

was another trick of the dark one to bring calamity and disaster upon me.

"Then the terror swept over me. Suppose you wouldn't have me because I was an Inupiat, and suppose I loved you more and more, harder and harder? All my old generalized terrors of love revived. I remembered the disastrous love affairs of the past."

Betty started to say, "Oh, you silly fool…." but my fingers on her lips won her silence.

"Had my desire for you been less, I might well have been frightened out of thinking about you. As it was, I found consolation in the thought that some love affairs do come out right. And for all I knew, maybe it was God's plan for my life that it was to take a positive turn. Some men are born unlucky, live unlucky all their days, but die lucky. Perhaps, I was such a man."

Betty could restrain herself no longer.

"Oh, you are, my dear. For me you are such a man. When I read the diaries I was overwhelmed by her loneliness, loneliness I've known. After he died she lived a widow's existence. Except for two brief affairs, possibly three, if you want to count that deceiving snake Irving Stone, She was alone for the next thirty-eight years. She was sustained by the memories of him. And I know why. For her, no other man could live up to his shadow.

"Page, after page, in her diary, she noted her loneliness and sadness. She was the consummate actor. She never let the outside world see her true feelings. Even with her husband she was always a happy, cheerful face. He never suspected the long hours of tears and sadness, the migraine pain that racked her head, the ache of a barren womb. When the struggles brought him down, she comforted him on her ample bosom, rubbed his temples and hummed to him like he was her child.

"She was a wise woman who knew that within every man there was a little girl who needed hugs, kisses, and comforting, once in a while."

Our love time was cut short by the crunch of gravel under a car's wheels. A few moments later, Sergeant Lewis stepped onto the deck. His heavy steps were filled with weariness.

"Sergeant, what brings you out this evening?" I asked.

"Excuse me for breaking in upon you. But could you come with me? It's Joe old Coyote, he wants to talk to you."

"Where is he?"

"I have him in the jail downtown. He was in Tides-In Tavern, drunk and raging like a mad man, breaking furniture, challenging every white man in the place to a knife fight. I had to book him for drunkenness and disorderly conduct. He's sobered up a bit now and wants to talk to you. Would'ya come?"

When we arrived at the tribal jail Joe was sitting quietly at a small table in his cell, playing solitaire. A broad smile lit up his face as Sergeant Lewis unlocked the steel door to let me into his cell.

It's walls, ceiling and floor were painted in jail house gray, a slightly lighter shade of navy gray.

"Call me if you need any help," said Lewis as the door clanged shut.

Joe's red eyes and emaciated face showed the effects of a three-week binge. At the moment, there was nothing I could do to cure that.

Joe smiled up at me and said, "A long time dead."

I took the chair across the table from him.

"I'm surprised to find you here, Joe. What's going on?"

His jaw muscles tightened, as he said, "Did you know they still haven't arrested those bastards who shot Tom? Nor have they done anything about those who set the fire that killed our elders. We all know who did those things, but no one can prove it."

"It will take time to convict them. It took years to convict the KKK man who shot Edger Evens."

While we talked Joe continued his game of solitaire, puncturing our conversation with long periods of silence.

"I can't sleep anymore. Every time I close my eyes I see Tom laying on the beach pleading for his life. He was my best friend. We dove in the Port Madison trench many times. He helped me bring up the cedar.

"I hear the screams of Chris George…Young and gentle Chris George who wanted so much to be a Suquamish man.

"And Old Running Bear, my teacher and my mentor, was an old man who deserved to die peacefully in his sleep, full of his years, not in those terrible flames.

"And what about Sun Dog, Bigjim, and Bill Eagle? Who will replace their wisdom? In one terrible holocaust of fire, the leadership of our tribe was reduced to ashes, only the sacred pipe survived."

"Not all the leaders, Joe. There is still you. While the tribe mourns the loss of six of its elders they'll be looking to you for leadership. The sacred pipe has been passed into your hands."

"What terrible thing were they doing that they should be killed for? They didn't deserve to die."

Joe's shoulders began to shake and his chest heaved as he fought back his anguish.

"They died because of me. It was my fault. If I hadn't carved that totem they'd still be alive."

I reached out to touch his hand as I said, "You're too hard on yourself. The volatile atmosphere was only waiting for an excuse to explode. If it hadn't been your totem it would've been something else, but it would have happened anyhow. Irresponsible firebrands always incite the fearful and the mentally deficient to violence, pushing them over the edge of common sense.

"The deaths of Tom and the others have had a sobering effect on everyone. We can honor them by using their deaths to bring reconciliation instead of recrimination. If not, they'll have died for nothing."

After a period of thought Joe said, "Do you know why I hate the Christian religion?"

"Oh, I'm sure you don't hate all Christians. You don't hate me, do you? I'm a follower of Christ. I can't believe you hate Christ."

"I didn't say I hated Christ. I said I hate the Christian religion. There's a big difference between the two.

"When I was a young child in Montana I was force to attend a missionary school. They baptized me when I was twelve. But I gave it up when I discovered that my Christian teachers were hypocrites. They said one thing and did another. They said God loved me at the same time they were stealing my people's land and destroying my people's way of life."

"You'll find hypocrites everywhere...In churches, in politics, in organizations like Elks, Lions, D.A.R., and every gathering of men or women. I suspect even the Suquamish Tribe has a few hypocrites beneath its blankets."

"Yes, that's true. And I'll tell you why...."

"You didn't ask me here to talk about human weaknesses. What's really on your mind?"

"Will you get me out of here?"

"Yes, of course. I'll do what I can."

Joe nodded his head. "Good."

Joe had something more he wanted to talk out, to get out into words, so that he could listen to his words and get a better grip on himself. Shuffling the cards he said, "As far as I'm concerned life is like a card game, all a gamble. God is a mad thing called Luck.

"How we happened to be born—whether white or native—is a matter of Luck. Luck deals out the cards, and as little babies we pick up the hands dealt to us. Protest is in vain. These are our cards and we have to play them. There is no fairness in it. The cards most of us pick up put us into the poverty class. The cards of a few enable them to become drug dealers and prostitutes. The playing of the cards is life. The crowd of players is society. The table is the earth. And the earth, in lumps and chunks, from loaves of bread to big red Mercedes, is the stake.

"And in the end, lucky and unlucky, we're all a long time dead.

"The stupid lowly live a hard life, for they're destined to lose from the start. But the more I see of the others, the apparent winners, the less it seems to me that they've anything to brag about.

"They, too, are a long time dead.

"And living doesn't amount to much. It's a wild animal fight. The strong trample the weak, and the strong, I've discovered, aren't necessarily the best.

"My tribal comrades are the stupid lowly. They do the hard work and are robbed of the fruit of their toil. Like the old women who weave their baskets on the Washington coast and get only pennies for their efforts. Yet they've finer qualities of truth, and loyalty, and square dealing than do the people who robs them.

"Most of the time, the winners are the crooked ones, the unfaithful ones, the wicked ones. And even they have no say in the matter. They play the cards that are given to them, and Luck, the monstrous, mad-god thing, the owner of the whole shebang, looks on and grins. It's Luck who stacks the deck and there's no justice in the deal.

"The little babies that come are not even asked if they want to take a turn at the game. They've no choice. Luck jerks them into life, slams them up against the gaming table, and tells them, 'Now play, damn you, play!' And they do their best, the poor little devils.

"The play of some leads to yachts and mansions, of others, to jail or the drug asylum. Some play the one same card, over and over, and make baskets all their days on the beach, hoping at the end, to pull down a set of false teeth and a coffin. Others quit the game early, having drawn cards that called for violent death, or starvation in the streets, or loathsome and lingering disease. The hands of some call for irresponsible and unmerited power. Other hands call for ambition, for wealth in untold sums, for disgrace and shame, or for women and wine."

I asked, "What about you, Joe? What kind of hand have you been dealt?"

Joe looked into my eyes and answered with a shrug, "As for myself, I feel I've drawn an unlucky hand. Though I can't see all the cards, I know that somebody or something will get me in the end. The mad god, Luck, is tricking me along to a tragic end.

"It can be an unfortunate set of circumstances, or in a month's time the fire bombers might be war dancing around my carcass. Or a log truck might run me down, or a sign fall from a building and smash in my skull. And there is disease, ever rampant, one of Luck's cruelest whims. Who can say? Tomorrow, or some other day, a HIV bug, or some other of the thousand or more bugs, might jump upon me and drag me down.

"You've heard about Morning Star, haven't you? She sat with me two weeks ago at the council fire and talked and laughed, a picture of magnificent womanhood. And in a week she was dead—cancer, heart attack, and heaven knows what else—at the end screaming in agony that could be heard a block away."

Morning Star's death had been terrible. It was a fresh, raw wound in everyone's consciousness.

"And when will my turn come?" Asked Joe.

I shrugged the answer, "Who can say?"

"Meanwhile, there is nothing for me to do but play the three cards I can see in my hand, and they are—Revenge, Drugs, and Whiskey."

I looked into his dark pool eyes and said, "I see there are two cards yet on the table. I wonder what they'll turn out to be."

"An ace and an eight most likely," Joe replied.

When it was time for me to leave, Joe smiled and said, "And Luck sat and grinned, knowing that we'd all be a long time dead."

CHAPTER TWENTY-THREE

"You look like you could use a cup." Sergeant Lewis said as he held up a steaming cup.

"Thanks, I sure do."

I sat by his desk, exhausted from the long hard night.

Outside the morning commuter traffic rumbled past. Cars and buses rushed to catch the Seattle ferries that would carry ten thousand or more people to a new day of work in the great city across the waters. In the vehicles were people with sleepy eyes, sucking on their mugs, longing to be blasted awake by their morning shot of espresso.

The face of Sergeant Lewis sagged with weariness.

"How's he doing?" Lewis asked.

"Just fine I think. When will you let him out?"

"Sadie won't press charges if Joe agrees to pay for the damages."

"If he doesn't have the money, let me know and I'll pay. Just be sure to let him out this morning."

"Fine by me."

Lewis looked into the cup cradled in his hands. "I've been thinking that maybe its time for me to leave Suquamish."

There was thoughtfulness in his manner like one that stood at a fork in the trail facing a decision, not knowing that it had already been made.

I understood his anguish because position makes cowards of us all. We do not want to risk what we have achieved. Everyone agrees that change is inevitable, perhaps even desirable, but few have the courage to change themselves because that risks pain and loss.

Can anyone blame the rich, young ruler for refusing to accept Jesus' command to sell everything he owned and give the proceeds to the poor?

Back in 1987, I was hiking in the Chugach Mountains east of Anchorage, Alaska. I heard a voice tell me to take a different trail. I didn't know that my trail would lead me into a desert that grew in proportion to my desire to reach the other side.

If I knew then what I know now, would I have taken that trail? That is a silly question, but it deserves an answer. With perfect 20/20 hindsight, I can firmly say the only choice was the timing because, sooner or later, this life or another, I had to travel the path that day for it's my soul's path back to God.

I had wandered far, and the journey back has required passing back through experiences that would train me for service in this life and beyond. Like a fiery furnace, experiences refined my soul, separating the pure metal from the dross.

In the past it had been easy for me to set my goals, develop my plans and work my plans, to dream and visualize success, fame and fortune.

Then I discovered that the map I was following was defective. Like the Klondike maps sold in Seattle and Vancouver, BC to the argonauts of the 1897 gold rush, my map was defective. It didn't show the desert.

When I came to the desert, I sucked up my courage inspired by golden visions and pressed forward trusting in divine providence to provide the essentials, visualizing the kingdom of God wherein fame and fortune would flow to me like golden nuggets from a mother lode in the Klondike.

It took years of wandering and oceans of tears for me to understand that I was required to wander in the desert like the ancient Hebrews until my goals and ideals passed away.

Many sincere people set the heavenly city as their goal, expecting to enter its pearly gates and walk its streets of gold, to sing in the heavenly choir, praising the Lord God throughout eternity in the company of their loved ones.

St. Augustine visualized that heavenly place as the City of God, not realizing he was mistaken. God isn't interested in recruiting human members for his heavenly choir. He's training us to be peaceful warriors who like knights-errant will serve him throughout the universe.

Physical exhaustion limits our vision. When we are old, tired, sick in mind and body, it's comforting to visualize a heavenly reward of rest and ease. But the heart of the matter is not what we desire but what God wills to be done.

Each person has different experiences. The good Lord customizes the refining process to meet the needs of each soul.

"What's wrong?" I asked.

"Oh, I'm just frustrated. There have been too many deaths and too much destruction. I know who's doing it, and so do you, but I can't stop them. Both the County Sheriff's Department and the FBI just brush me aside and ignore what I tell them."

"Why are they doing that?"

"It's a power thing. The Sheriff and County Prosecutor don't like to recognize any tribal jurisdiction because they think natives are nothing more than brown, beer-bellied idiots less deserving of legal rights and protection."

"So, what's new? Rednecks aren't a Southern monopoly. My God, Lewis, don't you realize that if it weren't for your efforts, the people of Suquamish would have no police protection? What about the FBI? Do they treat you the same way?"

"It's too early to tell. But it took nearly fifteen years for the FBI to get interested in the bodies that keep turning up on the Yakima Reservation. Hey, it's the same old problem, too much crime and not enough agents."

"All the more reason they should accept your help instead of ignoring you."

"Perhaps they will, eventually."

"Maybe the drug problem will bring them around. The lock-them-up and throw-away-the-key program has failed. After twelve years and sixty-seven billion dollars, our justice system is collapsing. Our jails are full and there are more drugs on the street than ever before. And on top of that, you can add the staggering public health costs for long-term care of addicted babies. In addition to strong law enforcement, we have to try other things."

"Do you have any suggestions?"

"What's the driving force behind illegal drugs?"

"Money."

"Huge amounts of money. So much money that the drug cartels are like Hydra, the multi-headed monster that confronted Hercules, cut off one head and two replace it faster than the DEA can swing its sword."

"So what's the alternative?"

"A while back I watched a TV documentary on a city in England, Liverpool I think, that was declared a legalized drug zone. Drugs were made available through government drug rehabilitation centers cheaply or at no cost to addicts.

"After ten years, the drug dealers had left town for more profitable fields. All drug-enhanced crimes such as theft, violence and prostitution had been radically reduced.

"But the greatest discovery was that after ten years of using drugs, most of the addicts dropped the habit and resumed useful productive lives."

"That will never happen in this country."

"It, or something as courageous, will have to be tried and very soon, for our civilization is on the verge of collapsing, not into an Armageddon that some preachers say is about to happen but into another dark age."

Dawn's ruby lips had kissed the eastern peaks and the sun was chiming ten when I sought the repose of my garden away from the outside world that was churning and spitting like St. Helen's caldera. But I was not alone in the garden. A visitor was waiting beside the yellow roses.

"Is that you?" Asked Pastor Jerry.

"Yes."

"I hope you don't mind my being here. Diane had to get some groceries for a seafood salad that she's taking to Dominique's potluck supper this evening. So I decided to come here."

"I'm glad you came."

Pastor Jerry shifted to the end of the bench. Patting the seat beside him, he asked, "Will you sit with me? I'd like to talk to you about something."

The sun warmed our spirits, also our bodies. It was wonderful to sit quietly, eyes closed, and let the sounds and smells find their way to our ears and nostrils.

The chirp, chirp, chirp of little English sparrows were heard as they bounced from limb to limb protecting nest, mate and territory. The honeybees buzzed about the herbs and flowers. And when we were very quiet, the gulp, gulp, gulp of fish feeding on the pond's surface floated to our ears.

Into our nostrils, waves of scents came wafting on the Indian summer breeze. First lilac, then honeysuckle, followed by sweet rose and then, with a swirling of the breezes, a potpourri of other fragrances stirred together into a garden medley.

"Diane said the statue in front of this bench is of a roaring African lion. Is that true?"

"Yes and no. Sometimes it is something else."

"I knew it," Pastor Jerry said, slapping his knee. "While I've been sitting here trying to visualize the lion, I kept seeing a helmeted man who looks like a Greek or Roman soldier with buckler and shield holding a double-edged sword above his head."

"That would be Mars, the god of aggression and war."

"How come I visualize that instead of the lion?"

"Perhaps, you must deal with Mars before you can see the lion."

"What are you talking about?"

"Nothing really. I'm just trying to help you understand what goes on in this garden. If you're willing, it's an experience that requires time, patience and sensitivity but the rewards are beyond description."

"What do you mean?"

"Well, as you know, time is movement. When we slow down and cease the hectic race, time slows down to nature's pace. As we recline on nature's bosom, our hearts begin to beat in syncopation with the mother's heart.

"Patience is accepting the diversity of God's creation and seeing the beauty he has given to all things, great and small, and accepting ourselves as well as our neighbors.

"Sensitivity is the opening of our inner senses to see the angels who protect us, to hear our guides as they lead the way through foggy mists, to feel the closeness of God, and to experience the world of the spirit, God's Kingdom, the City of God.

"That being said, I'll leave you alone for a while."

"Please don't go."

"I must if you are to experience what has been prepared for you."

Pastor Jerry reached out for my arm but I'd slipped away.

"Please don't leave me," he pleaded. "I'm…I'm afraid to be alone in this place."

"You're never alone," I replied as I walked up the path to sit beneath the oak tree and await their coming.

Later that afternoon, while sitting on the deck sipping some Glen Ellen Chardonnay, Pastor Jerry told of their coming.

"I smelled smoke from a fire nearby. I could hear the crackling of the flames and feel its heat. I called for you to come and get me, but you didn't. I became afraid. I kept calling. When you didn't answer, I became angry, angry with you and at my helplessness.

"When the heat became too intense, I tried to get away but was met by the warrior riding a red horse. He was a mad man swinging his sword around and around and shouting, 'Pay your debts or die.' I didn't know whether to fight or flee.

"Then the lion leaped between us as if to protect me. Little people began to appear beside me; I shouted to the lion, 'Protect my children.'

"As the lion roared and the horse reared, I looked around at the little people. Their faces were familiar. Gradually, I began to remember them, one by one. They were my children. I'd fathered them and raised them. And now I had to protect them.

"There was a little girl who was pretty of face but had twisted, bowed legs and could only hop from place to place as she cried, 'First Love is my name; forgetfulness has made me lame.'

"The lion roared, the horse reared, and the warrior swung his sword. Its cold steel struck full and clean through my neck removing my head from my shoulders.

"The sound of the battle turmoil ceased. Darkness covered its fury. I was certain that I was dead. Then you came for me."

We silently pondered the meaning of Pastor Jerry's vision.

"What do you make of it?" He asked.

"A friend once told me such visions can best be understood by comparing them to a movie camera. Turn the camera around and run it backward."

"What on earth does that mean?"

"Reverse the perspective. What you see out there is the reflection of what's going on inside you. The brown lion, the shining warrior, the red horse, the little people are performers acting out a drama. The playwright is your soul, a kind of soul self-healing where the physician heals himself."

"But…What does it mean for me?"

"Ah…That's something you must discover. Meditate on it and ask the Christ to reveal its meaning for you've just seen the opening scenes of a drama called 'The Revelation of Jerry Hanson.'"

"This is all new ground for me. Like in a massive earthquake, all points of reference have dissolved into quivering mass. I need your help to make sense out of it."

"Our Soul forces us to question the beliefs we hold most infallible, to test them in the fires of experience, to look at them from other perspectives. Let's begin with the lion. What comes to mind when you think about a lion? What's the nature of the lion?"

"To me, the lion's nature is to protect. I see the lion apart from his pride sitting under a shade tree scanning the horizon for any danger."

"That's a good start. Now lets look at the concept of protection as preserving, preserving the species, preserving our mental and emotional concepts which are like our little children."

"Why was I so afraid? I didn't know whether to fight or run away."

"In the urge to fight or flee, there is the idea that preserving our concepts will take peace from the earth."

"What about the warrior?"

"The warrior on the red horse has been given great power even the power to kill you by cutting off your head. This killing does not relate to your physical death but to your old ideas and memories. As you expand your awareness, you will reach the time when you'll sacrifice yourself 'for others.'"

"And, what about the yellow roses?"

"The yellow roses represent the adrenal center which is the storehouse of karma, our memories, and is thus the place of stimulus.

"When we fight for our beliefs and fixed ideas, it's little wonder that the rider of this horse was given a great sword for this center is also the place where all the concepts we live by, or otherwise express, are tested. Here they are either justified or are returned to the fiery furnace for remolding.

"Cutting off your head is a warning to be cautious of what you create, what you do, for should you abuse your creative abilities by overuse or non-use, you're being admonished to 'do the first works' or else the candlestick will be 'removed out of its place.'

"This simply means that some of your creative functions—such as sight—will in some manner become non-active."

"Are you saying I lost my sight because I was misusing my powers?"

"I'm not saying anything. I'm just trying to acquaint you with the symbolic language of your soul. The important question is…What is your soul telling you?"

"Okay. I can accept that. So what's the meaning of the pretty little girl who said her name was First Love and faithlessness had made her lame?"

"Can you remember your first love?"

Pastor Jerry fell silent, his hands twisted, thumbs unconsciously tracing the lines of his palms, the life lines, the love lines, the lines of his life, forward and back, up and down.

His answer came slowly, deliberately.

"When I was thirteen, I was in a hospital recovering from an operation. Complications set in resulting in an extended period of pain that drained me of all will to live. Deep into a dark and sleepless night, in the midst of my tossing and turning, I saw a point of white light appear above the foot of my bed. As I watched, it grew and spread into a vertical beam. It's beauty held me transfixed. Then a voice said, 'Ask God and he will help you.' I knew it was the loving voice of the Lord Jesus. I don't know how I knew but I did. I turned my life over to Jesus that very night. Without question, Jesus was my first love."

"What do you think that has to do with the little lame girl?"

"Taking the total vision into account, I'd say my soul was telling me that I've been unfaithful to my first love. But I love Jesus more than my soul."

"A man may love his wife dearly and still bring concubines and mistresses into his house. To echo Jesus' questioning of Peter, Pastor Jerry, do you love Jesus more than your ideas?"

"You know I do."

"Do you love Jesus more than your church?"

"But Jesus is my church."

"Do you love Jesus more than your theological concepts?"

"But Jesus is my theology."

"Your soul doesn't agree."

"Hi fellas."

Diane's perky voice preceded her arrival.

"Have you had a good day?" She asked.

Pastor Jerry, pursing his lips in reflection, replied, "Yes, a very good day."

"I'm sure looking forward to your salad," I said.

Diane blinked in confusion.

"Oh, are you coming to the potluck, too?"

"Yes, of course. Dominique came by earlier this afternoon to invite Jerry and myself. Would you like to meet a Christian witch, Jerry?"

CHAPTER TWENTY-FOUR

"No, thank you, I'm stuffed," Pastor Jerry moaned, tapping his bulging stomach. "The food is great."

The potluck dinner had been laid out on two long banquet tables brought over from the Tribal Center and set up in Dominique's backyard.

There was Diane's seafood salad, Betty's Southern fried chicken and Cajun shrimp, Sandra's corn casserole, Emmy Lou's crab cakes, Carl's French bread and Rachel's squaw bread.

Fruit pies and chocolate cakes were donated by Bruce's Bakery and Cantina. All were washed down with coffee or wine. A keg of beer squatted in a tub of ice on the porch.

Dominique had provided a gas-fired grill where quests could cook their specialties. Bruce Carlton labored lovingly over his beef ribs and polish sausages while Sue Old Coyote grilled salmon steaks.

It had been a magnificent outpouring of food and drink by thirty-three people, among whom were leaders from all sections of Suquamish society, native and non-native, Christians and Atheists, rich and poor. Many broke bread together for the first time in recent memory.

Dominique, a robust, full-figured woman in her fifties, had welcomed her guests with the announcement:

"I'm happy that you accepted my invitation. No business may be transacted this evening. Only fellowship is allowed. So let's eat and get acquainted."

And acquainted we became. The presence of food relieved the belly hunger, and the fellowship relieved the angst, that gloomy, often neurotic feeling of anxiety and depression that had gripped the village since the night of fires.

Dominique floated among her guests dissolving cliques before they could solidify, mixing combatants from the recent turmoil, silently teaching that it's hard to hate an enemy who is eating your beef ribs and praising them to other guests.

Late in the evening, long after the moon had beamed her silver light into the backyard, attrition thinned our ranks until, around midnight, only eight people remained, a portentous number arousing amazement in those who knew the potential of the mix.

A hand reached out and grabbed Pastor Jerry's hand. Its clasp was firm and its shake was strong, and it wouldn't let go.

A deep, threatening voice whispered, "Did you know your hands are covered with blood?"

Pastor Jerry tried to jerk his hand away, as he called out, "Diane?"

When she didn't answer, he asked, "Does anyone know where Diane is?"

The deep voice answered, "She's in the kitchen. Should I get her?"

"Would you please? Tell her to bring a washcloth."

"A washcloth won't do you any good."

"But you said I had blood on my hands."

"Indeed you do. The blood of innocent people! The blood of a twelve-year-old boy who was denied manhood, the blood of five elders of our tribe...."

Pastor Jerry began to shake.

"Diane?" He called again. "Diane, where are you?"

"Old Running Bear did you no harm, but you killed the last of our great carvers."

"I...I had nothing to do with those fires."

"Bigjim always taught tolerance and patience and what did it get him?"

Pastor Jerry reached out trying to feel his way away from the voice.

"And the others, did you ever meet Bill Eagle, our pipe bearer? Or Sun Dog who told the stories of our people?"

In his desperate attempt to get away, Pastor Jerry fell over a chair. Strong masculine arms lifted him to his feet. The strong hands refused to release Pastor Jerry's arms but pulled him face-to-face with the voice that intensified with anger.

"I know that you knew Tom Proudfoot. He rescued you when the motor on your boat conked out, and the tide had you in its grip. You showed your appreciation, you hypocritical bastard, by shooting him down like a mad dog."

Pastor Jerry frantically tried to twist free.

"Will somebody help me?" He pleaded in terror.

"How do you like being trapped without an escape? I've been thinking. What would be a fitting punishment for your crimes? And then it came to me."

The man took Pastor Jerry's arm and pulled him toward the door.

"Let me go," Jerry shouted. "Diane, for Christ's sake, where are you?"

"She can't hear you. There's no one here who will lift a finger to help you."

I pitied Pastor Jerry, knowing the panic of being blind and in a snake pit of your worst fears, helpless against their strikes.

It reminded me of the Tennessee railroad engineer who was blasting in a mountain tunnel when an accident killed his partner and left him stunned and blind. Help was slow to come. Rescuers, fearing secondary explosions collapsing the tunnel, waited two days for other engineers to arrive.

Meanwhile, the helpless blind man waited. When the sun went down, rattlesnakes, seeking protection from the cold fall air, slithered into the tunnel, their tongues seeking the warmest place.

The blind man felt them coming. He heard their bellies slithering over the rocks. He froze as they wiggled against his legs, his sides, even coiling up on both sides of his neck. They pushed and shoved to gain the top of his head that produced the greatest body heat. Soon he was wrapped with poisonous snakes like a mummy, unable to move, not even a finger to ease the darting tongues from his face.

It was the morning of the second day before help arrived. After they had eased the snakes off with long sticks, the blind engineer was carried out of the tunnel. A young man, confident and strong, had gone in but an old delirious, blind man with white hair and shattered nerves came out.

Like the trapped, blind engineer, Pastor Jerry also was trapped standing rigid with his hands balled at his sides. Joe grabbed Pastor Jerry's shirt and yanked him nose-to-nose so the hot blasts of fury could pommel into his face.

I pleaded, "Cool it, fellas. You're guests in Dominique's home. Settle this somewhere else at another time."

Joe released his grip on Jerry's shirt, nodded his agreement, and stepped back.

Pastor Jerry remained on alert in his darkness, expecting more blows. When they didn't come, he taunted, "What's the matter, you red devil? Don't you have the guts to take on a blind man?"

"Jerry, it's over," pleaded Diane. "There'll be no fighting tonight."

I turned to Dominique.

"Pastor Jerry came expecting to meet a Christian witch. I told him you were one."

"Yes," Dominique chuckled. "I've been told that what I do is called witchcraft but I don't like that word. It conjures up the old wives' tales of the dark ages, the kind of stories that inspired fearful Christians to burn old defenseless women at the stake."

"What do you call yourself?" Asked Pastor Jerry.

"Since I'm a follower of Jesus Christ who is my Lord, I am a Christian."

"But I hear you practice the dark arts."

"Meaning?"

"Divination, channeling…All those New Age things."

"Yes, I believe in the New Age and all its wonderful powers. Don't you, Pastor Jerry?"

"Of course not."

"But don't you believe in the second coming of Jesus when a New Age will be established and Christ will reign for thousand years?"

"Yes…of course," replied Pastor Jerry, hesitantly, sensing a trap.

"Then all Christians are New Agers."

"Oh, no, you don't," replied Pastor Jerry, wagging his finger blindly in the air. "You're giving a New Age twist to a fundamental Christian doctrine just to confuse and mislead people."

I interrupted, "Why waste time and energy in debating semantics? Truth is known by its fruit. Dominique, you've told me that the task of a Christian is not to debate but to heal our neighbor's wounds as Jesus instructed his disciples to do."

"Yes."

"You've spoken of the need for people to have their chakra centers cleansed and aligned. For one, I'd like to see a demonstration of how that's done."

"If you like," said Dominique.

"Oh, yes, I'd like to see that," chimed Diane, bubbling with enthusiasm as her eyes begged for agreement from the others. "Wouldn't the rest of you like to see it?"

"Yes, I'm sure we all would," I answered in the midst of murmuring agreements.

I nodded toward Pastor Jerry. Dominique took my suggestion.

"Pastor Jerry, would you mind helping me with my demonstration?"

Diane took him by the elbow, urging him forward. "Honey, go ahead. There's nothing to be afraid of."

"Well…I don't know," replied Pastor Jerry. "Why doesn't someone else be the guinea pig?"

"Honey," urged Diane, "by being the subject you can feel what's going on."

Pastor Jerry reluctantly nodded his head in agreement.

Dominique asked him, "Would you please remove all restrictions: your belt, bracelet, watch, rings, and empty your pockets? Oh, yes, please take off your shoes."

Diane and Dominique helped Pastor Jerry onto the long, narrow, massage table that set in front of the fern-bracketed French doors.

A pungent sweetness wafted in on the evening breeze funneling its way through a heavy growth of honeysuckle vines laden with clusters of coral pink and rich yellow flowers.

"Lie back with your hands along your sides. Just close your eyelids and relax. Diane is right beside you."

Dominique quietly went about her preparations. She placed a small burning candle and crystal between his ankles. Under the table she lit a large white candle that stood next to a large crystal cluster. She gently moved a small table net to Jerry's left shoulder. On the table was a small crystal and another candle, its flame danced joyfully.

On the wall behind the table hung a large banner of white silk fringed with gold tassels. In the center of the banner was a dove taking flight from an empty cross. A wide golden circle encompassed the dove and cross.

Dominique stepped out of her white sandals, "To keep myself grounded," she said, and stood at Pastor Jerry's left side.

Drawing her hands together in an upward sweep, with her palms open in expectation, she closed her eyes and prayed:

"Lord Jesus, we invite Thy presence. Surround us with the white light of Thy love and protection. Let this servant be a channel of Thy healing power for Pastor Jerry, here present."

Drawing a deep breath, she exhaled slowly. Dominique stood straight and tall like a Venus. With arms stretched wide she looked around the appreciative audience, her loose—fitting cotton dress draping her full figure. Joy and happiness radiated from her smiling face as she introduced the demonstration.

"There are seven major chakras in the human body. In Sanskrit, chakra means wheel like the spinning wheels seen by Ezekiel. The soul energizes the physical body through these chakras. Attached to each chakra is a vortex that could be compared to the funnel of a miniature tornado. With all the negative forces that surround our bodies, it is inevitable that these vortexes get knocked out of alignment resulting in stress and dis-ease to the chakra system."

Diane asked, "What's the effect on the physical body when that happens?"

"The chakra system is known to biological science as the endocrine system of glands that produce hormones. It is known that abnormalities in these glands bring on all kinds of sickness and discomfort, little things like a mild headache all the way up to serious things like terminal cancer.

"Conventional western medicines usually treat the endocrine system with drugs or hormone replacement. Since ancient times, the Chinese have treated this system by cleansing, balancing and alignment of the life force they call Chi. I like to think of it as the Soul. Like the electromagnet force of a magnet, Chi is composed of two opposing energies, an active energy that is called yang, the male energy and a passive energy that is called yin, the female energy.

"Active and passive, positive and negative, male and female are not moral qualities but are equal, although opposing, forces. Blockage in any of the chakra centers disrupts the flow of Chi.

"I'll first cleanse the ethereal body that surrounds the physical body and extends outward for about six-inches or so. Then I'll align the vortexes. After that, I'll balance and energize the chakras."

Beginning slightly above Pastor Jerry's head and a few inches above his body, Dominique, with her adjoining hands forming a paddle, swept over his body from head to toe several times.

"It is important to cleanse the ethereal body of disruptive energies."

She shook her hands off to her left side, wiping them of any contamination.

"The next thing, we must balance the four elements of air, earth, fire and water by inviting the attending angels to energize their assigned positions. This is done with the power of a pendulum and crystal."

She placed a wooden cross of sticks on Pastor Jerry's chest. In her left hand she held a small crystal suspended on a string over one tip of the cross. She held her right palm over the crystal on the small table and waved it in a clockwise rotation until the pendulum in her left hand stopped moving. She repeated the process at the four ends of the cross.

Setting aside the wooden cross, she aligned the vortexes with the dedication of a master physician, moving from one chakra center to the next, swinging her pendulum and sweeping her hand over the table crystal.

When she had completed the realignment of the vortexes, she positioned herself behind Pastor Jerry's head.

"Now I going to hold the point of this small crystal at the top of your head and another small crystal on your third eye. The third eye is between your eyebrows and slightly up on the forehead."

When she gently pressed the crystal points to his head, Pastor Jerry cried out in a wheezing voice, "Ahhhhhh," and his body became rigid and shook like he was being electrocuted. He continued to shake and wheeze, "Ahhhhhh."

After a few seconds Dominique, withdrew the crystals and Pastor Jerry's body fell limp.

He whispered in a rasping voice, "When you touched my head with those crystals, my throat tightened. I couldn't breath."

"Good," Dominique replied. "Chi is flowing again."

It took about thirty minutes to complete the process. Then Dominique helped Pastor Jerry to sit up slowly. But he was impatient and sat up too fast. Grabbing the edge of the table, he whimpered,

"Oh, I feel washed out, limp as a rag."

"Take it easy. You'll have your strength back in a few seconds."

As Pastor Jerry sat on the edge of the table, Dominique leaned over and whispered into his left ear.

"Tomorrow go to Charlie's garden and wash your eyes in his pond."

"Why?" He asked.

Dominique didn't answer. She turned to the group and said, "That's how I align and cleanse the chakra centers. As you can see, it takes about thirty minutes or more depending on the person's condition."

"How about teaching us something else?" Joe asked.

"Where's Diane?" Pastor Jerry asked, his voice and hands trembling.

Diane slipped to his side and whispered, "I'm right here."

"It's time for us to go home," Jerry said.

Diane, ignoring his plea, turned to Joe and said, "I haven't had a chance to get acquainted with this man. I'm Diane Hanson, Jerry's wife."

"I'm glad to meet you. My name is Joe Old Coyote."

"You're the woodcarver, aren't you? I think I've seen some of your work in the Seattle Art Museum."

"Yes, I had several pieces in the Pacific Native Arts section last year. Did you like them?"

"Oh, I sure did. I was so proud to see something produced by a Suquamish artist."

Pastor Jerry squeezed Diane's arm so hard his fingers brought red streaks to her arm.

"I really want to go…now," Jerry insisted.

Diane pried his fingers from her arm and stepped beyond his reach.

I could see by the white panic on Pastor Jerry's face that his world was filled with snakes.

I slipped to Pastor Jerry's side and whispered into his ear, "Protecting your children takes peace from the earth."

CHAPTER TWENTY-FIVE

"That's an interesting concept," Dominique said. "What does it mean?"

I replied, "By children, I mean the beliefs we live by. We create or adopt them. Wars result when we defend our beliefs or try to force our beliefs on others."

Joe said, "There are times when we must fight. If we don't fight to defend our freedom, we'll become slaves to others. Many wars have been fought in the name of freedom. Are you saying it's wrong to fight for freedom?"

"Not at all. What I'm saying is that beliefs, like physical children, are the most intimate part of our lives, by and for which we live and die. We hold them so sacred that we regard them as gifts from God. And that's what takes peace from the earth.

"All religions hold the belief that the teachings of their holy men, such as Buddha, Moses, Jesus, or Mohammed, came directly from God. Hammurabi used the same approach to gain support for his code of laws as did the Greeks, the Persians, the Chinese and the Romans. They all claim divine origin for their teachings and laws. For centuries, Kings ruled by divine right. Even our constitution sets forth rights derived from God."

Dominique said, "But you keep saying that beliefs take peace from the earth."

Pastor Jerry, until then silent, joined in, "It's our Christian duty to suppress erroneous thinking and immoral living."

I replied, "That's the root of the problem. Who's right? Who's wrong? Who shall be the judge? Wars only determine who's the strongest or the most clever. The winners write history. So we never know the virtues of the losers. Surely, you must agree that right and wrong aren't determined by who has the sharpest sword."

Pastor Jerry replied, "It's better for the sword to be in the hand of a righteous man than in the hand of a sinner."

Joe snapped back, "By that do you mean in your hand and not mine?"

Pastor Jerry began to counter, "But the Word of God is clear that…." He shook his head in frustration, then turned the conversation to Dominique.

"Dominique, I'm told that you're a Christian witch, is that true?"

She smiled and asked, "What do you mean by a witch? Are you thinking about the witches of folklore and fairy tales? They never existed except in the subconscious. Or are you talking about the fabrications by the twisted minds of witch hunters who prey on the fears and superstitions of ignorant people?"

Pastor Jerry wouldn't give ground. "The dark arts of witchcraft, sorcery, satanic rituals have long existed and are even practiced right here in Suquamish.

He paused, "But I don't want to be combatant this evening. I've never talked to a real witch before and would like to learn more about you. How is it possible for you to call yourself a Christian witch?"

"I don't object when people call me a witch. I enjoy watching their expressions. They're like the people who recoil at seeing a circus freak but can't resist a closer look.

"As you know, my backyard is surrounded by a tall cedar fence. Sometimes I don't wear clothes when I work in my garden. When I catch my neighbors peeking at me through the fence, it's fun to see their sheepish expressions when they realize that I've caught them.

"Am I a witch? I don't know. You tell me. Am I a witch because I use the ancient arts of divination to see the future? Then Jesus was a witch for he saw the future and Paul urged all Christians to prophesy."

"That's different," said Pastor Jerry. "Christian prophesy is a gift of the Holy Spirit, not satanic tricks used by gypsy fortune tellers to cheat gullible people out of their hard-earned money."

Dominique smiled and replied, "Our world is filled with wolves in sheep's clothing. Some are carnival hustlers; others are religious hustlers. It's difficult to distinguish between them.

"All that you call satanic tricks have their Christian counterparts. The psychic arts are valid whether used by Christians or non-Christians because they're the capabilities of the human mind and spirit. The difference is that the Christian gives the credit and glory to the Holy Spirit while others claim the credit and glory for themselves. The sword is neutral. It can kill or bless depending on whether it's in the hand of Satan or Christ."

Pastor Jerry confessed, "I hadn't thought about it in that way."

"All I'm saying is labels are misleading and deceptive. It's easy to pin the donkey's tail on someone and then claim victory. What we really need to fear, Pastor Jerry, is what lies within ourselves. If Christ rules our heart, we've nothing to fear from psychic powers."

"Do you have psychic powers?" Pastor Jerry asked.

"Yes."

"Can you give a demonstration to us tonight?"

Dominique looked from face to face, then said, "For most of the people here no demonstration is necessary."

Diane bounced with excitement, "Oh, please. I'd like to see you do something."

Dominique smiled warmly at Diane.

"Well…Okay. What would you like to see?"

Joe volunteered, "How about conjuring up some spirits?"

He had a clever smile on his mouth and a twinkle in his dark brown eyes.

"That's too easy," said Dominique.

"Oh, please," pleaded Diane.

"How about table knocking?" Asked Joe.

I said, "Fine by us."

Dominique set up a folding card table in the center of her hardwood kitchen floor while I pulled up four chairs.

"Should I turn off the lights?" Diane asked.

Dominique smiled, "No, it makes no difference to the spirits whether there are lights or not. A dark room with a few candles is pure Hollywood.

"Diane, why don't you sit here and Pastor Jerry, would you sit opposite her?" Instructed Dominique. "Charlie and Betty take the other two chairs; and the rest pull up chairs around us."

We took our places.

"Place your hands flat on the table with your fingers spread. Now…Bring your hands together until the tips of your thumbs meet…That's right. Now, slide your hands forward until the tips of your little fingers touch the little fingers of the persons next to you, forming a circle of hands on the table."

We did as instructed.

"Now, take a deep breath, relax your arms and shoulders, just let them rest gently on the table with your feet flat on the floor. Good. Now close your eyes and concentrate on your breathing. Try to keep your hands still.

"Don't be afraid. I've asked the Christ to surround us with his white spirit of protection. Only positive spirits will be allowed to communicate through the table."

We sat quietly for several moments, then Dominique closed her eyes and asked, "Is there someone present who'd like to communicate with any of the people at the table?"

Again several moments passed before one leg of the table slowly lifted off the floor then dropped with a thud.

Dominique said, "Good. We've established contact. Who do you want to talk to?"

The table rose and then bounced against Pastor Jerry's solar plexus several times.

"The one who is in spirit wants to communicate with you, Pastor Jerry. You may ask the spirit any question that can be answered by yes or no. If the answer is yes, the table will bounce against you twice, once if it's no. Think of someone who has passed over whom you think might want to communicate with you. Then ask, 'Are you so and so?'"

Pastor Jerry squinted in concentration.

"Are you my grandfather, Henry Hanson?"

The table rose and vigorously bounced against Pastor Jerry twice. Jerry's face beamed with excitement.

Dominique said, "You may ask your grandfather more questions, if you like."

Pastor Jerry asked, "Grandfather, are you happy over there?"

Two strong bounces.

"Is grandmother with you?"

There was a long pause, then one bounce.

"Do you know where she is?"

Two bounces.

"Is she in heaven?"

One bounce.

"Where is she?"

The table didn't move.

Dominique said, "Your questions must be phrased so they can be answered with a simple yes or no."

Pastor Jerry tried again, "Is she in hell?"

One bounce.

"Is she in purgatory?"

One bounce.

Dominique suggested, "Ask him, is she back on earth?"

Pastor Jerry hesitated then asked, "Is she back on earth?"

Two strong bounces.

"Is she someone I know?"

Two strong bounces.

"Who is she?"

The table remained at rest.

Dominique reminded him, "Remember, he can only answer yes or no."

"Is she present in this room?"

Two bounces.

"Is she Diane?"

One bounce.

"Is she Betty?"

One bounce.

"Is she Sue?"

One bounce.

Pastor Jerry's face twisted in confusion.

"Is she Dominique?"

One bounce.

"I don't understand," he said. "If my grandmother is present in this room but is none of the women, who can she be?"

Dominique explained, "Sometimes, after a lifetime in a woman's body, our souls return in a male body, and vise versa. Your father could've been your sister in a previous life, your sister could've been your uncle, and so on. Throughout many lifetimes, we experience a variety of relationships. You haven't asked about the men."

Pastor Jerry confessed, "This is getting weird. I'm not too sure I want to know."

"It's up to you."

He paused for several moments then said, "Oh, what the heck. Is she Charlie?"

One bounce.

"Is she the Old Man?"

One bounce.

Pastor Jerry froze when he realized that Joe Old Coyote was the last remaining male. Then he jumped up in agitation.

"Oh, no! It can't be."

Reaching out for Diane with trembling hands, he pleaded, "Please, Diane, let's go home…Now."

Three votive candles sat on a rough wooden plank beneath a poster that hung on the wall. Their flickering cast a sick yellow light on the nude black woman's oiled skin. Her dark eyes glared into the observer's eyes, daring the observer to look within her spread legs. Like a wild animal, she challenged the hunter to enter her lair. The steel blade of the knife in her hand glistened threateningly. She was the wild woman, the archetype most feared by men because she roamed uncontrolled within their unconscious.

Across the room, the dark one sat with flaring eyes fixed on the wild woman. He held an AK-47 assault weapon between his legs with the barrel pointed at the wild woman's privates. Gently, lovingly, he stroked the upraised barrel with an oiled cloth.

It was as if the gun was an extension of his penis. The weapon was his power to defend his masculinity against the onslaught of the wild woman who disguised herself as women-libbers, femi-nazis, NOW zealots…The braless ones who taunted him beneath silk blouses.

His eyes glazed over with ecstasy as he fantasized ramming his barrel deep into her lair and emptying his clip with rapidly fired jerks.

Gently, lovingly, he stroked the upraised barrel and whispered, "Soon, very soon, you whoring bitch, you will experience my power. You will submit to me and plead for more."

The sun's gentle hands caressed my cheek, warming it slowly and lovingly. Moving upward, he touched the lid of my eye ever so softly sending healing waves into my brain, inviting me to wake up.

I opened my eyes. Had they been violently closed to the outside world so that I could see the inner world, the world filled with beauty, and love, and many friends?

I watched the sun's hand move up the wall until it touched the crystal that hung in my window, the crystal that Sara Duggan had given me. Was that a month ago, or a year, or in another lifetime? I reached up and tapped it to watch a new burst of energy dance on my walls. Around and around she swirled, her skirt of seven colors flaring then contracting.

I heard a chair creak on the deck. Peering through the French doors, I saw Diane sitting quietly in the morning light looking into the garden and observing her husband as he sat on a bench beside the 'Sundowner' roses. She watched as Michelangelo's David, his foot on the fallen Goliath, materialized in the morning mists.

Diane jumped at my silent approach. I handed her a mug of fresh black coffee.

"Oh," she said. "We've barged into your garden again. I hope you don't mind."

"No, not at all. I quite enjoy your company. It's a wonderful way to begin the day. Jerry is a lucky man."

Diane dropped her eyes to look into the blackness inside her cup, like the blackness that filled her spirit.

"He doesn't think so. Ever since his accident, he treats me like I have some vile disease. He used to be such a passionate lover."

"You don't have to explain to me what…."

"Some people think I was wrong to pose for those pictures, but I wasn't. They were a very private part of our lovemaking. Posing excited me because I knew it excited him.

"Couples make love in many ways. But that's a private matter. Like one's underwear. They're perfectly okay to wear, but no one wants them to be hung on a line for every passerby to ogle. You understand, don't you? You don't think I was wrong, do you?"

"Diane, I agree with everything you've said and done. What's missing in all this flap about your pictures is who stole your pictures and put out those flyers? Everyone seems focused on the titillating things, the things people can click their tongues at while their groins are warmed."

Diane smiled. Patting my hand, she said, "Dominique told me that you'd understand."

"Speaking of Dominique, how did Jerry take last night?"

"That table knocking really upset him. He couldn't sleep. He kept me awake prowling around the house, bumping into doors and chairs, cursing everyone and everything. I thought if he could spend some time in your garden, it would calm him down."

"I'm sure it will. Jerry is in the grip of a spiritual hurricane that is blowing away all his children. The garden can be the eye of his hurricane where, for a few minutes, he can find a little peace. Is there any hope that he'll see again?"

"Dr. Wells and the other ophthalmologists at the University Eye Clinic have done all the tests but can't find anything wrong. They just don't know why he's blind or what to expect."

A movement in the shadows next to the north wall caught my eye. Uncertain, but suspicious, I slipped along behind the moving shadow, careful not to be seen. Creeping silently up behind the lilac bushes, I saw him sitting beside Pastor Jerry. He was talking softly. I crept closer to hear what he was saying.

My God! It was my voice. He was imitating my voice!

"It was all a trick, wasn't it?" Asked Pastor Jerry. "She set me up, didn't she? How weird can you get? Joe Old Coyote as my grandmother! Come on now, only a fool would believe that."

"Of course, it was a trick. They were all in on it, even Diane."

"No, not Diane!"

"Yes, Diane. Why do you think she's been going over to Dominique's house so much lately? They're getting to be good friends, aren't they?"

"What are you saying?"

"Oh, nothing. But you should see how they light up when they're together. Their eyes never leave each other, and always smiling in that special way. You know what I mean. You didn't see Dominique give

Diane a warm hug and kiss when you left last night. And it wasn't just a sisterly peck."

Pastor Jerry squirmed in agitation.

"I don't believe it," he said. "I just don't believe Diane is that kind of woman. I know her too well."

"Do you really? Haven't you ever wondered why she was so willing to exchange pictures with those other women?"

Pastor Jerry replied thoughtfully, "She did like to linger over their pictures when she thought I wasn't looking. I remember one night waking up to find her gone. I found her down in the den looking at the albums."

"Exactly! That's what I'm talking about. She has always had…A thing for other women. Dominique could sense that. That's why she's been so friendly to her. She hasn't been that friendly with you, has she?"

"No, but…."

"Dominique is a very desirable woman. Can you imagine what it'd be like to have two women make love to you?"

Pastor Jerry fell silent.

The dark one pressed the thought.

"You've the makings of a beautiful setup. Why don't you encourage Diane to see more of Dominique until they do it? Then she'll be ready for a menage a trois. You've done that before, haven't you?"

"Well…No, not really. I thought about it once back in Dubuque, Iowa."

"Who suggested it, you or Diane?"

"Well, Diane…."

"I thought so. Men get so caught up in their fantasies that they're oblivious to their partner's needs.

"In your case, blindness is better than a blindfold. Can't you visualize lying naked in bed, not knowing what will happen? You hear and sense them moving about. They tie a cord, first around one wrist then the other. Your arms are stretched up as they're tied to the bedpost. You're at their mercy. All the time your senses strain to detect what they will do next. Will it be the sharp chill of an ice cube on your nipples or the wisp of a feather as it's slipped along your thighs? Then their warm, naked bodies slide in beside you, one on each side, and they press their…."

"Stop it! Don't say another word. True love doesn't grow in the soil of illicit passion. Diane and I love each other too much to destroy that love. I just don't believe there's anything going on between them."

"Well, you'll have to wait and see then, won't you? I hope you won't wake up someday and find Diane has run off with Dominique."

"I said shut up! Diane is not that kind of a woman."

"Your marriage will be nothing more than ashes, like your church."

"What do you know about that fire?"

"I know the Indians didn't do it."

"Who did it?"

"What do you know about your friend Clara Goodwill?"

"Haven't heard from her since I started the Church of the True Faith."

"What would you say if I told you that Clara was behind all the fires. That she had her gang burn your church to the ground. That she murdered those people in the sweat lodge. That she is the leader of a secret militia group that call themselves The Servants of God?"

Pastor Jerry's stomach churned with dark green bile that boiled up into his throat until he spit out his fury.

"That poor misguided soul! I won't be surprised if she had something to do with Sara Duggan's death. She came unglued after Henry left her for that native woman and she discovered that she had inoperable breast cancer. She has poured out her misery on the whole village ever since."

A smile crept over the dark one's face as he said, "Wouldn't it be wonderful if you could rebuild your church? At such times as these, Suquamish needs a truly Bible-based ministry, one that will preach the good news of Jesus."

"That's out of the question. I'm broke and alone."

"Doesn't the Bible say that with God nothing is impossible? If you have faith, whatever you ask in prayer will be granted. Can't you envision the joy of seeing the Church Of The True Faith rise from its ashes? Because of your blindness, you can preach even greater sermons. Like Job, your sufferings can be stepping stones to an even greater ministry than before."

Again the dark one almost had Pastor Jerry convinced, but not quite.

Pastor Jerry said softly, "I've been thinking a lot about why I wanted to have my church. I can't deny it. My Ego was puffed up by power and fame. Then the Lord struck me blind and reduced my church to ashes forcing me to rethink my motives. As long as I gained power, prestige, and property from my ministry, I was serving my Ego and not my God."

"What are you saying? Are you going to just roll over and die?"

"Yes…I'm going to die. I'm going to let my Ego shrivel up and blow away. From now on, my ministry will be one of service to others with no personal gain."

"That's ridiculous. Who's going to pay your bills—your mortgage payments, the heat and light and all the rest?"

"I don't know. But I know, if God shows the way, he'll also provide the means. My greatest challenge is to have the courage to step out into the unknown. Perhaps it is possible to have a ministry without a building."

The dark one slowly stood up, his arms hung dejectedly from his stooped shoulders. Looking up, he saw me behind the lilacs. His eyes flared red for a moment, then went out as a gray cloud dampened the sun. The dark one walked away.

Upon reaching the fishpond, he turned and sneered in a voice from Hades, "I'll still see you in hell."

Then the dark one disappeared in the rainsquall that poured down from the sky as if heaven itself wanted to wash away his evil presence.

Pastor Jerry recalled Dominique's whispered instruction, 'Wash your eyes in the pond.' He groped his way to the pond's edge and knelt down. With wide sweeps of his cupped hands, he splashed the blue water into his face and eyes again and again until his hair and shirt were dripping wet, and the rain poured down on him like a baptismal fountain. He felt clean and whole.

When the rain lifted, Diane appeared out the mist with all the majesty and beauty of Venus. She spoke not a word as she reached out for Jerry's hands. He stood up and didn't resist when she guided his hands over her shoulders and around her neck. They kissed the kiss of lovers who have survived the great test. The kiss of oneness from which would come the strength to step out together into the unknown future, arm in arm.

Pastor Jerry brushed the hair from Diane's face. Looking deep into her eyes he said, "I can see for the very first time, I can truly see what a beautiful woman you are."

The rainbow rose into the eastern sky and a golden eagle soared above the garden.

CHAPTER TWENTY-SIX

Arm in arm Betty and I walked along the beach of Agate Pass talking the way lovers do. Wisps of tender sensitivity reaching out to probe and explore.

She grew quiet.

I asked, "What's the matter?"

She replied, "I had a dream last night that refuses to leave me. I need to tell you. May I?"

"Yes, please tell me."

"I was alone walking through tall redwoods and madrona trees. It was night but the moonlight was so bright that I had no trouble finding my way. I felt a force drawing me forward but I didn't know where I was going.

"I moved so lightly that not a leaf rustled under my feet as I floated through the mists. I wore a long, white dress trimmed with lace frills and ruffles at neck and wrist. My hands and face radiated in the moonlight.

"A sadness hung over me like a heavy blanket threatening to press my spirit into the ground. I floated up a knoll and looked down upon the pathetic, burned-out ruins of a great house. The rain that had poured down earlier in the evening had let up and the clouds separated allowing the full moon to bathe the moss-covered red rocks with its silver light.

"The night air was filled with the sweet scent of roses as I stood on the ridge alone and sad. Then I became aware of a man standing nearby, a sullen melancholy look about him. I slipped my arm around his but I couldn't feel his arm not even when we exchanged the knowing squeeze.

Then I realized that I was a spirit and he was in flesh but our hearts leaped nevertheless.

"He said, 'Boojims, I had hoped you'd come but wasn't sure if you could.'

"I whispered, 'I can only stay for a short time.'

"He asked me, 'How are things with you?'

"'I'm content.'

"He said, 'I've been standing here looking at these ruins and recalling our dreams for this place.'

"'I think that's what drew me.'

He looked down at me and smiled, "There is a twinkle in your eyes."

"I said, 'You were such a wonderful builder! Always building something. And the ranch was the biggest building achievement of your life though most thought of it as a rich man's fancy.'

"'But it all turned to ashes.'

"'But our dreams live on.'

"'Mate, those were wonderful dreams, dreams built on love, our love. It's sad how our dreams turned to ashes. Why do you suppose that happened?'

"'That's what we're trying to find out, isn't it?'

There was a slight chill that came with the stirring of a breeze. I put my arm around Betty's shoulders.

"There is a lot we don't know about ourselves! What a difference mere passion seems to make! Yet who am I to say 'mere.' If our passions had been different, we would've never gotten together. Yet how true the words, her wall was no stronger than my attack. We give and live; we withhold and die."

Betty asked softly, "I remember a little Greek idyll. How on warm summer nights I would ride up to that beautiful lake to swim in the nude.

"I especially remember one night in particular. The moon was full and its soft silver light bathed my glistening body as I stood on the dock with my head back and face raised to allow my long, satin hair fall down my back.

"I remember that my hair was so long it tickled my behind," Betty giggled playfully.

"Upon request, I pulled back my shoulders and lifted my chest to permit feasting upon my boo'ful full breasts. Oh, such a sight was meant for the gods not for mortal eyes!"

"Then we hurried into our shrine in the trees where I rode his stallion until dawn began to break over the eastern mountains."

We grew silent as we savored the memory.

She whispered to him, "After your death, there were others."

"Yes, I know."

"There was...."

"It doesn't matter, Boojims. I know your life was sad and lonely after my death, and I'd never begrudge you one thrill of living. Life holds so few real thrills."

"The thrills that come to me out of the past are of us and our little Greek Idyll. I never married again because I preferred to be your widow than the wife of any other man ever born."

"Boojims, will you tell me what it's like on the other side?" He asked.

"I'll tell you that it's like standing on the edge of a world so new, so terrible, so wonderful, that you're almost afraid to look over into it."

"Boojims, you mean all the world to me."

"Yes, I've always known that."

"I was afraid I would have to live this life without you?"

"Oh, mate. In my dream you asked if we'd ever be together again and I said, 'I had come to tell you that we'll be together again soon.'"

"'When?' You asked.

"I smiled coquettishly with a twinkle in my eyes. Throwing misty arms around your neck, I looked deep into your eyes and purred, 'Some day soon you'll turn and there I'll be.'

"You threw all caution to the wind as you attempted to encircle me with your arms and kiss me full upon my lips. We kissed the way that we did the first time on the bungalow porch so many, many long years ago in another lifetime. But you melted away as the moon ducked behind a bank of clouds withdrawing its light, leaving me alone in the darkness."

The crackling of the fire brought me back to the present. I blinked my eyes to confirm my place.

The Old Man was sitting by the beach fire, poking it with a long stick.

Looking across the flames, he said, "You've been given a gift, a remembrance to encourage you on your journey. By the way, Charlie, have you solved the riddle?"

"Yes, I think I have," I said.

I settled around the beach fire as I told my discovery.

The ability to watch my little girl walk by had been a long time in coming. Yes, I understood that within me lived my mother's daughter. Her bent, her perversion, were from the cradle like a seedling that grows from beneath the mother log. I had come to realize that my little girl had been twisted and bent by those early experiences.

My wise old friend had helped me to realize that the power within me was greater than all that befell me. He helped me to appreciate the truth that, with every birth, there are really twins, an outer child and an inner child. His or her parents have shaped everyone's inner child. All men have their mother's daughters within them as all women have their father's sons.

Over the months of sharing many fireside chats with my wise old friend, he helped me to see how society conditions men to view women as either virgins or whores.

He taught me that, at the extremes, women see men as either tough macho-types or weak, nice guys. The macho man hides his neediness and vulnerability beneath a tough exterior and behind a big-penis ego. The nice guy strangles his resentment and confusion and finds himself drawn into relationships with sexually addicted women who exploit or abuse him.

My wise old friend showed me how men grow up with a confusing combination of fear, respect, and anger toward women, and with a profound desire for women's acceptance.

"As a nice man," the old man said, "you don't want to be like the macho-ego men who view women as vessels in which to satisfy their beasts, but you find yourself rejected by women who desired the macho beasts."

The old man told me that the sad thing was that it had taken me a long time to come to love the woman within me. I recognized how male sexuality hurt women. I didn't want to hurt women because I loved them and needed their love. As a nice guy, I had a tremendous need for women's approval and when I didn't receive it, I built up anger inside toward the macho-ego men.

I was still struggling to control the pain and anger caused by Sara's verbal castration. I had frozen my emotions inside an ice cube that could only be melted by a woman's love.

My wise old friend said, "When you competed with Sara's penis fixation, you walked in her father's garden. For Sara, it was a power trip born of her need to control her father's beast that had ravished her as a little girl and by that, to win back her father's love. That was Sara's problem, not yours. To a healthy, whole woman, the size of a man's penis is immaterial, of no relevance to a man's capacity to love and be loved."

"I had never realized that for a normal woman, the size of a man's penis wasn't important."

The old man said, "Until men realize that, they'll remain vulnerable to be used or exploited by sadistic women. Your need was to know and love the woman within so you could love the woman without."

When I stood aside and watched the women of my life pass by, I recognized no pattern of physical shape or size, no smile the same, or color of eyes or hair. There were tall women and short women, some were plump and some were skinny, all different, and all unique, all were beautiful in their way. All began as lovers and all ended as enemies.

Within me was my mother's daughter as within them resided their father's son.

How easily that phrase tripped from my lips! How difficult for me to acknowledge its truth!

I will always remember Suquamish as where the hands of God's two sons came together to form a crucible in which I underwent my transformation, my rebirth. In Suquamish I died and was born again.

A year later, during a night when all were asleep, a massive cold front surged down from the north. It roared out of the Gulf of Alaska into Puget Sound, mounting the warm moist air like an enraged bull. Black clouds boiled up along the leading edge. Flashes of lightening heralded its arrival; rolling thunder drummed its attack.

The people of Suquamish shivered and quaked in helpless terror. Little children wet their beds and cried, lovers clutched in desperate embrace and panic-stricken dogs and cats cringed beneath decks and porches.

FLASH! CRACK! SHAKE! And RUMBLE!

Zeus, the Thunderer, joined forces with Neptune of the ocean storms, to terrorize man, beast, birds and fish.

Beneath the offshore waters, mother earth's skin responded with a sharp jolt as her plates dove one beneath the other. One second later, the earth beneath Suquamish echoed its response. Layers of clay, wet from the winter rains, became gigantic slides on which Clara Goodwill and her house and all the other waterfront homes were deposited onto the beaches of Agate Pass, there to await the arrival of giant Tsunami and her cleaning maids.

In a brief two minutes it was over. Mother Earth had completed her cleansing. The storm front had moved on and the waters retreated through the Strait of Juan de Fuca. The ground ceased its quaking.

In the brief span of 120 seconds, the world had changed. Waves, economic waves, seismic waves, social waves, waves beyond comprehension, swept over North America on to Central and South America, Europe, Asia, and back again with staggering blows. All life on the face of the earth was changed in 120 ticks of the clock.

Panic, riots, looting, rapes and wars followed quickly on their heels. But first, there was the silence, the silence of shock and disbelief.

Across the sound, Seattle's crumbled skyscrapers smoldered in the night. Few tragedies in recorded history, written or oral, exceeded the catastrophe that had fallen upon Puget Sound and along the whole of America's west coast. Our radios told of its effects in Oregon and California, the panic on Wall Street, but that was beyond the ability of our shocked senses to absorb.

The people of Suquamish emerged from their ruins to a new world that had suddenly become old. Kitsap Peninsula had become an island again isolated from the rest of the world, all bridges and ferries had been swept away, the Narrows Bridge joined its sister as did the floating bridge across Hood Canal. The jumbo ferries, *Puyallup*, *Wenatchee* and *Tacoma*, slept with the fishes beneath 1,000 feet of salt water. Power and telephone lines were severed. Radios and cellular phones were the only link to a world that was struggling to rise to its feet, far too wounded to bring help to Suquamish. The horrors and tragedies that came over the airwaves became too much for us to endure. Mercifully the batteries soon ran out, generators fell silent for lack of fuel, and Suquamish returned to the time before white civilization arrived.

The rest of the story that I'm about to tell, if my power holds, pushes all that has gone before off our sensory screens. It is the story of how in the end after Adam had gone into extinction the meek inherited the earth.

After the cleansing, there was silence. When the survivors emerged from the ruins, they....

THE END

CONCLUSIONS

Suquamish, February 10, 2000
Reviewer: Paul Roland from Ashland, Oregon

As a playwright and screenwriter, I'm especially fascinated by a novel that presents rich and exciting characters in a situation that's rife with mystery, passion and a compelling plot. Jerome Lofgren has managed to tweak this reader's imagination in a way that made it impossible for me to set the book aside, and equally impossible to read it only once. I predict this story will be given at least one more lifetime in motion picture houses around the world. Paul Roland, Ashland, Oregon.

ABOUT THE AUTHOR

Jerome V. Lofgren has been a Presbyterian Minister, Navy Chaplain, Packaging Equipment salesman, Marketing Specialist, President/Founder of a High Tech Plastics Fabrication Company serving Aerospace and Defense Industries, Commercial Real Estate Developer, President/Founder of a Computer Consulting Company and Owner/Manager of an Anchorage apartment complex.

Since 1983 he has phased into a writing career and have completed a novella, six novels and over 60 short stories. He lives and writes in Poulsbo, Washington.

Made in United States
Troutdale, OR
12/04/2024